INEQUALITY

A.J Dighiero

Inequality

ISBN: 0692754822

ISBN 13: 978-0692754825

www.ajdighierobooks.com

Acknowledgments

It may be my name that appears on the front of this novel, but behind this work has been a group of people who've been with me every step of the way. This book could not have been completed without their unending help and support. Each of these people, in their own special way, have enriched the novel you're about to read. I give my sincerest thanks to…

Marlon Williams, for his unwavering support throughout this two year adventure that became this novel.

Karen McGregor, for all the love and support you always gave me throughout this process.

Liza George, for her continued support throughout the story development process.

Katherine Dempsey, for her amazing editing and support.

Thomas Raube, for his amazing artwork. For more of his work, please visit: http://euderion.deviantart.com/

And last, but never least, Daniel Nievas— whose friendship and support can never be replaced.

Chapter 1

The meeting had been dragging on for several hours. None of the elected officials who had gathered would be satisfied until every single piece of intelligence had been carefully analyzed and taken into account. Kalduron, the leader of the Thespian army, had been explaining to them all of the information that had been gathered on the target ship. This was a situation that required meticulous planning; no one could afford even the slightest chance of failure. Melthuron, the newly elected Prime Consort and leader of the two Thespian species from the planet of Demora, had gone missing. He was a rather young Thespian, a famous scientist, and had won a decisive victory after an election that had a voter turnout of more than 90 percent—the highest voter turnout of any election in Thespian history.

All of the Intel that had been gathered by an intergalactic coalition of human and Thespian and forces pointed to that ship. Kalduron could feel the pressure inside the conference room. It was almost as if it were weighing down his body. Sweat began to flow down his green, hairless face. Melthuron had to be found by any means necessary. Even if he had to search every inch of the galaxy, every little planet on every solar system, he couldn't afford not to find him. His planet was still recuperating from a bloody civil war that had plagued his home for more than one hundred years. Both species had fought over Demora's land and resources in what had been the worst catastrophe either species had ever faced. Each side had believed the war would only last a couple of years at most; no one could have foreseen just how long and devastating it would actually turn out to be. Kalduron was a veteran of that war and one of the oldest Thespians still alive. Even though a peace treaty had been drafted and a new government created, one that was inclusive of both species, the hatred between them still ran rampant. Kalduron knew that if Melthuron wasn't found, it would be his species who would pay the price. They would most probably be blamed for his disappearance, and a coup could sweep the nation faster than the war had begun. After all, Melthuron was beloved by his people and respected by all, and Kalduron had been his main opponent during the election. It wouldn't just be easy to blame him and his species for

Melthuron's disappearance; it would be the most logical thing to

assume.

"And that is all the intelligence that we have been able to

gather," Kalduron said as the hologram displayed every file that had

been compiled. Behind him stood four soldiers dressed in the same

military gear that Kalduron was wearing.

It was as if those soldiers were wearing darkness itself. The

armor they were wearing was darker than the farthest reaches of

outer space. It was designed to protect their bodies from head to toe,

leaving no trace of skin exposed. This pitch-black armor was made

out of a light metal alloy produced in Demora. It was lighter than

aluminum yet thousands of times stronger than titanium, making it

easy for soldiers to move about without feeling much stress on their

bodies. The helmet was also just as dark as their armor, with a rather

intimidating design. The front side of the helmet contained a lower

front face shield that protected the mouth and eyes with its dark,

reinforced metal alloy. The inside of the helmet was equipped with a

high-definition display that served as its interface and visual center, capable of displaying the outside world to its wearer as if it were seeing the world through their own eyes.

The equipment they were wearing hid their identity from everyone in the room, as was tradition in the Thespian army. They were nobody, just agents on a mission that had to be completed at all costs. The meeting had been going on for hours, and it was finally Kalduron's turn to introduce the soldiers who would carry out this mission. He looked around the room nervously as he began addressing the diverse group. A drop of sweat slid down his face; it was time.

"Dear leaders, I firmly believe these brave soldiers standing before me are the right choice for this mission; none live who are more qualified," Kalduron said. He paused again for a moment, looking over the four soldiers he had chosen to carry out this important mission. Pride filled him. "In all my years serving in the Thespian army, I have never worked with finer soldiers." He said with confidence.

"If Melthuron is in fact being held at this location, these soldiers will bring him back safely. Of this I can assure you. Thank you,"

Kalduron concluded with complete faith in his choice of soldiers. Kalduron and his soldiers remained still, waiting for the elected officials to voice any opinions or concerns.

A moment of silence overtook the room before a voice spoke out from among the group of officials. "Could your soldiers be so kind as to remove their helmets? I believe all of us here would like to see their identity before sending them on such an important mission," a female voice said, with distrust in her voice. It was the Thespian official Tei-va, a shorter, long-haired Thespian who had served in the Thespian senate since the establishment of Demora's new government.

Kalduron nodded his head at the soldiers, giving them permission to obey her request. The four soldiers proceeded to remove their helmets, showing their identities to everyone. There standing before them were four Thespian soldiers, one female and three males. The female soldier, although looking rather feminine in bone structure and appearance, was anything but fragile. She had short, black hair that was slicked back, and light green skin. The male soldiers, on the other hand, displayed strong male facial features such as a longer, more pronounced faces with more squarely shaped chins and darker skin tones.

"Why how convenient!" Tei-va exclaimed, before standing up to address everyone. "I don't believe for a moment Kalduron has the well-being of our elected leader in mind." Raising her voice, she said angrily, "All of these *elite* soldiers are Thespians from his species, whereas Melthuron is from my own species. I cannot ignore the history between our two species; therefore, I cannot let an old enemy of my people take charge of this mission."

Although the two species appeared similar from afar, when seen together up close, distinct differences were apparent. Tei-va's species was shorter than Kalduron's by an average of two feet, and the diameter of their eyes was also larger. Kalduron's species developed violet irises, whereas Tei-va's species had a mixture of green and blue eyes. The skin color of both species remained the same light green; although in both species there were different tones of green. Being descendants from large-brained reptilian-like hominoids, both species had lost their scales and over time evolved more pronounced hominoid features. Their body proportions remained similar. They had long arms and long legs when compared to their small torsos, although over time Kalduron's species had evolved into a slightly more proportional body shape with a slightly longer torso. Their faces had changed a great deal over the course of their evolution. Both species shifted from their ancestors' flat, elongated, hairless head and face to a much shorter, broader face and head. Both species shared an evolved thick head of black hair on their heads to protect their evolving brains from their planet's powerful ultraviolet radiation. Their teeth, however, remained stubbornly sharp and thin like their common ancestor. Both species also still sported their ancestors' full predatory-like retractable claws in their hands and feet.

Tei-va stared deeply into the female soldier's violet eyes as her hatred simmered, making it very obvious to everyone where she stood on the matter. "I cannot trust these so-called Thespians to carry out this mission, for they may be the ones who orchestrated his kidnapping in the first place!" she screamed loudly, looking directly into Kalduron's bright violet eyes. Her deep blue eyes filled with even more hate as she stared him down, hating him and everything his species represented. Although peace had been achieved and a new Thespian government established, the hate between the two species continued to cause problems in the new government.

Her accusations, however, would not go unchallenged. "That is simply preposterous!" Kalduron responded, looking rather angry yet trying his best to maintain his composure. He took a second to calm down, clearly insulted by her defaming words. Kalduron hid his disdain.

"With all due respect, ma'am, Melthuron is the democratically elected leader of all Thespians, both your species and mine. I am bound by military oath to protect him and all Thespians no matter which species they belong to," Kalduron calmly explained. "These talented individuals have served as military spies for decades and have the most experience of any other soldiers in executing similar missions. They have worked together countless times during the civil war and saved millions of Thespian lives…from both species. They are the most decorated, faithful war heroes whose reputations I will not allow you to tarnish. And if I may add one more point: they have never failed a mission. If anyone can bring the

Prime Consort back safely, it is them," Kalduron concluded. Although his tone indicated respect, Kalduron's stare showed disdain for Tei-va and her words. He attempted to continue but was swiftly interrupted.

"My fellow leaders, if there was ever a time to be weary of his intentions, the intentions of his traitorous species, it is now!" Tei-va responded. "If we all take a moment and reflect on this, I find it rather convenient that only two days after Melthuron was elected, right before his term of office would begin, he disappeared without a trace. Doesn't his disappearance grant you temporary leadership, Kalduron? If I remember correctly, according to our new constitution, you would be next in command if anything where to happen to the prime consort."

She quickly glanced around to look at his soldiers, growing angrier as she stared them down. "You, sir, are known to have publically criticized Melthuron during his campaign; you opposed him at every turn. You also chose to run against him, viciously attacking Melthuron from every conceivable angle. It was a borderline smear campaign." She took a deep breath before continuing. "I won't let you personally sabotage this mission. I'll be dead before I let you become Prime Consort," she shouted as she pointed her finger at him.

"I will never trust you, and neither should this council. Intergalactic members, please take into account the concerns that I have brought forth, and vote accordingly. Thank you," Tei-va concluded. She sat down, smiling at Kalduron with contempt.

Kalduron and his soldiers remained silent on the matter, for it was not their turn to speak.

"What a terrible display," a voice said, coming from the other side of the room. "The issue at hand is important to the entire galaxy. Accusing your fellow Thespian of treason before our congregation is ill advised, Tei-va. Don't forget that it was the rest of the galaxy that funded the reconstruction of your world. I advise you to keep your petty vendettas to yourself." A brown-haired human with a well-groomed beard suddenly stood up from among the group of officials, ready to address the members. He looked unamused by her performance.

"Elected leaders, my name is Ramos. Although I believe Kalduron only wants to find and bring his leader back safely, I understand where Tei-va is coming from even if she is being…quite indecorous," he said. Although Tei-va wanted to interrupt him, Ramos quickly cut her off, promptly continuing his speech. "To ease concerns I am sure are shared by others like Tei-va, I offer to Kalduron's band of what I am sure are very capable soldiers, a worthy addition." He then turned toward the person sitting next to him, a tall man by human standards. He stood up, standing approximately seven and a half feet tall, easily towering over the six-foot-tall Ramos, yet he stood with respect. He was a very well-built man with dark hair and even darker eyes and dressed in human military gear. "Please state your name and background for all of us here today," Ramos instructed with confidence.

"My name is Salvador. I currently serve as Ramos's personal body guard, and I am a veteran of the intelligence gathering agency of Earth," the human soldier said in a respectful tone.

"In addition to adding one more member to this group, I propose we add my military's recording technology to their armor.

This would ensure that even if the mission goes awry, we will know exactly what took place," Ramos said.

"Do these measures alleviate some of your concerns?" Ramos asked.

Tei-va still looked displeased. "I don't trust you at all, Kalduron, but with these measures I am somewhat more reassured. Although I would love to see all of his soldiers expelled from the mission, we just don't have to time for such novelties. I vote in favor—"

Before she could continue, Kalduron decided to intervene in an attempt to reestablish control of the conversation. "Well, if we are done here, I must brief our soldiers before executing the mission," Kalduron said, eager to get out of that drama-filled room.

"Yes indeed, let's proceed," Ramos said, smiling as he turned to face Tei-va. "All in favor of executing the mission under these conditions, please raise your right hands now." The voting was swift and unanimous. All elected leaders gave their vote in favor of the newly proposed measures. Kalduron was relieved to be done with the meeting. He finally had the permission he needed to begin the mission. "Thank you, leaders," Kalduron said before turning around to face his soldiers. "Soldiers, please join me in the prep room for briefing before deployment. I have no doubt that our leader will be returned safely," Kalduron said as he began to walk out of the room. Salvador quickly followed, joining the marching soldiers outside of the conference room.

As the door shut behind him, Kalduron turned to face his soldiers. "Civilians with political power have always gotten in the way of my military operations," he said while staring down at his group, focusing his gaze directly at Salvador.

"Over two hundred years. Over two hundred damn years and I still have to cater to their inadequate, inexperienced leadership," Kalduron said angrily. His eyes burned with dissatisfaction toward the whole thing. He stopped for a second as he marched in front of Salvador. He was now standing just inches away, face to face with him. "Human…do not hold my team back, or I will make sure you don't return. Are we clear?" Kalduron said as he stared him down.

His threat, however, seem to fly right past Salvador, who proceeded respond swiftly with a confident tone. "Yes, Commander." He was clearly not intimidated by Kalduron's words.

Kalduron seemed pleased by his response as he turned around and began to walk down the corridor once again. They made their way down the corridor for a couple of minutes, turning into the outermost room in the ship. As the door opened, weapons and devices of all kinds were displayed on various metal shelves, all organized based on function and type. A small ship was attached outside with an entrance from inside the room. This was the ship that would be used to fly close to the target ship for infiltration.

With the door closing behind him, Kalduron began the briefing. He quickly touched the wall, initiating a holographic screen that contained diagrams and highlighted areas of the unidentified ship. He stared at the female soldier briefly before turning his attention back to the screen, looking proud of her as he introduced her.

"This is Seleece. She will be in charge of this mission once my briefing is over. You are all to follow her orders as if they were my own." He then stopped, his attention now shifted to the screen in front of him. "As we are all aware, we cannot be sending wireless transmissions from inside the ship or into the ship, so once you are all aboard, you will follow her command without question," Kalduron said.

"Yes, Commander!" they all chanted in unison.

Pleased, he reverted back to explaining the plans. "As far as our intelligence agents have been able to gather, this is a small ship; roughly fifty rooms, ten thousand square meters." He paused as he pointed to a corner of the spherical ship highlighted in green. "You shall enter here at the ship's docking area. Our intelligence agents have been able to hack into their systems, and they will allow you to enter without being noticed by the ship's main computer," Kalduron said, now looking a bit nervous. He paused to take a deep breath. "Once inside, you will search every room of this ship for signs of Melthuron, while making sure you are not discovered by anyone."

Kalduron shifted himself over to the right side of the room. "Stealth, not muscle power, is the vital part of this mission," he said as he came within reach of various military devices that were stacked together. With two fingers, he picked up a small, white cube and placed it on his shoulder. Within seconds, it changed shape, flattening on his shoulder and attaching itself completely to his body, covering his entire shoulder. "Courtesy of Thespian army researchers, these new devices will be your wave absorbers, which will ensure no waves of any kind are emitted from your communication, weapon, and other devices that you will be carrying with you on this mission," he said before taking the device off and placing it back on the shelf.

"Along with these devices, you will be equipped with the standard cloaking device that blocks body heat, so thermal scanners won't be able to detect you. And, of course, the famous Thespian battle armor and helmet, the crown of our Thespian technology. The helmet makes it possible to control all of your gear with your thoughts from the built-in computer."

Kalduron suddenly stopped his speech and glanced over at Salvador. "Time is of the essence, so once the briefing is over, Seleece will give you a crash course on how to operate all of this gear before deployment. For your sake, let's hope you are able to pick it up in time," Kalduron said before returning his attention to the screen. "This area here, highlighted in red, is where you will make your escape. It is located on the opposite side of the ship and will be where one of our ships will be waiting to pick you all up exactly forty minutes after you board the unidentified ship. You will use this docking area, not the one you entered from, for your escape. You have exactly forty minutes; no more, no less," Kalduron explained while staring at Seleece. He knew by the look on her face that she had a specific question in mind. "There will be no time to go back and exit from where you entered, so each room is to be searched along the way to the exit, maximizing your time."

Seleece was about to ask her question, but Kalduron was way ahead of her; after all, he knew her better than anyone.

"If, after all of these measures, you are still somehow discovered, disable any and all who have taken notice of you before they have a chance to alert the whole ship." Kalduron paused. Something was making him angry. He clenched his fists as he looked up at his soldiers with disappointment. "The use of deadly force is not authorized unless Melthuron is found," he said in a frustrated tone. Kalduron was clearly upset with that directive; in fact, it infuriated him. Kalduron's original plan was to launch a full-scale takeover of the ship, but his proposal had been rejected by the council. The elected leaders had earlier pointed to intergalactic laws prohibiting the use of force on a ship without probable cause, so he was prohibited from launching a military takeover of the ship. Previously, all attempts to get in contact with beings aboard the ship had failed, but according to their laws, that was not enough to launch a raid on the ship since it was flying in intergalactic space not actually claimed by any government. His frustration with this decision was obvious. "If Melthuron is found, I don't care if you send every single soldier or civilian to an early grave," he said, with no apparent regard to any potential life on that ship, Thespian or otherwise. Kalduron was not known to let pressure get the better of him, but these circumstances were much different. With the honor of his species questioned by a member of his own government, along with the frustration the bureaucracy had caused him, he was starting to crack. Infuriated, Kalduron shouted slowly, dragging each word out for emphasis: "DO NOT FAIL ME!"

Kalduron's shout pierced their ears before sending shockwaves down their spines. Although his Thespian soldiers had worked with him countless times in the past, they had never seen him like this. His honor had been attacked, and the pressure he felt to find Melthuron could also be felt by everyone else in the room. With peace on the line and the threat of another civil war, the soldiers knew they could not fail under any circumstances. Kalduron quickly calmed himself long enough to ask, "Any questions?"

He promptly received a "No, Commander!" from everyone.

"Oh yes, one last thing," he said. "If Melthuron really is aboard that ship and you do not bring him back to me alive, do not bother coming back. Desertion would be better for all of you than what I would do to each and every soldier who fails." He shouted, "One hour until deployment!" and left the room. A moment of silence ensued.

"All right then," Seleece said, while quickly walking to the front of the room. She turned, facing the rest of the group, but focused her attention on the newest member, Salvador. "All right, listen up, human. The tallest one here is Melron, to his right is our medic Lenduin, and last but surely not least is Caal'dor," she said. Wasting no time, she made her way to the right of the room, quickly grabbing two Thespian helmets. "Now that we are better acquainted, let's teach you how to operate this piece of equipment. We don't have much time," she said in a kind, yet commanding tone. An hour of training went by.

Suddenly, Kalduron entered the room with an anxious look on his face. Everyone was now fully geared in Thespian armor, holding their helmets against their waists. They were standing in single file, waiting for deployment orders. Kalduron was pleased to see this.

"Can he operate the helmet properly?" Kalduron asked, hoping everything had gone according to plan.

"Yes, Commander," Seleece responded diligently. "Salvador learned quickly," she said. Even Seleece, one of the best soldiers in

Thespian history, was impressed by Salvador's progress. It usually took the average soldier twice as long to get on the hang of such complicated technology, but Salvador just breezed right through the training like a natural.

"Place this inside your helmets," Kalduron said as he tossed one device at each of them. It was the technology Ramos had mentioned. It would record everything that would go down in the mission. "Excellent!" he said as they all inserted the small devices inside their helmets. Although they were of human origin, these devices had been formatted to work flawlessly with Thespian technology. "You are all now authorized to begin the mission. Find our leader and bring him back to me safely. Go!"

At that very moment, the most important mission in all of their lives had begun. They quickly made their way toward the small ship, turning on its cloaking device before blasting off toward the target. Although it only took a few minutes to arrive at the target ship, to them it felt like hours. The pressure they were all feeling was immense. Although they did not show it externally, deep inside they were all more than anxious to find Melthuron. The future of Demora

depended on it.

Chapter 2

Seleece's ship was now positioned just outside the unknown ship's docking area. They stood completely still, waiting for Kalduron's order. Kalduron, who was back at headquarters, had just spoken with the team of hackers to disable the ship's sensors on command to allow for a successful, undetected infiltration. "Can you all hear me, over?" Kalduron asked his soldiers via transmission.

"Sir, we hear you loud and clear, sir! Over!" Seleece immediately responded.

"I am placing a ten-second countdown on your helmets. Once that timer reaches zero, that is when you have the go ahead," Kalduron said as the timer became visible to them. A big red number "ten" was displayed inside everyone's helmets. "Come back with our leader safely, soldiers. Drol'ar Agnar!"

"Drol'ar Agnar!" they chanted back in unison. It was Thespian tradition to chant that phrase. It meant "glory and success" in old Thespian.

Seleece and the others grew tense as the countdown timer started in their helmets. Nine, she clenched her right fist. Eight, they all stood up. Seven, their cloaking devices turned on. Six, Seleece turned to face her group. Five, "We will find him!" she roared, confident in herself and her crew. Four, three, their ship door opened. Two, they ran toward the end of the ship. One, the ship door opened. Zero. The hacking was successful. They were inside, completely undetected by anyone aboard that ship. "Deep breath," she thought as she focused. Seleece then turned on their ship's autopilot from her helmet, catching a glimpse of it before it flew away. Now there was no way of turning back.

They were now standing against the wall in the ship's docking room, observing everything around them. As far as they could tell, the room was clear. As they looked around the room they noticed nothing unusual about it. It was a small room, perhaps about the size of their ship's docking room; no more than four hundred square feet. Their backs were now facing the stars. They could be seen from the ship's reinforced glass behind them, millions of them in every direction. The walls inside that room were as white as snow, completely uniform, with no visible cracks or spots. The room even appeared to have been recently cleaned, as there was no sign of anyone ever having been in it before. It was spotless. Toward the end they noticed a control panel next to the door.

"Let's proceed, everyone," Seleece commanded telepathically via her helmet. With her small blaster in hand, she made her way silently toward the panel, reaching over to inspect it. She noticed that all security measures were activated. It seemed the new wave absorbers were working as expected, for their presence had not being detected by the ship's security system. With this reassurance, she extended her left hand outward, pointing with two fingers toward the door, giving the signal to press on.

The door opened, and they quickly and uniformly followed her lead. They entered a corridor that was completely empty. Not a single soul was present as far as their eyes could see. The corridor was lit with two sets of circular lights. The walls were painted a chrome-like gray, like most other standard ships. Their helmets, which were equipped with very sensitive motion detection technology, were not picking up any movement in the corridor. This did not sit well with Seleece or any of the others, who at this point expected to see activity. Pressed for time, they put their concerns aside and strode forward silently, entering the first room. There was nothing; no one. The room was completely empty. There were no windows, no chairs, no tables; nothing but absolute silence. Acknowledging this, they exited the room quickly, proceeding to the second room.

Seleece raised her right hand, signaling her crew to stop. They positioned themselves against the wall, ready to storm inside and take anyone who may be there by surprise. She gave the go ahead, and they stormed inside. "What's going on?" she thought. This room was also completely empty, with the same white walls staring right back at her. This ship was starting to make Seleece feel uneasy; she felt a heaviness in her stomach. "Why are there no signs of anyone on this ship?" she thought, troubled by the position they were in. There they stood in an unknown ship with no sign of life, no sounds, no movement, just a chilling silence. Seleece could feel it; something was very wrong. But things only got worse: they saw the same thing again and again. She looked around the fourth room, growing more anxious as the sheer emptiness of the next few rooms turned everyone's stomach just a little bit more. Again, no sign of life anywhere, no matter which room they checked. To them, time now seemed to move even faster as they checked every room available. Ten rooms later, progress remained stagnant. There was no sign of Melthuron, no sign of his supposed captors, no sign of anyone.

They continued to check room by room for the next two rooms, finding nothing but beds, showers, appliances, even warm food on a table, but nothing else. It was as if everyone on this ship had vanished into thin air. Seleece then raised her clenched hand, telling everyone to remain still. They now stood at the end of the corridor, with all the rooms behind them already checked.

Twenty minutes had already passed. They only had another twenty-five minutes left before their time was up and the mission was over. "This isn't getting us anywhere," Seleece thought as she glanced around the empty, gray corridor. She knew every second counted on this mission. The longer they were there, the more dangerous the situation would become if they were found. Following orders from her superiors was important, but it seemed like they would not find anything at the rate they were going. There were still many more rooms to be checked.

Right then, her mind was made up. Using her helmet, she telepathically sent a message informing everyone that the plan changed. "We don't have the time to search every room in this corridor. I have a feeling we will find nothing here," she said in her message, trying to remain calm in front of her crew. She then pointed to the ceiling, showing everyone the way they would take. "This looks like a big enough vent for us to fit in. Let's not waste any more time on this part of the ship; we are going directly to the ship's control room," she communicated.

"Are you sure about this, Seleece? I know we haven't found anything yet, but this wasn't part of Kalduron's plan," Lenduin responded.

"That's an order," Seleece commanded.

"Yes ma'am!" her fellow Thespians responded.

But Salvador did not seem to agree. "No!" Salvador exclaimed vehemently. "We had clear instructions. We should continue the mission as commanded by Commander Kalduron and search every single remaining—"

"Quiet! You will do as I command!" she interrupted, flexing her commanding muscle as she took out her short range blaster from her armor's back compartment. Seleece would not allow disobedience. She quickly raised her blaster in Salvador's direction. "Do not disobey me, Human, or I will make sure you never return home," she said.

Salvador did not like this plan in the least, but he had little choice but to comply given the circumstances. Everyone's weapons were now aimed straight at his face.

"Go ahead, make my day, Human," Melron said in a menacing tone.

The room grew tense and even more silent as everyone stared at Salvador, awaiting his reply. The pressure to complete this mission was at an all-time high.

"Yeah, please give me a reason to find out what a human brain looks like," Caal'dor added in a cocky tone, itching to shoot the questioning soldier.

It seemed like Salvador had no choice. He unclenched his fists, accepting his orders. "My sincerest apologies. Please lead the way, boss," Salvador said.

"Oh no, by all means...after you," she responded, with distrust clear in her voice.

"Yes ma'am," Salvador responded as he took out a small laser from his suit's back compartment. He made his way toward the ventilation shaft and quickly burned off the cover of the vent. He stopped to look at them one more time before beginning to pull himself up into the shaft. One after the other, they quickly followed in Salvador's footsteps, pulling themselves effortlessly inside with just one arm, making no sound at all. As they crawled quickly down the air shaft, their helmets suddenly picked up movement in one of the rooms a couple of meters down from their location.

"Stop," Seleece commanded. "My sensors indicate movement

directly below us. Let's check it out." Before she could give the order, however, Salvador rushed into the room in an attempt to escape Seleece's control.

"No! After him!" Seleece exclaimed, wasting no time in following him quickly to into the room. But as she entered the room and looked around, Salvador was now nowhere to be found. Somehow he had completely disappeared.

"How could he get away so quickly!" she said. "More importantly, how is he invisible to us?" Melron asked telepathically via his helmet.

"That's a good question. We should be able to see him even when he is cloaked since our helmets are all linked," Caal'dor responded.

"Damn it! Where is that deserter? He couldn't have gotten far," Lenduin said as he glanced around the whole room, livid at their failure to keep Salvador under control.

"There's only one way in and one way out of this room. Caal'dor, you watch over the way we came in; Melron, I want you to—"

But she didn't finish. Her eyes had noticed something farther away toward the end of the room. It was a rather large container, and there was something big inside it.

"When I get my hands on him, I'll—" Melron stopped in midsentence, noticing the cylindrical tank at the far end of the room. Before he was able to say anything, Seleece made her way swiftly toward it, wasting no time with their idle chattering. She stopped just a few feet away from it; she couldn't believe yes. She put her anger aside for the moment, shifting to a confused but curious.

"It's some sort of life form I have never seen before...just what the hell is that?" she said via her helmet, profoundly amazed by what she was staring at. The alien's face was perfect. It had a long, strong jawline with high cheekbones and a perfect rounded chin. The small nose was set above beautiful full lips, and it's small, almost oval-shaped ears were slightly pointed but served to complement its appearance further. It was about nine and a half feet tall by the looks of it, with perfect, spotless blue skin. It had no visible reproductive organs of any kind. It had two arms and two legs like most other intelligent alien species in the galaxy. She walked around the container, noticing that this alien had no navel area anywhere on its body.

"No navel area? How is that possible?" she thought as she continued to examine the mysterious creature.

Most life forms had some sort of left over imprint from their birth, such as a belly button or, in the Thespians' case, a back scar. But this alien showed no sign of anything close to that. When the others reached Seleece, they were equally in awe and profoundly confused as to why it was here in the first place.

Lenduin's jaw dropped, unable to be seen from behind his helmet. "What kind of alien is that?" he asked, completely taken by surprise.

"I have never seen any species like it before," Melron added, staring straight into the alien's face. "And what is that doing in this room?"

"Hell, I'm just glad we didn't find Melthuron in this container," Caal'dor said shakily, trying to be funny while being creeped out.

"That's one hell of a science project," Melron laughed, equally disturbed by what he was seeing.

Seleece had made up her mind. "We are busting it out of here," she said. Her team did not expect to hear that.

"But ma'am, what about Salvador? We have more pressing matters at the moment than this…this alien," Caal'dor said.

"We will figure that out later. This alien, whoever it is, has been illegally imprisoned on this ship. It is against our code to ignore this. We don't know if it will be friendly, so all of you must proceed with caution," she said.

The rest of the crew wondered whether it was the right decision, but having nothing else at the moment they could do, they followed her orders promptly.

Seleece quickly walked over to the control board in front of the tank, hoping to figure out how to safely get the alien out of its liquid cage. She looked at the screen in front of her and touched it. The screen quickly lit up, displaying different numbers, statistics, and figures; that was when Seleece noticed something unusual. "Wait…why is this in Thespian?" she thought, growing concerned. Her stomach sank as she began to wonder just who they could be dealing with in this ship. "Could Melthuron's kidnappers be Thespians?" she thought. If so, the situation now made even less sense to her. "Why would this interface be in Thespian? This ship is not of Thespian origin," she said out loud, this time not using her communicator. "Do not drop your guards, everyone, I don't know who is on this ship or what is happening here, but the mission to find Melthuron is still—" But before she could finish, she was interrupted by a loud blast.

Melron had been shot. The force of the blast violently launched him several feet forward, thrusting him against the reinforced window. His tough Thespian armor was broken by the sheer force of the blast, turning off his cloaking device as he fell to the ground, unconscious. Wasting no time, they raised their weapons and formed a circle, covering one another's blind spots while trying to pinpoint where the blast came from.

"Melron! Melron! Are you all right?" Seleece shouted desperately while trying to remain focused.

"Don't worry, Seleece...he shouldn't be dead. Poor guy is just having a bad day," a voice said in a sneering tone, taunting them before laughing loudly. Suddenly, about thirty feet away from them, a cloaking device turned off, revealing the shooter. The shooter was in full Thespian armor, with a blaster pointing in their direction. The shooter then took off the helmet, showing his smiling face to them, looking extremely satisfied with his shot.

"Salvador! You damn traitor!" Seleece screamed with rage while staring him dead in the eyes. The only thought running through her mind was vengeance. "Kill him now!" she screamed

loudly as everyone pointed their weapons directly at him.

"Now, now there…let's not be hasty!" Another voice said in

a soft, mocking tone. "I don't think it's in your best interest to

initiate a fight that you cannot win," the voice said, this time in a

more serious, threatening tone.

"Who's there? Show yourself! You are under military

arrest!" Seleece screamed while shifting her gaze around the room.

But there was no sign of her mysterious foe in sight. Her helmet

wasn't picking up any signs of life other than the alien behind her

and Salvador, so they were now at an even bigger disadvantage.

Whoever it was, it was now obvious to Seleece that they had planned

this ambush. They seemed to have the technology to nullify their

gears' capabilities, which was probably why they had not picked up

any signs of life until now. But now this mysterious being could

attack at any second. By the time they could figure out where the

shot had come from, half of her team could potentially be taken out.

Even worse, none of them knew just how many more were out there

in that room, staring at them ready to attack from within the shadows. The situation could not be worse for Seleece and her team, and they knew that very well.

"I said show yourself!" Seleece screamed out to her enemy.

"Or we will find you and eliminate you just like we are going to do to this damn human!" Lenduin exclaimed as he looked around, frantically searching for the source of the new voice.

"Well now, you would fail your mission then wouldn't you?" the voice exclaimed. He removed his cloak and revealed his identity to the group. They couldn't believe their eyes.

They didn't want to believe it, but it was impossible to deny. The being standing before them was none other than Melthuron himself standing next to Salvador with a warm smile.

"Me...Melthuron?" Seleece asked, uncloaking herself and taking off her helmet. She stared at him in complete disbelief. There was no doubt it was him; the resemblance was uncanny. He was a shorter Thespian, about six foot two, with light green skin and long, red hair that was pulled back into a pony tail. He was wearing a long, badly stained white lab coat that appeared to have not been washed in a long time.

"Ah!" Melthuron exclaimed joyfully, his smile widening. "You must be Seleece!" he exclaimed.

Seleece could only stare back as he continued. "I am so pleased that such a famous soldier like yourself could join me aboard my ship! As I'm sure you have earlier witnessed, I tried to tidy up a bit before your arrival. It was just such a mess. You see, I've never been much of an immaculate guy," he said as he walked closer to them.

"His ship?" she thought to herself, trying to figure out what was going on. Nothing was making sense.

"Mr. Prime Consort, sir, we have come to—"

"Silence, soldier!" he screamed at Lenduin angrily.

Melthuron now stood just a couple of feet away from Seleece, admiring her. She stood a full two feet taller than him, towering over the six-foot-two Thespian, but feeling felt powerless in his presence. "Oh my! Magnificent! What a fine product of genetic engineering…don't you agree, Mr. Salvador?" Melthuron asked without taking his eyes off of her.

"I guess," Salvador responded in an unenthusiastic tone without shifting his gaze from them, his blaster still pointed in their direction.

"Ah, why do I ask you anyway? You're just a small-brained lackey! You're not a scientist…but I digress. Welcome, all, to my ship!" he said. "Now, if you would all be so kind as to get away from the container and hand over all your weapons, we can continue to have a nice day together…how does that sound?" Melthuron concluded while smiling, eagerly awaiting their response.

But with their weapons still raised, they chose instead to remain still, staring them down both down with their fingers ready at the trigger.

Seleece stared at Salvador and then shifted to Melthuron; her hands firmly clenched the short-ranger blaster. She was ready to shoot either of them at any moment. She proceeded to reply in a loud tone, with a stare as cold as ice, "Tell us what you are doing here, Mr. Prime Consort, and why you are working with a human." She was hoping that talking could buy them some time. But Melthuron grew furious with her questions, clearly insulted by her defiance.

"You will do as you are told, you lowly soldier! Do you have any idea who you are talking to?" he raged before snapping his fingers.

The situation was now much, much worse. They were now completely surrounded. Dozens of robots became visible, all pointing their weapons directly at them. The sheer number of them was too overwhelming; they would have no chance of coming out alive if a battle were to break out at that moment. They would be killed in a matter of seconds, and the mission would fail.

Melthuron then let out a small laugh. As quickly as his laugh began, it ended, and he became serious. "I do not work with a human. That implies he is an equal in some way. He works for me!" he said while signaling them to hand over their weapons. "I've been told I'm a patient being, but I've never liked to repeat myself," he said to them.

Caal'dor and Lenduin just stared at them, waiting for Seleece's order.

Having no other viable options left, she unwillingly lowered her weapon slowly as she stared at Melthuron with disbelief.

"Damn it, damn it all!" Caal'dor screamed as he lowered his weapon after her. Lenduin followed, stubbornly tossing his weapon a few feet in front of them.

Melthuron clapped his hands at them, happy to see them comply. "There we go! Don't you all feel more relaxed now? There was just so much tension in this room! Weapons make me feel so…uneasy," Melthuron taunted them as he walked toward the room's exit.

Seleece was now staring around the room. Time seemed to slow for her while she breathed in, slowly trying to calm herself and focus her mind in an attempt to calculate her next move. After what seemed like a brief second, she was ready. She looked at Melthuron while he was walking away, and said in a calm tone, "We have done as you asked, Melthuron. Could you at least enlighten us by explaining why you are here?" She tried to sound hopeless, to make it sound as if they were defeated. Getting him to talk could perhaps provide more information about what was going on.

Melthuron turned to face her, grinning. "I don't see a point in explaining something so complex to such simple minds," he responded condescendingly. "No! You know what? I will enlighten you all with one detail. All of this was according to my plans," he said. Melthuron stopped for a moment to admire the alien in the tank. His eyes grew bigger as he let out two small, chilling whispers. "Just like him"—he pointed to the alien in the tank—"you are all mine now."

"All…all yours?" Caal'dor responded, his voice shaking as he wondered what horrible things would be done them.

"Yes, well I don't like spoiling good surprises! But I promise you this: you will not have to wait long to find out," Melthuron responded. "I hope you are not under the illusion that you successfully boarded my ship without me enabling you to do so, or that you got this far without me knowing every step you took."

"You did manage to arrive at this room, which, frankly"—he paused briefly as he quickly glanced at the container—"I didn't intend you to find!" He looked directly at Seleece. "But leave it to Seleece to surprise me! You have lived up to your reputation as a calculating soldier," he said, halfheartedly praising Seleece for her efforts. "But do not be concerned, everyone. Your discovery of this room has only caused me minimal delay. My experiments shall continue as scheduled!" he said.

"So, he didn't intend for us to find this room," she thought to herself. "This must mean that alien is probably the cause of his disappearance. Melthuron had never been kidnapped in the first place. That must be why Salvador was so against us finding out about this room, because that alien thing was imprisoned here. But why? Why would he disappear without telling anyone where he went? Could he be purposely trying to stir up confrontations between the two species again?" she wondered as she stared at him.

Melthuron then turned around and began to walk away again. As he reached the door, he instructed Salvador calmly, "Anesthetize them and bring them to the lab. I have much work to do," he said in a low, sinister tone, sending chills down their spines.

"Very well, sir," Salvador responded as he took out a tranquilizer gun from his armor's back compartment.

As Salvador began walking toward them with the anesthesia ready in his hand, Seleece looked at Caal'dor with confidence burning in her eyes. "Do it now!" she screamed, hoping he knew what to do. He did. In flash, there was a loud explosion near the tank's control board. The bomb she had secretly placed close to it earlier while observing it blew it to pieces, completely destroying the device and breaking the cylindrical container along with the machine itself. Being aware of how strong the blast would be, she had skillfully placed it close enough to the machine to destroy it and make a hole in the ground as a means of escape, but far enough so that minimal damage would be done to the alien inside. If that alien was as important as she hypothesized, bringing him back to Kalduron safely was now as vital as it was to rescue Melthuron when the mission began. This was their only hope of escape, however slim the chance. She knew that even if she didn't make it, the others also had chance to escape and relay what had happened with their commander. With little time to act, Seleece screamed while sprinting toward the unconscious alien.

"Grab Melron, and let's get out of here now!"

Even with all the odds stacked against her, she had no choice but the gamble with this escape plan. She ran as fast as her legs allowed, dodging blasts quickly due to her amazing reflexes. As she drew closer to her target, she slid down the floor, avoiding a few more hits before reaching him, but it was too late. By the time she was close enough to grab him, Salvador managed to shoot a decisive blow with his blaster, sending her flying into some of the robots before colliding with the wall on the other side. This all happened in mere seconds, and by the time Seleece had taken that armor smashing blow, Melthuron had made it back the room.

"No!" Melthuron screamed loudly as he noticed the fiasco that had taken place in his absence. He looked terrified at the sight of his experiment being released. "How could you let this happen, you blundering idiot!" he screamed at Salvador violently. "Do not let my experiment wake up! Put it under anesthesia now, before it's too late!"

"Yes sir!" Salvador responded quickly as he ran toward the unconscious alien.

"And do not harm it! It is worth more than anything else in the entire universe!" Melthuron commanded as blasts were being fired from every direction.

Caal'dor and Lenduin were busy returning fire. While Lenduin had his force shield up, Melron was focusing his shots in the robots' direction. Salvador ran. He ran as fast as he could toward the unconscious alien. He was now standing right in front of it. He quickly kneeled down, turning the alien's body around to apply the anesthesia carefully on the alien's neck. Lenduin and Melron wanted to stop Salvador before it was too late, but they were taking too much fire; there was no chance for them to get a proper shot. Their shield wasn't going to last much longer. Salvador rushed to quickly find vein-like structure around the alien's neck to apply the anesthesia. But as his hand reached the alien's throat, its eyes opened.

The expressionless alien stared at Salvador, with its left hand clenched tightly around Salvador's wrist.

"Shit!" Salvador screamed as the alien stopped him. It easily overpowered him, stopping him dead in his tracks. As Salvador struggled in his attempt to put the alien down, the alien easily pushed him back and began to slowly get up. The alien was now standing up, staring back at Salvador; its white eyes were fixed on his face. It seemed to be a great deal stronger than Salvador was. As Salvador continued to struggle, the alien did not give an inch, but it seemed unwilling to harm him.

"Let me go, you damn…thing!" he screamed nervously as he struggled to free himself from the alien's iron grip.

The alien looked confused. It then looked around the room and noticed the battle that was taking place, but it seemed to struggle to make sense of it all.

"I said let me go!" Salvador shouted again before throwing a punch directed at the alien's face. As this struggle was taking place, Melthuron took out a tranquilizer syringe from his pocket and ran toward the alien, hoping he could stop him before it tried to escape. The alien effortlessly moved his head away from the punch. It then placed its right hand on Salvador's head. It looked as if it were getting ready to do something.

The alien's hand was huge. It engulfed Salvador's head completely, with its fingers locking place behind Salvador's face.

"What are you doing?" Salvador screamed nervously as he moved around, frantically trying to get loose from the alien's tight grip. Salvador grabbed the alien's arm and tried to push it off, but his efforts didn't faze the alien at all. It just stood there, completely expressionless as it held Salvador captive. The alien's cold, expressionless stare sent chills down Salvador's spine. But suddenly, the alien tilted its head back slightly. Its eyes slowly began to glow, emitting an almost blinding white light that overtook the entire room.

"Uh, what's this?" Melthuron asked as he stopped midsprint; he couldn't see anything. "Aaaaaaah! Noooooooooooooo!" Salvador screamed out in pain as the alien's eyes continued to glow brighter and brighter. The light was getting stronger and stronger until suddenly, the alien let go, and Salvador fell to the floor, unconscious. The alien's eyes quickly returned to normal.

"You are mine!" Melthuron screamed enthusiastically as he leaped at it from behind, his hand almost reaching the alien's throat. But it was too late. Before the syringe could pierce the alien's skin and inject the crippling anesthesia, the alien disappeared before Melthuron's eyes. Melthuron then proceeded to collide with Salvador's unconscious body, slamming Salvador and himself into the ground from the force of the jump.

The alien moved extremely fast. It appeared in front of Seleece almost instantly after Melthuron's jump. In fact, it moved so fast, that not even the robot's sensors could pick up his movement. It was almost as if he did not move at all, but rather appeared somewhere else. It took the robots a few milliseconds after it appeared to process where it had gone. The alien glanced at her quickly, observing her as it placed its right hand on her shoulder. The robots quickly aimed their weapons at them.

Melthuron could be heard screaming desperately from a short distance. "Stop it at all costs; do not let it escape!" he screamed as loud as he could, nervously looking at his experiment. The robots quickly followed their master's orders, taking aim and firing relentlessly at them with full power. However, the alien's speed was so great that right before their blasts could hit it from even that short of a distance, it disappeared, taking Seleece along with it.

Chapter 3

Seleece was waking up. She slowly opened her eyes, and what she saw surprised her. "What! Where am I?" she said out loud, still rattled by the battle that took place in what seemed like just moments ago. It seemed they had traveled a great distance away from the ship somehow. A beautiful, clear blue sky was staring back at her, and there was a feeling of grass gently caressing her neck. As she began to slowly sit up, she felt a sharp pain in her abdomen from the blast she had taken, stopping her from being able to stand up.

"Ow...damn that really hurts," she said while trying to ignore the pain. She placed her hand where it hurt; trying to get a feel for the damage she had taken. It seemed she had a few broken bones and maybe some internal bleeding, but her enhanced genetic makeup made it possible to could feel less pain than normal Thespians, which made it easy for her to ignore what would otherwise be intolerable pain. Luckily for her, it seemed the wound wasn't fatal, and with prompt medical attention she would probably be back to normal in no time. She wouldn't know for sure until she was medically evaluated. The armor had done a good job of protecting her; without it she would have surely been killed by the strong blast.

However, her armor had been severely damaged along with any recordings of what had taken place on Melthuron's ship. She had no hard evidence of what happened. As she tried to figure out where she was, the alien appeared in front of her, staring at her. She was taken by surprise by the alien's sudden appearance, instinctively trying to reach for a weapon but had none to use.

"Who are you?" she asked, emotionally and physically drained from everything that happened.

The alien's only response was a blank stare. It then kneeled down in front of her, overlooking Seleece's wounded area.

"Who…just what are you?" she asked, getting nervous as the alien continued to stare at her with a blank expression. The alien looked at her before uttering a few words that she couldn't make out. Maybe it was another language, but she had never heard anything like it before. The alien attempted to communicate with her again, but was unable to say something that she could understand.

Rather than trying to communicate again, the alien placed its right hand on her head just like he had previously done to Salvador, and his eyes began to glow, emitting the same blinding light once more.

"What are you doing?" she exclaimed. Seleece was scared but unable to fight back due to her injuries. There was little she could do. This time, however, the alien did not hurt who it was touching. Instead, it seemed as if it were trying to get a feel for her wounds. Seleece felt a small pain throughout her body, but strangely enough, she didn't feel like it was attempting to hurt her. She felt complete calmness for a brief second before the alien moved its hand away. It then placed its hand on her head just like it had done with Salvador, but she wasn't scared. She couldn't explain it, but the alien's presence actually made her feel calm.

"Apologies provided," the alien said with a very strange accent before moving its hand away.

She looked at him somewhat confused, although she understood what the alien was trying to say.

The alien was now squinting at her. It looked as if it were trying hard to do something.

"I think you mean 'my apologies,'" Seleece said with a feeling of relief. For reasons she couldn't explain, she didn't feel like the alien was going to harm her; it was as if the alien had communicated with its feelings, or with its mind while it had touched her.

"Yes, I do apologize for the confusion you are now experiencing," the alien said. "Never in my existence have I spoken what you call this…Universal language," the alien explained.

She found this odd, because Universal was the language spoken by most of the intelligent species in her galaxy. It was developed hundreds of years ago in an attempt to make communication easier between different planets after they had come together to form what was now the Intergalactic Alliance. Although she had never seen an alien like this one before, it was not rare for new species from other planets to join the alliance.

"Never?" she questioned. "Then how come you seem to know it? Even if you sound weird when you speak it, it's quite clear that you have learned it. Everyone knows Universal in this galaxy. It's the law," she said.

"I do apologize. It took me a moment to reorganize this brain in a way that enabled me to speak this—"

"Where are we? What happened to my crew? And how long have I been unconscious?" she asked swiftly, quickly interrupting the alien.

"This is my favorite planet from your galaxy; it's the small fraction of this universe I could take us to under such circumstances," the alien said. The alien's voice was almost robotic in nature. It displayed no emotion; its face had no expression whatsoever. "It's of great curiosity to me that this was the only place I was tied to. To answer your question, it has been thirty of your minutes since we arrived here."

This answer only made Seleece more confused. Even though this alien was now speaking Universal fluently, what it was saying made her feel as if it were still speaking a different language. "What is it talking about?" she thought to herself, wondering if this alien was crazy. "Yes, but where are we? What happened back at the ship!" she exclaimed in frustration while thinking of her crew, the mission, and the position she was now in.

"Yes, my apologies again," the alien said in a soft, monotone voice. "According to your memories, you refer to this planet as CB19."

Her jaw dropped. That was simply impossible; it couldn't be true. "That can't be true...stop lying," she responded. She was dumbfounded, completely taken by surprise by that answer.

"I do not lie. I have never lied," the alien responded.

"Well, you're lying now! How can what you say even be possible? This planet is light years away from where we were! There is absolutely no way we made it all the way here in thirty minutes," she responded.

"You are correct. It didn't take us thirty minutes to get here. We have been here for thirty minutes," the alien responded.

The alien had to be messing with her. CB19 was a planet located just outside her solar system, about ten light years away from Demora. It was simply physically impossible for them to be there. It would have taken days to reach it from Melthuron's ship. More importantly, there wasn't even a ship around as far as her eyes could see, unless the alien had hidden it somewhere.

"It has to be wrong or lying," she thought to herself. "OK then, if we are where you say we are, how did we get here then? Where is your ship?" she asked.

"Yes, I will provide an explanation. But first, let's remedy your physical state. It seems your body has sustained tissue damage along with broken bones," the alien said as it placed his left hand on her wounded stomach once more. Its eyes began glow again. Soon after, she felt a strong, but deeply relieving feeling sink into her wounded area.

The alien was healing her, and Seleece couldn't believe it. She felt better and better with each passing second. Until that very moment, this had been unheard of. There had never been any life form capable of doing something like that, at least any life form that had been discovered so far. "How can anyone be able to do something like this? Not even the best technology in the galaxy could do this so quickly and efficiently," she thought. It truly was amazing; a few seconds was all it took. When the alien was done, she was able to stand up without any pain

"It will require a couple of hours for your body to revert to its original state, but you should be able to move with minimal pain now. Your body won't have any trouble," the alien said.

"What have you done to me?" Seleece asked, her face expressing gratitude.

"Do not fear," the alien responded, unable to understand the smile she was giving him. "In simple terms, I have used some of my energy to boost the rate at which your body heals."

"Thank you…that's…that's amazing," she responded. It was now quite obvious why Melthuron was being so careful with the alien earlier; it was powerful. Seleece couldn't let this being fall into the wrong hands. With this in mind, she was ready to figure out what to do next.

"Now please tell me what happened back at the ship. How did we get here and where are the others?" she asked. Seleece needed good news. She was hoping the answers the alien provided would give her the break she so desperately needed. But the alien looked back at her as expressionless as ever as it began to explain what had happened.

"I gained consciousness in this body right before the being you called Salvador attempted to take it away from me once more," the alien said.

"Wait…what do you mean 'in this body'? What are you talking about?" she asked. The more the alien spoke, the more confusing the situation became. "Yes, this is not my body," the alien responded calmly. If it was true, it was as if that situation didn't bother it one bit. It was just as emotionless about that notion as everything else it had talked about so far.

"I assume from Salvador's memories the one you call Melthuron has placed me in it somehow, although I am not sure how anyone of your kind would know how to do so." The alien stopped for a moment, placing its hands in front of his face as to observe them. It closed its hands and then opened them again, as if it were trying to get a feel for them. It almost looked as if it weren't familiar with them. It just stared at them. "This body seems to hold me well, although we are not in complete sync yet. Its limitations are still unknown to me."

"In sync? This body? What is it talking about?" she thought to herself, beginning to question this alien's sanity. Perhaps it had been brainwashed by Melthuron, or perhaps it had gone insane from captivity. Who knows how long it had been in there, being experimented on. Whatever the reason, it was still a powerful species of alien. Gaining its trust and having it as an ally was a must for Seleece under these conditions.

"I'm diverging from the main point. I apologize once more," the alien continued, interrupting her thoughts. "As I searched Salvador's mind, I discovered that you had been previously shot by Melthuron's machines, so I teleported to you and took us both away from that place before they harmed both of us further."

"Teleported? Wait, what about Melron, Caal'dor, and Lenduin? What happened to my crew?" she asked with great concern.

The alien stared blankly, showing no emotion as it gave her the devastating news. "I cannot say with certainty what has become of them. I took us here right before they had chance to cause you or me further harm. However, I am positive I witnessed them taking heavy fire before I brought us here. Their souls have most probably left their corporeal bodies."

Seleece knew what the alien meant by that, but she was hoping to hear something else; anything else. "What do you mean by that?" she asked him while trying to seem calm.

"According to your memories, you call this death," the alien responded.

She dropped to her knees. "No! No! No! No! No!" she screamed out in great pain. To her, those guys were family. They were like her younger brothers. They had served more than one hundred years together, saving one another numerous times. They had always been together. Her crew was all she had, all she knew. The news devastated her. For the first time in more than fifty years she couldn't contain her pain. She clenched her fists. Tears began to flow down her green cheeks. "Damn it!" Damn it all!" she screamed, relentlessly pounding the ground in a frenzy as tears continued to stream down her face.

She didn't stop. She continued to punch the ground, crushing the grass and pulverizing rocks that stood in her way; her fists growing bloodier with each blow. But she couldn't feel any physical pain. At that moment, the only thing she felt was grief. The only family she ever had was dead. The alien just stared at her, showing no emotion as she used the ground to cope with her loss. She then stopped for a moment, staring at the crushed grass and broken rocks underneath her face.

She breathed in, grief stricken, and said in a whisper, "I failed the mission, I failed my brothers, I failed everyone." For a moment, everything stopped. Her mind drifted to another place and time, the time before the mission started. "We will find him!" she had said to them, confident. "They always followed my lead," she thought. "I won't let their sacrifice be in vain. Melthuron…you will pay for this!" she screamed as she stood up, making up her mind.

"We are going back there right now," she said in a strong, commanding voice. "I will bring Melthuron back with me even if he's half-dead. He will pay for his crimes," she said with rage in her voice, but sadness in her heart.

"No," the alien responded.

She looked at him with resentment in her eyes. "No? What the HELL do you mean by 'no'?" she lashed out, enraged by the alien's response.

The alien only stared back, saying nothing in return. If what the alien said was true, she needed it to get off that planet right away. She would have to reason with it.

"Melthuron caged you, ran experiments on you, and you don't want him to pay for what he has done to you? To me? To my crew?" she asked as she stared at its bright white eyes. The alien didn't seem to care; it only stared back as indifferent as ever.

"Because of him, our government, our society could be at the brink of war. My species is being blamed for his disappearance. Hatred between Thespians is resurfacing," she paused to look at him in the eye, hoping to change his mind. "You and I, we can make this right. Please help me get to Melthuron's ship," she pleaded sincerely.

The alien only stared back looking unconvinced, then responded off topic, "All of these events have never happened before. I am just quite curious about why; I want to understand it."

"This isn't going anywhere," she thought to herself.

"This alien continues to talk nonsense, but if it was able to get me here, it can get me back to the ship. I just need to convince it somehow." She thought for a moment, trying her best to figure just how to do it. Perhaps taking a different approach would yield better results. "Yes," she thought.

"Well, you said you were imprisoned in this body. Don't you want to figure out how to get out of it? Perhaps the answer lies in Melthuron's ship?" Seleece said to him, attempting to convince the alien once more. "If you help me get there and search the ship, we can also try to figure out how to get you out of that body. We can find your original body. If he has placed you in this body, then surely he knows how to reverse process."

The alien stared off for a moment, perhaps thinking about what she said. "Yes, I have hypothesized that very notion already," the alien said. "However, if I am killed in this body, I don't know what will happen to me. Since my soul has never been in a corporeal body before, it could undergo the same process as all other souls go through in the universe."

The alien still made no sense to her. Souls, bodies, it was all nonsense. Whether it was brainwashed to think these ideas or it had gone mad from captivity, it didn't matter at all. Seleece had no choice. She was stuck on this planet, light years away from Demora, from Melthuron's ship, and the headquarters. This strange alien before her was her ticket out of there, and she had to convince him under any means necessary.

"You have a greater chance of success if I help you," she said. "Let's help each other out. If you take me to Melthuron's ship, I will help you," she concluded, trying to sound sincere. She had no intention of indulging the alien's crazy ideas, but perhaps she could still use it to her advantage.

"Yes, perhaps that is true," the alien said in a monotone voice. "What course of action do you propose?" said it asked, placing its trust in her.

"Yes!" she thought to herself, eager to leave this planet.

"How did you get us here from the ship so quickly? Can you

take us anywhere in the universe?" she asked, wondering just what this strange being was capable of.

"Hypothetically yes," the alien said before closing its eyes. "I can take us anywhere that feels natural to me in this body." The alien looked focused. "But I…I do not yet grasp the reason why I am incapable of doing it," the alien responded.

Why would it be incapable of doing it? She thought to herself. That just didn't make sense. But then again, nothing made sense to Seleece at that point.

"Well, how did you get us here then?" she asked, questioning whether or not this alien could actually teleport like it had claimed. Why could it be able take them to this desolate, faraway planet, but not anywhere else?

"That is the question," it replied. "That is the question?"

"What? Stop wasting time!" she responded. The alien almost seemed surprised by her outburst. It clearly didn't understand what was at stake, or it didn't care, it just continued to stare at her.

"Yes, yes, I understand now," it said, repeating itself over and over again. "Perhaps there is a way I can do it, but I require your help. Well, not *your* help in particular. Really, anyone could—"

"What is it? What can I do?" she swiftly interrupted. "I have no crazy abilities; I don't see how I could—"

It placed his hand on her head, and began to take deep breaths as it closed his eyes. "It seems that if I want to do anything while stuck in this body, it must feel natural to me. I have not yet grasped why. I need you to think of our destination. I need to feel it, be familiar with it, and connect with it," the alien said. But this time it was sure. Seleece was ready to do anything.

"Perhaps this will actually work. It just seems as crazy as everything else," she thought.

"It will," the alien responded.

"You can hear my thoughts?" she thought, amazed again by what he was capable of doing.

"I don't hear them. We are bonded together right now, and I can feel them. You could feel mine as well if you learned how."

"Never mind that," she thought. "So I just need to think of our destination and you will get us there?"

"Yes," the alien replied.

"In that case, we should head to my home first to get some supplies. I need new weapons and armor, and you need some damn clothes," she thought.

"Very well, let's proceed," the alien said.

Seleece began to focus on what she had to do. "My home, my home…home," she thought, but nothing was happening. She thought about it again. "My home. I want us to go to my home." Still nothing. "Why didn't you take us there yet? I have been thinking about it just like you told me," she said, confused and frustrated. It was all starting to feel like nonsense once again.

The alien took a step back, removing its hand from her head before opening its eyes. "I will not be able to feel this place if you just tell yourself to go there. I need you to show me. I need you

visualize it and show me how it makes you feel when you are there,

what it's like to be there. Just share your feelings about this place,"

the alien explained. "If you can do that, I believe I can get us there.

But just repeating the words 'my home' in your mind does not seem

to give me what I require."

She looked back at the alien, annoyed. "Fine," she said,

grudgingly.

The alien stepped closer once more, placing its left hand on

her head before closing it eyes.

"My home," she said in her mind. She visualized what it

looked like. It was an apartment, on the fortieth floor of the building.

It was a very tall, black building, where many of the habitants were

also of military background, or families of deceased veterans. It also

housed the very politicians she was sworn to protect. It was close to

the capital, where the majority of the population were actually from

the other species. The city itself was never friendly to her kind, but

her home was the only place where she did not feel the hate. Her building was closed off from the public; her apartment signified safety. She felt safe in her living room; at peace in her bedroom. She remembered reading her favorite books there and preparing her favorite meals in the kitchen. Her apartment was a home. It was a haven from the outside world.

"I understand you," the alien said to her. "Your apartment...your life in that city," it said. "Let's get you home," the alien said as they disappeared.

Chapter 4

"This must be the place you thought of," the alien said as it moved its hand away.

They were now inside of her apartment. When Seleece opened her eyes, she couldn't believe it. It had actually worked. Her apartment was just as she had left it before the mission; nothing seemed out of place.

"I don't believe it! I can't believe it actually worked!" she said as she walked around the living room.

Her Serverbot picked up movement in the apartment and switched on, welcoming Seleece home. It was a silver-coated, personal server model robot with two arms; a small, sturdy body connected to a big wheel at the bottom, and a small head at the top. "Welcome home, master Seleece," the robot said at it rolled over to her. "How may I be of service?"

Seleece didn't respond. She was still amazed by what the alien was capable of doing. "I just can't believe it worked," she said. "You are really something else."

"How may I be of service," the robot repeated.

"Oh yes," she said, snapping back to the room. "We have no time to waste. Serverbot, fetch my guest here some clothes that fit, and be quick about it. I hope you don't mind feminine clothing," she said to the alien as she walked over to the home medical center.

"Yes, master Seleece," the robot said as a blue light emitted from its left eye, scanning the alien's body. "Would you please follow me, dear guest?" the robot asked as it rolled toward the bedroom.

While the alien followed the robot into Seleece's room on the left side of the apartment, she walked over to the home medical center located on the right side. She stopped near the wall, staring at the machine in front of her. "Activate medical center," Seleece said.

Shortly after, the voice recognition software recognized Seleece's voice and turned on. "Welcome back, Seleece. It has been five days since your last scan," the automated voice responded.

Wasting no time, Seleece commanded. "Medical center, proceed with full body scan."

"Scanning," the automated voice responded as a red light was projected onto her entire body, searching for anything out of the ordinary.

The floor under her began to rotate, allowing for a full body scan. After a full ten seconds, the body scan was completed. Briefly after, the screen on the wall displayed various stats including heart rate, different hormone levels, and other vitals.

"Abnormality detected in abdominal region," the automated voice pointed out as the other stats were zoomed out, replaced with a diagram of the selected area. "Out of the ordinary cellular reproduction detected in highlighted area, calling nearest medical center for further analysis."

"Override," Seleece said.

"Warning. It is advised to contact medical—"

"I said, override!" Seleece screamed at the medical center.

"Override successful," the voice said.

"That unusual cellular reproduction must be from the alien's abilities," she thought to herself. "I still can't believe what this thing is capable of doing. Just what was Melthuron doing on that ship with this strange life form? Healing, teleportation; just what else could this alien be capable of doing? At any rate, I can't just let it run loose," she thought. "It must be kept in check at all times."

However, all of that would have to wait. Seleece knew that she had little time to waste with such questions; she had to return to Melthuron's ship and complete the mission as quickly as possible.

"That bastard. He will pay for everything he has done," she vowed.

As she turned around, the Serverbot was coming out of the bedroom with the alien. "We currently have no clothing to fit our guest," the robot said to her.

"Is that so, Serverbot? All right, that's all for now, initiate shutdown," Seleece commanded the Serverbot.

"It has been a pleasure serving you," the robot replied, before shutting down.

"Let's get ready for our mission. Do you know how to shoot a weapon?" she asked the alien.

The alien just stared back with the same expressionless face. "I have never used a weapon before. I've never had the need to since I've never had a body before."

"Well, we are gonna have to change that," she responded.

Seleece still didn't believe it never had a body to begin with. How could that even be possible? If that was true, what would that even make it? It must have had a body; maybe this one was it. Although Seleece was not aware of any alien life form like this in this galaxy, perhaps it was possible that Melthuron had found him outside this galaxy somehow. Its memory must have been altered by Melthuron somehow. That was the only possibility she could come up with. Anything else just seemed too outrageous to even contemplate.

"You will be the only backup I'll have. I'm gonna have to teach you how to use our military gear," she said while analyzing every aspect of the alien's body. "It seems my armor could fit your body, but unless we try I won't know for sure. Follow me," she said as she walked toward her bedroom. As she walked closer to the transparent door, it automatically slid open, allowing them to enter. The alien followed quickly, also seeming eager to get started.

It was a big room, perhaps twice the size of her living room. The room was somewhat unkempt, with clothes scattered all over the bed. A large, holographic picture of herself hung on the wall that was directly parallel to her bed. It was taken ten years ago and showed her in full uniform, receiving a gold medal for her life-saving performance during the civil war. The Thespian awarding the medal was none of other than Kalduron himself.

Near her bed on a nightstand stood a small, holographic picture of Seleece and her group. Lenduin, Caal'dor, and Melron all stood together with her in full Thespian armor, with their helmets in their hands. As she glanced at it, she began to remember the first mission they had together. It was during the first years of the Thespian civil war, more than one hundred years ago. She stopped for a moment to glance at it. Her mind drifted away for a moment, remembering so many things that had happened that very day.

"I won't let your deaths be in vain," she vowed to herself.

"Seleece?" the alien said in its monotone voice. "May I ask what you are doing?"

"Nothing," she replied. She was too proud to show emotions again. The only thing on her mind was revenge. Melthuron would pay for his crimes.

"Let's see," she said. "Will this fit you? Try it on," she said as she began taking out pieces of armor from her armory and throwing them on her gigantic bed. As she took out a Thespian helmet, she looked at it and said, "I want you to try this on first. If it doesn't fit, then none of the other parts will matter much."

The alien picked it up quickly and observed it for a minute. It was an exact replica of the helmet she had been wearing before. However, the alien almost appeared somewhat confused by it.

"And what is it I am required to do with this?" the alien asked.

She was a little confused. "Does it really not know what to do with a helmet?" she thought. "Don't you know anything?" she said while making fun of the alien. Had this thing never seen a helmet before? How could a being with such amazing abilities not know basic things like what a helmet was?

With little time to waste, she quickly picked up another helmet to show him what to do. "Place it on your head like this," she said while putting her own helmet on. The alien looked at her for a moment before saying, "Very well," and attempted to do the same.

It seemed to fit the alien just fine. Hopefully, it would have an easy time learning how to use it.

"Ah, it fits! Great!" Seleece exclaimed. "Now comes the hard part," she said as she took a deep breath, seeming a little stressed out by what was coming next. She was going to have to teach another non-Thespian how to use this equipment. Salvador had managed to learn the basics, but maybe she wouldn't be as lucky this time. Perhaps Salvador was already familiar with the technology before Seleece attempted to teach him. "Yes that makes sense, that's probably why he was able to learn it so quickly," she thought. But as long as it took, she had no choice but to teach him how to use it.

"I'm going to have to show you how to use it. It might take a while, but we have no choice," she said. "We can't have you getting shot or killed or captured again now can we," she teased.

The alien didn't respond. "May I touch your head again?" it asked.

"What? Why?" Seleece responded a little confused. "We are not ready to leave yet; we still have a lot of work to do before we go."

"No, that is not the reason why," the alien responded. "I do not require lessons to learn such information. If you recall, I am able to learn such information from memories. If you let me feel your memories, they will become part of me and I will learn whichever knowledge you require," the alien explained. "That will also hold true for your previous question regarding what you call guns."

"Why, how clever you are. I wish I could do that," she said with a hint of envy. "All right then, tell me what to do," she said.

The alien walked up to her, placing its right hand gently on her head. "Be at peace," the alien said. "Close your eyes and begin to remember everything you want me to learn. Picture it in your mind, remember how you felt when you yourself were attempting to learn this," the alien said.

She did as instructed, closing her eyes and focusing on the helmet. Seleece began remembering the first time she had tried one on, more than one hundred and fifty years ago. It was her first day at the military academy. She remembered Kalduron instructing her on how to use a helmet.

"Put it on and think of the interface. That will turn it on," Kalduron had said to her all those years ago. First, she pictured the interface in her head, and then remembered all the commands she had first learned. She remembered how frustrating it was to get the helmet to do what was required, and remembered how frustrating it was when she couldn't get it to turn on the cloaking device. "That was really annoying," she thought.

Her mind then shifted to the first mission she ever had. Caal'dor, Lenduin, and Melron were with her, standing outside the enemy weapons facility. It was during the first year of great Thespian civil war and their mission was to sabotage the production of weapons, armor, and enemy robot soldiers. Back then she was just a newcomer, and her old commander stood in front her. She remembered how he communicated his orders to her through the helmet, telling her and the others that deadly force was authorized.

She stopped for a moment, opening her eyes. "Was that enough?" Seleece asked as she moved the alien's hand from her head. She didn't want to remember that mission. She just wanted to forget about it and everything that had happened that day so long ago. "Well, was it enough?" she asked, frustrated.

"I believe I understand," the alien said as it opened its eyes. "But, Seleece, perhaps you should—"

"Just grab a helmet and turn it on," she interrupted, trying to avoid whatever the alien was going to bring up.

For the first time, the alien seemed to understand what she was thinking and how she was feeling. Instead of asking further questions, the alien proceeded to pick up the helmet and placed it on its head, using what Seleece remembered to turn it on. The display inside the helmet worked just like the memories had shown. The alien seemed to feel quite familiar with it.

"Do you understand how it works? Did I provide you with everything you need?" Seleece asked, hoping she would not have to start remembering anything else.

"It would seem to be the case," the alien responded as it took of the helmet. "Yes. Everything looks and feels quite…familiar," the alien said in its monotone voice before placing the helmet down on a table. "What else do you require me to learn?"

But it was as if she were no longer there. The alien's words were lost in a cloud of thoughts as she began to think about this upcoming mission. After remembering that mission all those years ago, she was hoping this time it would turn out differently.

"Seleece," the alien said as it placed his hand on her shoulder.

"What?" she replied as her mind drifted back into the room.

"What else do you need me to learn?" it asked once again.

"Oh yes," she said distracted.

Even the alien could tell she was not well. Not only was she reminded of a mission that she did not want to remember, but the stress of this mission was also beginning to take a toll on her. She was distracted, nervous, on edge.

"Now I just have to teach you how to shoot properly," she said trying to shake it off like she was fine.

But she wasn't. As soon as the alien placed its hand on her head, the feelings she was desperately trying to hide began to flood the alien's mind. The alien was struggling to feel her memories. What Seleece was trying to show the alien was clouded by a fog of emotions that the alien could not filter out.

"Seleece, you must focus. All I am able to feel are your—"

"Shut up!" she screamed as she violently pushed his hand away from her. She knew what the alien was going to say. She desperately wanted to hide it, to forget about it. This mission came first. "Forget it! Just take me to the ship," she replied.

"Are you sure about this?" the alien asked.

She didn't respond. Instead, she walked to where she had placed the armor and picked up the black chest piece.

"Here, try this on," she said in a calmer tone while looking away. "You put it on like this," she said as she showed him what to do.

She easily picked up the chest piece from the floor, making it look like it weighed nothing. It was made out of a very strong metal alloy that was found only on Demora. This metal alloy was five times as strong as titanium but lighter than aluminum. Armor like this had saved her and her crew numerous times in the past, but without the helmet it was nothing more than a way to avoid a quick death. The helmet was linked to all the other pieces of armor, giving the user swift mind control over all of the armor's functions.

The alien picked up a chest piece from the floor, trying to fit it around its body like Seleece had demonstrated, but it didn't fit.

"I cannot get it around the contour of this upper body," it said as it continued to struggle with it.

She was afraid of that. Although the alien only had about half a foot on her, the alien's shoulders were much bulkier than hers. It wasn't going to fit.

"Damn," she said. "I guess you will just have to be extra careful. Don't get shot," she said with a frustrated voice as she started putting on her gear.

"Perhaps that is for the best," the alien responded. "I do not wish to use your weapons or cause any souls damage in this universe. Let's just proceed with the goal at hand," the alien said.

"Here, at least take this," she said as she tossed him what appeared to be a small microchip. It was quite small, but the alien had no problem catching it. "You may not be able to use the armor for protection, but this device will still render you invisible to the naked eye," she said while the alien observed it. "It's an older-model cloaking system, but it does not need the armor in order to work," she said. "Just place it on your shoulder and let it scan your body."

"Like this?" the alien said while placing it directly on its shoulder. The small microchip attached itself to his shoulder and turned on, emitting a blue light that scanned its whole body.

"Just touch it to turn it on and off," she said. "It's better than nothing. I am taking a guess here, but the only reason we were able to be detected by Melthuron was because of that traitor Salvador. He must have rigged our gear before we deployed somehow," Seleece explained. "But this time my armor won't be linked to their technology. We should go undetected," she said.

"Let's go over the plan," she said as she picked up the most powerful gun in her collection, the C1 blaster. It was a rather small gun when compared to the standard blaster, but it actually packed twice the power. It could easily blow a hole through most reinforced walls. Aside from Melthuron, anyone else whom she found in that ship would meet their death. She was growing more and more infatuated with the thought of revenge. Handing down her own form of justice was all she could think about. She placed the weapon on her back, which was magnetically held by her armor. She then proceeded to grab stationary bombs and grenades and placed them inside her armor in one of the small back compartments. Before she closed it, she peeked inside one last time to make sure she wasn't forgetting anything. Something caught her eye.

"I can't forget this," she said as she picked up the last remaining piece of gear. It was her favorite weapon enhancement:

the electroglove. She quickly attached it to her right hand. She flashed a wicked smile at the thought of using it on Melthuron.

"I will bring him back alive, but I will enact my own form of punishment first. For their sake," she thought to herself. "He will not escape me this time. The next time we meet will be the last," she said as she walked up to the alien, ready to discuss the plan.

"First off, which part of that ship can you teleport us to?" she asked. She remembered the layout of that ship very well from Kalduron's briefing.

"Any location within that ship is an acceptable location," the alien responded. "Yes, I feel it," the alien said as it focused.

"Huh? Feel what?" she asked.

"The spaceship. I feel all of its molecules. It seems I am able to teleport to anywhere that my energy has been attached to. In short, anywhere on that ship will be fine," the alien concluded.

"So if I can just visualize the exact room where I would like for us to go, can you make it happen?" she asked.

"Yes," the alien responded.

This was great news to her. If they could go anywhere on that ship, the control room would be the best location to start. If they started there, they could turn off all security systems, kill the lights in the whole ship, and search the ship in a much safer way.

"Yes, that is the best course of action," she thought to herself. But suddenly, something else crossed her mind. What if they could teleport to exactly where Melthuron was? Teleport to the exact room, perhaps right behind him.

"Wait, can you sense Melthuron in that ship? Can you teleport us exactly where he is?" she asked the alien, hoping it could be done. If the alien was able to do that, they could just attack him right away with a surprise assault; he wouldn't know what hit him.

"I am unable to complete such a task under these conditions," the alien responded.

Seleece was frustrated to hear this. "And why not?" she asked impatiently.

"It is technically quite possible, but my ties to the universe are greatly diminished by being stuck in this body," it said.

"Again with this nonsense. No, Seleece. Now is not the time," she thought.

"But why…why can you teleport to place but not to a living being? I just don't understand…just try it!" she exclaimed in frustration.

But it wasn't possible. The alien just stood there, confused by her outburst. "I cannot do it under these circumstances," the alien repeated once again. "It is out of the question at this time."

Seleece was very disappointed. This could have made her mission much safer and much faster. "Well then, how many times can you use this ability?" she asked.

In order to use the alien in the most optimal way, she needed to know exactly how its abilities worked. "If you can take us one room at a time, we can avoid having to move around. This will limit the chances of being detected," she explained.

The alien didn't respond at first. Instead, it seemed preoccupied with something else. It looked at its hands for a moment, placing them in front of its face as if it were pondering something. The alien's face was still expressionless, so she couldn't tell what it was thinking.

"I regret to say that I cannot accurately answer that question at this time," the alien said. "I do not yet know the limits of this body. We may be able to attempt that, but I do not know how far this body will let me go," the alien said with a calm tone "I will never know the limits of this body unless I test its boundaries more. But I believe it to be possible," the alien said, this time sounding a bit more confident.

Seleece was pleased. "Well, all right then! We are getting somewhere!" she said enthusiastically.

"But we have not moved yet," the alien responded.

"That's not what I…never mind. Our plan will be as follows: First, we will go to the control room. From there I will disable all of the ship's security systems. Afterward, you will teleport us from room to room until we find Melthuron, providing you are able to take us room to room. If you can't, then I guess we will have to do it the old fashioned way. Once we find Melthuron," Seleece paused.

"Once we find him," the alien said.

"Once we find him, we…we will bring him back to Kalduron and the mission will be completed," she said as she thought of them. It sounded like a good plan, but the alien did not seem to agree.

"I will not allow you to have him until I have figured out how he has placed me in this body and how to reverse it," the alien responded with a calm tone.

"I promise you we will figure that out. But first we will have to—"

"You shall not have him until that is done!" the alien said as its eyes began to glow a menacing white. The alien was not messing around; it was serious. It had no intention of letting Seleece do whatever she wanted with Melthuron. "Are we in agreement?" the alien asked.

"But of course! You have yourself a deal," she responded without much hesitation. Seleece knew she had to tread carefully; she couldn't run the risk of losing her ticket to finding Melthuron. "We both want Melthuron. I believe we can come to an agreement. No need to get so worked up," she said, hoping the alien would believe her. "You can have him first. You can do whatever you need to do. But then he is mine," she said.

"Those are acceptable terms," the alien's said as its eyes dimmed.

"If you have gathered all of your equipment, let us proceed," the alien said as it placed its hand on Seleece's head before closing its eyes.

"All right, walk me through this," Seleece said as she closed her eyes, eager to get going.

The alien, however, remained silent for a moment; something wasn't right. "Is something wrong?" Seleece asked. Seleece was now very weary of the alien's abilities, especially the mind reading. She couldn't let it find out about her plan to double cross it, so she had tried her best not to think about it at all while they were connected. But perhaps she had failed; perhaps the alien had just found out. She had to keep calm.

"What do you need me to do?" she asked.

"It seems his ship has moved," the alien responded with his thoughts. "No, it hasn't just moved. It's currently traveling at an accelerated rate," the alien communicated telepathically as it continued to struggle.

It hadn't caught on to her plan; she was safe.

"But I can feel it. I should be able to take us there," the alien said out loud. "However, I will have to take us to the room from which we left first. It seems I cannot take us anywhere else while the ship is moving at its current speed. Once we are inside, however, I should be able to take us to the control room as planned," the alien concluded.

"All right, let's get going," she said before turning on her cloaking device.

The alien followed, using its other hand to turn on its cloaking device.

"I won't fail this time. You are mine!" she roared as they vanished from her apartment.

Chapter 5

When she opened her eyes, they were no longer staring at the wall of her apartment. The eerie look of the battle-torn room gave Seleece a familiar, uneasy feeling.

"We made it," she thought to herself as she took out the C1 from her back and stared toward the far end of the room. About twenty yards away stood the hole she had made with her bomb not even an hour ago. There was rubble all around the room.

"Good. It seems we have gone unnoticed so far," she thought. "Let's keep it that way." There was no sign of Melron, Lenduin, or Caal'dor anywhere in that room. Her helmet wasn't picking up any signs of movement either; they appeared to be alone.

"No one is here," she communicated telepathically. "All right, now take us to the control room," she communicated to him while thinking of what the control room looked like. "The control room should be something similar to this," she thought as she visualized a control room from a different ship.

"This is the control room from a ship of similar size and model. It should help you with what you need to get us there. Can you feel it?" she asked telepathically as she focused on picturing everything she could about that room. She visualized a room half the size of the one they were currently in. It had a wide rectangular window that let people see out into space, typical of every control room she had seen before. The control room would have to contain some sort of control panel. In the middle of the room they would probably find a circular, maybe rectangular hologram machine. That was the standard. This was often used when engaging in battle with other ships, as it had the capability to display other areas that would be critical while in battle.

"Yes, I am able to sense a room like that on this ship," the alien thought as its eyes began to glow.

"I will take us there now."

Before she could even reply, her gaze shifted to a new wall that was now just inches in front of her. They were now standing in the control room. The alien took its hand from her shoulder and opened its eyes. A big, reinforced glass window was standing right in front of it. Millions of starts could be seen in every direction, moving away from them as the ship continued to travel to its destination. They were lucky; the room was empty. Seleece had expected someone to be in the control room overlooking the ship's trajectory, but there was nobody in sight. It seemed logical to conclude that the ship was on autopilot.

"Let's see where this ship is headed," she thought as she walked toward the control panel.

"And where the hell is everyone again?" she anxiously thought as the same eerie feeling began crept into her mind. Her gaze shifted to the left side of the room where a map was showed the destination of the ship along with an estimated flight time. "So according to this map, this ship is traveling toward…Earth?" It was surprising at first. However, it was now obvious to her that Salvador wasn't the only human who worked with Melthuron.

"Well, Melthuron has been working with the humans, so this is not surprising. The real question is why. Why are they working together? What is Melthuron's purpose?" she pondered as the ship continued onward. There could be hundreds of different reasons why Melthuron could be doing this. None could be ruled out, but Seleece knew that it wasn't the time to ponder such questions. With little time to waste, she walked up to her ally and pointed to her shoulder, signaling it to communicate telepathically. The alien quickly placed its hand on her shoulder, linking them together.

"I will now disable the security systems," she said telepathically. "Once that is done, we can begin searching room by room as we have planned."

"Very well," the alien responded. "But do not forget our agreement. You will not take him until I am done."

"Don't be so concerned. He is yours to do with as you wish. He will answer for all his crimes, especially the ones committed toward you," she quickly responded. She walked up to the control panel on the left side and turned off all of the security systems.

"Security systems now offline," the main computer said in Universal.

"Yes! All right," she thought. "Let's get to it."

The alien appeared behind her, placing its hand on her shoulder. "Which room first, Seleece?" the alien said telepathically.

Seleece vividly remembered what Melthuron had said: "Anesthetize them and bring them to the lab."

"Melthuron had spoken about a lab. You should take us there first," she responded as she turned on her electroglove. "If you want to find out what Melthuron has done to you, the answers you seek could potentially be hidden away in his lab." She began to picture what she thought Melthuron's lab could look like. The room most probably had tanks just like the one the alien had been imprisoned in. That seemed to be the most logical piece of equipment Melthuron would have. After all, keeping the alien contained had been Melthuron's utmost priority based on what she had carefully gathered from their conversation. Seleece also knew it probably housed all sorts of machines, chemicals, and containers; a lab was never complete without them.

"A laboratory, yes I understand. I sense a room like that on this ship," the alien said as it focused. "Let's begin."

As fast as ever, they were now standing inside what seemed to be Melthuron's lab. It was a big room, perhaps twice the size of the control room. The walls were as white as the other rooms, with many different tables, glassware, and machines scattered throughout the place. As Seleece began to look around, the alien teleported itself toward the end of the room; something had caught its attention. There were four tanks, exactly like the one the alien had been imprisoned in. At first glance, they appeared to be empty. On closer inspection, however, the alien noticed some drops of liquid on the floor around each tank.

"What is the alien doing?" Seleece thought as she moved swiftly toward the alien.

The alien was standing completely still; it didn't make a single sound or movement.

"My helmet isn't picking up any movement in this room or any of the ones close to it," Seleece whispered as she looked at the tanks in front of them. "I think we should continue our search. There seems to be nothing useful here," she said as she placed her hand on the alien's shoulder, trying to get its attention.

"These tanks…they were once filled with liquid," the alien said.

"Liquid?" she asked. As far as her eyes could tell they were all empty. There seemed to be nothing inside of them at all.

"This one here," the alien said as it touched one of the tanks. "I can feel the leftover drops inside it."

Seleece quickly switched to thermal vision. The alien was right. She could see the temperature difference between the drops and the glass itself. Every tank, at one point in time, had been filled with some sort of liquid. The liquid was completely clear, just like the liquid in the tank that had contained him.

"Melthuron must have had some sort of experiments contained in these three containers. I believe the question is, what could it have been?" the alien said.

Seleece began to grow more concerned. "Could it be more aliens?" She thought.

"Perhaps Melthuron has captured more of your kind," Seleece responded with concern in her voice.

"That simply cannot be the case. I am the only one of my kind; none exist like me anywhere in the universe," the alien responded calmly.

But she didn't believe it. "How could that even be possible? There must be more of them," she thought to herself. To Seleece, the right question wasn't if they were out there, but whether or not Melthuron had more of them. Perhaps the alien was right, and Melthuron only had one. But she couldn't rule out the possibility of more aliens like this one. Maybe Melthuron was planning to use these experiments as weapons. And if so, for what purpose? After more than one hundred years, Demora had finally achieved peace.

Why would Melthuron create weapons now? Seleece planned to ask him personally.

"Well, whatever the case may be, whatever was in those containers is no longer here. We need to keep looking," she said.

What Melthuron was planning, whomever or whatever he had been experimented on, she knew she had to stop him.

"Yes, finding Melthuron is still our top priority," the alien responded. But its gaze remained locked on the containers; it was clearly thinking about something, perhaps analyzing something she had missed.

"Let's take a quick look around to see if we can find any useful Intel," she said.

But the alien continued to stand still.

"Alright…care to share what's on your mind?" she asked.

The alien remained silent.

"Fine. I'll start searching through everything on that lab bench over there," she said as she walked away.

As the alien remained still, Seleece began to turn that room inside out. She opened every box and searched every drawer. She found nothing worth examining. If there was ever anything important in that lab, it seemed Melthuron had taken it with him.

"There's nothing useful here," she said.

The alien didn't respond.

"Didn't you hear me? We need to go. We still have much more ground to cover," she said, frustrated.

Suddenly, her helmet's display lit up. "Something is moving outside this room," she thought. The alien also caught on. It quickly appeared next to her.

"I just felt movement outside of this room," the alien said telepathically.

"Yes! Take us outside this room…now!" she responded.

The alien quickly teleported them outside, placing them against the wall. There were two robots carrying boxes.

"Damn it!" Seleece thought in frustration. "Are you able to read memories from a robot?" she asked telepathically.

The alien thought about it for moment. "I do not believe so," the alien responded telepathically as the robots continued marching down the corridor. "I should be able to do it, but I don't know if I can do it at this moment in time," the alien responded telepathically.

"What? Why no—"

But suddenly she felt something. It was the alien's emotions. It was brief, almost as if it didn't happen. But at that very second she felt a slight sense of pain and confusion. It seemed the alien wasn't so heartless after all. The feelings quickly vanished, maybe because the alien didn't want her to know.

"I understand," she said telepathically.

The alien ignored her comment as it teleported them closer to the robots.

"I vow on my life that we will figure out what Melthuron has done to you. That I promise," she said telepathically.

The alien didn't respond. Its stare was fixed on the robots. The robots suddenly entered the docking room.

"Quick ta—"

But Seleece couldn't finish her sentence. The alien had teleported them inside.

"The docking room?" she thought as she remained vigilant. As her gaze began shift around, she saw a familiar face standing about thirty yards away. Seleece's rage bubbled to the surface. It was Salvador. He was helping the robots load some boxes into a crate.

"That traitor…he's mine!" she thought to herself as she pulled out the C1 blaster.

"Calm yourself," the alien said. "These…these feelings are clouding your judgment."

Seleece knew the alien was right, but she didn't care. "I'm going to kill him for what he did to my crew!" she screamed to herself as she took aim with her blaster. As her finger began to pull the trigger, the alien quickly stopped her.

"Wait! Do not harm him," the alien said telepathically as its eyes began to glow. "I will search his memories for any information about Melthuron. I need you to take care of the robots so I may do so without being interrupted," the alien concluded before disappearing.

She wasted no time. Within seconds, the robots had been blown to pieces by her C1's powerful blasts. Salvador was taken by complete surprise.

"What? Who's there?" Salvador screamed nervously as he took out a short range blaster and ran toward the end of the room, rattled by the powerful blasts.

"Well, well…I see you have no way to track our movements this time," Seleece said in a taunting voice as she remained hidden near the entrance of the room. "You are not wearing any armor…what an easy target!" she said as she let out a small laugh, enjoying the predicament he was in. "Finally, some justice will be served," she thought as she pointed her blaster at him.

"Show yourself!" Salvador screamed as he began shooting his blaster in the direction of her voice, frantically trying to pinpoint her location. It was a futile effort; all of his shots missed his invisible target.

Quickly after, the alien responded with a calm voice.

"Human, do not be alarmed. If you comply with my request, I will not let Seleece hurt you."

Salvador was shocked by that name. His expression shifted from surprised to scared. "What? Seleece? But how! She should be dead," Salvador said as he fired a shot, this time in the direction of the alien's voice, hoping he wouldn't miss this time. But the shot hit nothing but the wall, making a small hole. "You are bluffing! She should be dead! There's no way!" he screamed as he began to grow more nervous. The gun was shaking in his hand.

Seleece relished this moment, the moment she had been waiting for since his betrayal.

"You can't beat us! Lower your weapon now or I will kill you!" Seleece screamed back at him, enjoying their little exchange.

But Salvador was not about to comply. "Oh no, Seleece, I will find you!" he said as he began shooting around the room in every direction, hoping that he would hit at least one of them.

The alien, however, was completely unimpressed with their exchange. "That is quite enough," the alien said as it appeared in front of him. The alien grabbed Salvador's weapon. "I will not allow you to harm anyone here. I will now take this weapon away," the alien said as the weapon vanished out of Salvador's hand, disappearing from the room.

"What the hell?" Salvador said as the alien removed his its cloaking device, revealing himself. Salvador's face was now riddled with fear. The alien's white eyes seemed to stare deep into his soul. "It's…it's…it's you! Just what the hell are you?" he said in a shaky voice as he tried to step back, looking straight at him with fear.

"Do what it says or I will keep the promise I made to you back at the ship," she said as she removed her cloaking device, her gun pointed straight at him.

"No…no! I won't allow you to get in my head again!" Salvador screamed as he tried to run into the docked ship to escape. But he couldn't make it; the alien was too fast. The alien quickly appeared in front of the door, blocking the ship's entrance.

"I apologize for this, but you really only have one option. Please comply and no harm will come to you," the alien said, striking even more fear into Salvador's heart.

"No!" Salvador screamed as he stepped back, turning around to face Seleece.

"You better shoot me now! I'd rather die than live to see what happens to me!" he screamed.

Seleece couldn't hold back her urges anymore. "Gladly," she said in a low tone as she fired a powerful blast into Salvador's direction, ignoring the alien's previous request. Right before the blast could blow him to pieces, the alien teleported above him, touched him and swiftly teleported him toward the end of the room. Her blast blew a huge hole in the wall that led to the corridor.

"I told you not to harm him," the alien said in calm voice. "Please understand, this situation is not necessary. You can either comply willingly, or only minimally delay this process. The only choice you have is how it will happen, not if it will happen," the alien said.

"Just tell us where Melthuron is and what he's planning," Seleece demanded.

Salvador, however, still seemed unwilling to cooperate. "I will tell you nothing!" he screamed at her while looking straight at the alien, watching its every move.

"I see. You don't have to tell us anything out loud, I will find out for myself," the alien said as it placed its right hand around Salvador's throat and lifted him off the ground easily, as if he were a feather. "But you chose the less comfortable option, and that is on you," the alien said, as it held Salvador four feet above ground, choking him slowly.

Once again, Salvador could do nothing as the alien completely overpowered him. The only thing he could do is struggle, struggle against an opponent he knew he had no chance of defeating.

"Let...let me go!" he tried to scream while being choked by the alien's grip. He placed his hands around the alien's arm in an attempt to free himself, but the alien's overwhelming strength did not give an inch.

"I will say it once more," the alien said while its eyes began to glow a menacing white, almost blinding Salvador. "Let me in your mind, or I will force the information out of you. I will make sure no harm comes your way. Not from Seleece, Melthuron, or anyone else," the alien promised him as it set him back on the ground, releasing its tight grip from Salvador's throat. The alien had made its point.

"Aw! Why did you let him go?" Seleece asked in a slightly disappointed tone, taunting Salvador with her weapon. "I was enjoying the show," she said as the alien turned to face her.

"Because my wishes have been communicated. Besides, Salvador is not our true enemy, he is just afraid," the alien said in its monotone voice. "He is afraid of me, afraid of you, and afraid of what Melthuron will do to him if he gives us any information," the alien said.

Seleece didn't say a word.

"I don't see any point in harming other living creatures. Nothing, absolutely nothing in the universe deserves to be treated with such ill intent. That is why I released him," the alien said before turning around to face Salvador once again.

"This is the last time I ask," the alien said. "Let me in your mind and I will protect you. No one will be able to harm you," the alien said sincerely as it placed its hand on Salvador's head, hoping he wouldn't struggle this time. But it seemed that was not about to happen.

"Don't you touch me!" Salvador said in a defiant tone, slapping the alien's hand away from his head with anger and fear in his eyes.

"You chose this," the alien responded as it delivered a fast and powerful kick to Salvador's stomach.

There was a huge amount of force behind the alien's kick. It sent Salvador flying through the room and into the wall. Salvador felt his ribs shatter.

"I apologize for having to resort to such tactics. It seems I will have to force the information out of you," the alien said before teleporting in front of Salvador.

The alien then lifted him up off the floor again, ruthlessly holding him up by his arm. Salvador now seemed to be in great pain. He was having a hard time breathing and was completely unable to move. The only thing he could do was gasp for air as he was left to the alien's mercy.

The alien quickly placed his other hand on Salvador's head and began to search his memories for anything he knew about Melthuron and his plans. Seleece could only stare as this was taking place; she was shocked by how quickly the alien changed the way it dealt with him.

"Anything useful?" Seleece asked the alien, this time in a more reserved tone.

The alien did not reply. A few seconds went by before the light from the alien's eyes began to fade. The alien softly placed Salvador on the floor, looking at him with an expressionless face. The alien then kneeled down, placing its hand against Salvador's wounded stomach.

"I do apologize for doing this, but you left me no choice," the alien said.

"What...what are...you doing now," Salvador struggled to say as he tried to catch his breath.

Seleece was surprised he was even awake after receiving such a strong blow without any armor protecting him.

"I am healing you," the alien said as its energy began to flow into Salvador's stomach.

Seleece could see a dim white light around the alien's hand as it healed him. Slowly, Salvador's breathing returned to normal.

He could feel his strength slowly returning with each passing second.

"I realize this process was uncomfortable for you, but you failed to comply with my request. You will be back to normal in a day's time. For now, I recommend as little movement as possible while your body continues to heal."

"So, what's the verdict?" Seleece asked, hoping for some good news. "What is Melthuron doing? What is his plan?"

"This being does not know anything about Melthuron's plans," the alien said as it walked toward Seleece, leaving Salvador alone to heal. "What I was able to gather is that Melthuron left this ship before we arrived. He doesn't know where or why Melthuron left."

"Damn it!" Seleece yelled at the top of her lungs. "He is always one step ahead of me!" she yelled out in frustration. Just like that, she was now right back where she had started.

"What about my fellow soldiers? What's become of them?" she asked the alien, hoping for any good news at all.

"Yes, that," the alien replied. "He was unconscious for quite some time after I obtained information from him the first time. He did not witness anything other than the heavy fire they were under before he lost consciousness. See for yourself," the alien said before placing its hand on her head.

She could feel it all. Everything the alien had learned from Salvador, every emotion Salvador had felt, all of his fears. She felt everything the alien had learned.

"That is all I know," the alien said telepathically. "It seems Melthuron is quite secretive about his work. This being knows nothing about me either."

"I see," she responded softly. That experience had changed her. She had learned a great deal about Salvador in those few seconds. Although no one could see it from behind her helmet, a tear began to roll down her cheek as she tried to cope with what seemed to be the obvious fate of her friends.

"We must keep looking for him, for all our sakes," the alien said.

"Yes, but where would we even begin? We have no idea what he is planning. We have no clue as to where he is," she responded telepathically. Perhaps a new approach would be necessary.

"We should report everything we have learned to my superiors at once. My helmet has recorded everything that has taken place here. With you by my side, we have enough evidence to show that Melthuron has in fact not been kidnapped, and that he is a threat to us all," she said as she turned to face Salvador, who was still recovering from the alien's bone crushing blow. "We will take him with us as further proof of what has happened," she concluded.

"Hmm...yes. I agree to these terms," the alien said telepathically as it teleported both of them to Salvador's position. "But Salvador will not be harmed in any way. Is that understood?" the alien communicated telepathically.

"Yes...you've taken that desire away from me," she responded. The alien could feel that she was no longer looking to spill Salvador's blood. Seleece just wanted justice, and killing a soldier who had just been following orders no longer qualified as justice, regardless of what he had done to her crew.

"Just touch his arm and think of where we have to go, and I will get us there same as before," the alien said.

"All right, listen up. You are coming with us, Salvador," Seleece said as she kneeled down, taking reinforced steel handcuffs from her armor's back compartment. "You are aware of their shocking mechanism if you attempt to remove them, so don't struggle. Just come along quietly," she said in a low tone before placing him under arrest.

Salvador didn't utter a single word. He was unable to fight back such a crippling blow.

"All right, he is now safely restrained. Take us to the Interplanetary Coalition headquarters," Seleece said while picking Salvador off the floor with one hand, thinking of their next destination. The alien quickly touched her shoulder, establishing a link between them again, this time with much less effort.

"That's rather odd. It is getting much easier to establish a link between us," it said telepathically.

"Just take us to this location. Can you feel it?" she asked while remaining as focused as possible, ignoring the alien's comment.

"Yes, I can sense it," the alien responded. "This destination does not appear to be moving, so I believe I can take us to any room inside it. Just tell me which one," the alien said.

She focused on the meeting room where all of the elected leaders had gathered, where the first meeting had taken place. "I will find you," she thought as they disappeared from Melthuron's ship, ready for the next phase of her mission.

Chapter 6

Kalduron was now standing in front of all of the leaders. Over two hours had gone by since his soldiers had boarded Melthuron's ship. They stood before him, anxiously waiting for Kalduron to update them on the mission. Kalduron was now dressed in full Thespian gear; his helmet in his hand. He had made up his mind. He was going to invade the target ship, no matter what those government bureaucrats said. But maybe there was still a chance to influence get them on board. He knew he had to play it smart.

"We have lost all contact with our soldiers," Kalduron said to them with shame written all over his face.

"What? How could this happen!" one of the leaders shouted out anger.

"Our lack of data indicates that their armor was either destroyed or turned off. We can't seem to pick up any feedback from them," he said.

"Well, I can't say I didn't warn you!" Tei-va exclaimed

condescendingly. "Your so-called best soldiers failed the mission…or was it perhaps that they thwarted it?" she asked, this time with a much more serious tone. "The fact that they failed the mission can only mean one of two things, they are either dead or—"

"How dare you!" Kalduron screamed back at her. He was sick and tired of her disgusting accusations. This time his demeanor toward her was completely different; he was no longer going to take this from her. With his team possibly captured or dead, with the possibility of a civil war looming ever closer, the time for formalities was over.

"If people like you would have stood aside and let me invade that ship in the first place, with the full force of the Intergalactic Alliance military, none of this would have happened!" he screamed back at her menacingly.

"We would have been violating intergalactic law," she replied smugly. "I wouldn't expect an old barbarian like you to understand. The law is the law, Commander Kalduron," she said.

But before Kalduron had a chance to respond, Ramos decided to step in to diffuse the situation once again.

"Both of you need to calm yourselves," Ramos said. "Frankly, Tei-va, I don't see what good your accusations are doing other than stirring up bad relations between your species," he said. "And in regard to you, Kalduron, your team has failed. Accept some responsibility for this failure. We will come up with a solution, but your outburst is both unnecessary and uncalled for given the circumstances. All of us here are facing bigger problems than your petty vendettas," he concluded, putting both in their respective places.

Neither of them had had anything to say; they just remained silent. Before any further discussion could take place, the alien, Seleece, and Salvador appeared in the middle of the room, surprising everyone.

"What? Who are you?" Kalduron screamed, almost instantly reaching for his weapon. He then noticed that the restrained person was Salvador. He quickly pointed his weapon at them, ready to shoot.

"Please lower your weapon, Commander," Seleece said.

Kalduron was shocked at first, but he instantly recognized her voice. Before she was able to take off her helmet to reveal herself to them, relief filled his heart as Kalduron exclaimed out loud, "Soldier! Report! Where are the others?"

"Seleece?" "It's Seleece!" different voices murmured in the background as they stared, awed by their sudden appearance.

"And who is this strange alien you bring with you? How did you even get in here?" Kalduron said as he stared at the alien.

No one in that room except Seleece had ever seen an alien like it before. With its blue skin, white eyes, and giant stature, no other life form like that had ever been seen before in the galaxy.

"This is an ally, sir. I understand these are strange circumstances, but I must talk about Melthuron first," she said as she put her C1 blaster away.

"Yes, where is the prime consort?" Tei-va questioned her with a concerned look. She looked as if she had seen a ghost.

"The prime consort's whereabouts are still unknown, ma'am," Seleece responded as she turned to face the alien. "This alien here, it's—"

"That, my dear Seleece, is still my experiment. I hope you haven't damaged it in any way," a voice said, coming from behind the door. As the door slid open, a familiar face walked into the room, accompanied by three Thespian soldiers in full armor. It was Melthuron, smiling and waving at everyone as he walked inside with his bodyguards swiftly following behind. He was still wearing the same, stain-ridden lab coat that he had on earlier.

"Melthuron!" Seleece screamed as she took out her C1 and pointed it at his face. "Don't you move a muscle or I will splatter you all over the floor," she threatened with hatred written all over her face. Almost instantly, Kalduron paled as he heard those words, completely speechless by her sudden outburst. Although he did not yet understand what was going on, in his mind he trusted Seleece.

"Something must have happened at that ship," he thought to himself as he remained shocked from his sudden appearance.

Melthuron just stared at the alien for a minute before addressing Seleece directly.

"Oh my," Melthuron said as he taunted back. "Whatever happened to Mr. Prime Consort?" He questioned her with a wicked smile on his face. "I rather liked it better that way; it showed me that you knew your place in my presence," he said.

Seleece only stood still, with her gun pointed directly at Melthuron.

"My goodness! Why do you look so angry, Seleece?" he said as he looked at the alien.

Before he could continue, Tei-va interrupted nervously, "Mr. Prime Consort…it is so great to see you unharmed!" She was attempting to diffuse the situation. "How dare you! Put your gun down, you stupid soldier! Who do you think you're talking to in that manner? That's the Prime Consort!" she screamed at Seleece.

Seleece, however, did not shift her gaze away from Melthuron. "My apologies, ma'am, but I do NOT take orders from you," she said defiantly, with her weapon still aimed at Melthuron.

The rest of the elected leaders could only stare as this was taking place, profoundly confused by everyone's sudden entrance.

"Oh, please. Cut the act Tei-va," Melthuron said as he walked toward Seleece.

She didn't flinch.

"You know, for hours now I have been curious about one particular thing," Melthuron said as he walked closer.

"What do you mean?" Seleece replied in anger.

"I do wonder how it all went down around here."

Her blood was almost boiling from anger. "How it all went down? What the hell do you mean, you traitorous bastard!" Seleece screamed out in anger, growing more furious by the second. Just the sight of Melthuron pissed her off. His smug attitude, how calm he was after everything he had done…she couldn't stand the very sight of him.

"I'm Tei-va and I hate you Kalduron!" Melthuron said as he attempted to mimic Tei-va's voice. "No way! No way will you get to call all the shots! I'm a stubborn politician!" he said as he laughed even more.

"I am Ramos. The keeper of peace. Both of you stop fighting, pretty please!" Melthuron teased as he paced from side to side.

"Did I get it right?" Melthuron asked as he stared at Ramos, directing his question at him.

"Yes, you nailed it Melthuron," Ramos responded.

"What?" Seleece screamed at him. "What are you talking about?"

"Well, it's really quite simple," Melthuron said in a more serious tone. "Those two were on my side to begin with," he said, sending shockwaves of confusion throughout the room. "I am sure you and Ramos gave quite a performance, bravo! Worthy of an award I am sure," he said.

Ramos just looked at him, completely unamused by Melthuron's little speech.

"All right, fine, but why is the alien with her? Wasn't it supposed to be in your lab? None of this was part of the plan," Ramos said as he began to walk toward Melthuron's guards, with Tei-va following quickly behind him.

"Yes, well, even the best of plans can be delayed by the most unforeseen of circumstances, Mr. Ramos. I do hope you understand," Melthuron responded.

The room went completely silent. The other leaders had no idea what was going on.

"Working together?" Seleece thought. "Why would a human official work with Melthuron? What could they be after?" Suddenly her thoughts were interrupted.

"Both of you stop right there! Nobody move!" Kalduron screamed as he pointed his weapon at them, ready to shoot if they so much as flinched.

"And what makes you think you can give us any orders?" Melthuron said as he turned to face him, with his back now toward Seleece.

"We have over one hundred well-equipped intergalactic soldiers stationed at this base," Kalduron said with his gun still pointed at them. "I have already notified them to make their way here. You have nowhere to run, and you are outgunned. Please stand down now, Mr. Prime Consort. The same goes for the two of you," Kalduron said in a low and menacing tone.

"Well, I didn't realize I was so outgunned. What about you two? Did you know about this?" Melthuron responded calmly, still completely nonchalant about the whole thing. "If you are referring to those soldiers stationed at the docking room, they are all dead!" he said, grinning.

Kalduron was shocked.

"No…that can't be," Seleece thought as she tried to remain focused.

"So you are Melthuron," the alien said.

"Oh my! It spoke! That is just simply amazing. How did you manage to learn so quickly? I have so many questions for you! You have more than exceeded my expectations," Melthuron said as he marveled at his creation. His eyes almost glimmered with excitement as he admired his own handiwork.

"I am glad to have found you here! Mr. Ramos…what was that saying you humans like to use…kill two birds with one stone?" Melthuron said as he walked closer to the alien. "How do you feel? You must feel confused or perhaps tired? Maybe a little sick?" Melthuron asked as he approached the alien slowly.

"I thought you two said you were going to shoot," Melthuron said as he called their bluff.

"This is unnatural," the alien said. "How did you place me in this body, Melthuron?"

"Oh no! Don't you worry about that! It's not really important. Those are just boring details," Melthuron said as he stopped right in front of the alien, just a few feet away from Seleece and Kalduron.

"Could it be true?" Seleece thought as she heard their conversation. "Was that really not its body? Who and what was this thing?"

"Focus!" Kalduron screamed at Seleece, trying to snap her back to attention. "Under these suspicious conditions, I, Kalduron, supreme commander of the Thespian army, place you under military arrest, Mr. Prime Consort. If it turns out that you are innocent of all charges brought against you in court, I will personally resign from my post," Kalduron said, with his weapon still raised in their direction. "Soldiers, I order you to stand down and drop your weapons, or you will be arrested as well," he said.

Melthuron's soldiers, however, did not flinch or utter a single word. They just stood there like robots, awaiting an order from their master. Melthuron completely ignored Kalduron's demands, and instead shifted his gaze toward Seleece.

"You really couldn't have brought it to a better place," Melthuron said to Seleece. "You have saved me the trouble of looking for my experiment. Now I can do two things at once," he said.

Suddenly, Melthuron snapped his fingers. In an instant, Seleece was quickly teleported to the left of the room, completely surprising her.

"What are you doing?" Seleece said as she appeared several feet away from where she was standing, with her gun still raised as if she were still pointing it at Melthuron. One of the soldiers was now standing right where she had been less than a second ago, with a blade in his hand.

"Those soldiers of his...they are not regular soldiers," the alien said. "That one tried to attack you."

Seleece didn't even see him coming.

"Yes, you were just too slow to see it," Melthuron said as he pointed his finger toward Kalduron.

But when Seleece turned to see what he was pointing to, it was already too late. Kalduron was bleeding from a stab wound. He had his hands around his stomach, trying his best to slow the bleeding down.

"Sir!" Seleece screamed as she ran toward him as fast as she could. He had been stabbed by one of the soldiers. It seemed they had purposely avoided any vital organs to make sure he didn't die right away.

At that instant, chaos broke out. Numerous screams could be heard throughout the room as everyone else noticed what had taken place.

Melthuron smiled. "Leave no one alive except the alien, Seleece, Salvador, and Kalduron," Melthuron commanded as he began to walk toward the door.

"Oh, and try not use your blasters too much. I rather like this room. I wouldn't want to have to remodel the whole place once we are done here," Melthuron commanded as one of his soldier's teleported in front of him, protecting him from their enemies.

The alien quickly teleported above Melthuron in an attempt to grab him, but Melthuron's soldiers countered it perfectly. Before the alien could place its hand around his neck, the soldier teleported next to the alien and delivered a swift kick to the alien's stomach. The alien was able to block the soldier's kick with its left arm, but the blow was still strong enough to push it several feet backward. In the meantime, the other two soldiers began slaughtering the leaders one by one, without any mercy.

None of the officials stood a chance. Some attempted to run out the door, but they weren't able to get far. The soldiers were so quick, that in less than five seconds more than half of the leaders had been killed at their hands.

"Take cover behind me!" Seleece said as she tried to shoot at one of Melthuron's soldiers, missing him as he teleported out of harm's way.

They all seemed to poses the same abilities that the alien had, and that was making it almost impossible to fight them. They were just too fast, even with her enhanced reflexes and all her weaponry at her disposal, they were impossible to hit.

"Damn it!" she said as she ran toward the other end of the room, where the last of the leaders were attempting to hide. "Stay behind me!" Seleece said as she took out a plasma shield and held it in front of her.

The green shield turned on, engulfing her and the remaining leaders inside it, forming a green, protective bubble between them and everyone else in the room. Seleece was controlling the size and shape of the shield through her helmet, making it big enough to protect them while giving no room for any of Melthuron's soldiers to teleport inside. "Don't touch the shield!" she said to the few leaders still alive. Just five, five out of the thirty leaders remained alive.

Suddenly, the alien teleported in front of her, standing just right outside her shield. "I need you to get Kalduron out of here...NOW!" Seleece screamed at the alien. "Then I will make the shield small enough so you can enter and get us all outta here as well. Go!" she screamed.

"Well, that is a good plan indeed. Your prowess in the midst of battle is impressive," Melthuron responded as he applauded Seleece. "Leave it to you to come up with such a little maneuver in such a small amount of time. Why, I am very impressed, Seleece! You are very good at thinking on your feet," he exclaimed with a smile. "But let's look at where we stand, shall we?" he said as he walked in front of the wounded Kalduron, smiling as Kalduron struggled to stand.

"Have you gone mad, Melthuron? Why are you doing this?" Kalduron asked as he struggled to keep himself off the floor, breathing heavily in the process.

"Quiet now. I was in the middle of a thought," Melthuron responded as he rubbed his chin. "Hmm...where was I...oh yes, that's right! Let's see, you have one alien with abilities; I have three soldiers with the same abilities. The alien has no weapons; my soldiers have all kinds of fun toys I personally designed for them. Seleece, you simply can't win," he said in a giddy tone.

"Incorrect assessment," the alien said as it teleported behind Melthuron. "She now has an ally by her side. I will stop you, although this course of action is regrettable," the alien said as a blaster appeared in its hand.

It was the one he had taken away from Salvador. The alien tried to shoot down Melthuron's soldiers, but each shot missed its mark as the soldiers teleported themselves and Melthuron away.

"Now!" the alien screamed as it appeared right outside her shield. She began to expand the shield when suddenly there was an explosion that destroyed the floor beneath them.

"No!" Seleece screamed as they fell several feet into the room below. The force of the blast caused her to lose her focus, causing the shield to lose its shape and break apart as they began to fall. Under them stood one of Melthuron's soldiers, presumably the one that had destroyed the floor that they had been standing on.

He opened fire on the leaders, mercilessly eliminating all but one of them with deadly precision. Their bodies had been completely disintegrated by the blasts. Nothing remained but empty space where their bodies once stood.

The alien managed to get to one of them before the shot could kill him, managing to teleport him out of the ship. Seleece continued to fall down into the room below but managed to land with her legs and arms in front of her, protecting her head from damage. She quickly got up and fired several shots at Melthuron's soldier, each time missing the mark as he teleported away from each shot.

"Damn it all!" Seleece screamed as she ran for cover. She quickly tossed a tech grenade, hoping its electric shock would disable their helmets and provide some breathing room from the fighting. It worked. With the brief second of concealment she gained, she quickly turned on her invisibility cloak. She was now completely invisible to her enemies. Her heart was beating faster than ever before. Seleece now stood still behind a generator, hoping to remain undetected until she could come up with a plan. Her breathing grew heavy as she held her blaster in her hand. She managed to remain somewhat composed as she turned on her helmet's heat vision, allowing her to easily pinpoint her enemy's position.

"That's weird. Their bodies are unusually cold," she thought as her eyes remained glued in the soldier's direction. Sweat began to run down her face as a bit of fear entered her mind, but she stayed focused.

Suddenly, Melthuron and his remaining soldiers quickly appeared in the room, shifting their gaze around in an attempt to find her.

"Where is she?" Melthuron asked one of his soldiers impatiently.

"She has gone invisible, master," his soldier responded with a lifeless voice, similar to the alien's.

"I want you to get Kalduron to my lab immediately," Melthuron commanded.

"Yes, master," the solider said as he quickly disappeared into the room above to carry out his order.

Almost as quickly as he had disappeared, he reappeared again right in front of his master.

"Kalduron has disappeared. The alien must have taken him to safety."

"I see," Melthuron replied calmly, not at all concerned with Kalduron's escape. "No matter. He was not my primary concern. I will have him soon enough regardless of where he is!" Melthuron said. He walked forward a little, letting out a confident laugh. "Oh, Seleece! Seleece, oh my dear Seleece!" he said as he stepped closer to the generator. "There's only one place to hide in this room! Why don't you come out now and save me the trouble of playing hide and seek?" he said as he pointed to the generator. The soldiers quickly moved closer.

"I must commend you, Seleece, really!" Melthuron said as his soldiers got in position, awaiting Melthuron's signal. "You have exceeded my expectations in every way. You even managed to temporarily save not only Kalduron but that human official as well! Truly amazing work," he said as he began pacing from left to right. He placed his hands behind his back as he paced, continuing his speech. "I swear, nothing seems to be going my way today! I am willing to bet most would be rather annoyed if they found themselves in such circumstances, but not me! This will change soon. You and the alien are what I want above all else right now. You will not escape again!" he said gleefully.

Suddenly, a voice was heard from the back of the room. "I want to know why," the lifeless voice said, coming from behind the generator.

As fast as ever, the alien appeared in front of Melthuron, just ten feet away. Just as quickly, all of Melthuron's soldiers appeared in front of the alien with their guns raised, protecting their master fearlessly.

"Why have you trapped me in this body, Melthuron? What is your objective?" the alien asked.

"Why, welcome back!" Melthuron said with a big smile on his face. "I just can't believe how much you have—"

"Answer my question now, Melthuron," the alien said. "Why did you place me in this body? How could a lowly being such as you do this to a being such as me?" the alien asked.

"Why how demanding of you! To be quite honest, I don't see why the 'why' is important," Melthuron responded in a low tone.

"So this alien has been telling the truth this whole time. What the heck is that thing then?" Seleece thought to herself while raising her weapon, ready to strike at the right moment.

"What does matter is that you are now the focus of my research. I want to know just what you really are!" Melthuron said with a smile. "Something like you…such cosmic beauty…I have never seen anything like it. I am just dying to know," he said while making an excited hand gesture.

"Know what exactly?" the alien asked, emotionless.

"Oh come on! You are so fascinating in every way. You must know that. As far as I know, you are the only one of your kind in existence…maybe ever! How could that not excite me as a scientist?" Melthuron grinned with excitement as the alien looked back at him, expressionless.

"I mean, how do you reproduce? Do you even reproduce at all? How old are you, really? Did you evolve into what you are, or have you always been like that? These are just some of the exciting questions your existence has brought up!" he said, his excitement building with each question. "You are a mystery, and a great one at that," Melthuron continued. "But like all mysteries"—he paused and pointed his finger at the alien—"I will solve you!"

Melthuron quickly touched his wrist, activating some sort of gadget. "Aaaah!" The alien screamed in pain as a shockwave coursed through its entire body, knocking the alien to the ground.

"You didn't really think I was just going to chat with you and let you just poof out of my sight again, did you?" Melthuron asked before letting out a loud laugh.

"But when…when did you do this?" the alien said as the shock continued to paralyze it.

"Oh, I didn't do it, he did," Melthuron responded as he pointed to one of his soldiers. "Back then when you two had your little squabble, I had previously devised this little gadget to seamlessly attach to your skin on contact. I have yet to come up with a name for it though! Perhaps the Crippler? Bah! I have never been good at naming my inventions! Now then, let's get you back to the lab. I have lost enough time with you already as it is."

Melthuron walked up to the alien, taking out a tranquilizer syringe. It was now or never.

"I won't let you!" the invisible Seleece screamed as she fired a shot at Melthuron, missing him by a thread as one of his soldiers removed him from harm almost instantly.

"Seleece, my dear Seleece," Melthuron said calmly. "Apprehend her...NOW!" he screamed out in anger.

One of his soldiers quickly appeared behind where the blast had come from, but there was nothing there.

"What?" Melthuron said right before his soldier was electrocuted by Seleece. The soldier quickly fell to the ground, dropping his weapon. "Quite impressive. How did you manage to fool—"

"That's enough!" the alien screamed as it struggled to stand while continuously being electrocuted. The alien quickly ripped the device from its skin. As fast as ever, the alien quickly appeared behind Seleece and placed its hand on her shoulder. "Wait, don't do it!" Seleece screamed as her view of the ship disappeared.

Chapter 7

"Where are we?" Kalduron asked as Seleece and the alien appeared.

"I brought us to the planet you call CB19," the alien responded softly.

"What! Why? Why did you do this? We could have ended this right then and there. We had him in our sights!" Seleece screamed angrily while attempting to punch the alien in the gut out of frustration.

The alien quickly teleported behind her and placed her under a firm arm lock.

"We don't have time for such nonsense," the alien said while firmly holding her arm in place. "This is precisely why I did it," the alien said while effortlessly overpowering her. "I have been injured. There was no way we would have won that battle…not even if we had a hundred more soldiers with your skill level," the alien said.

"It would have been foolish to stay and fight as we are now; you know that. If Melthuron had been successful in recapturing me, we would have all lost everything," the alien concluded softly.

But Seleece's anger continued to blind her. She couldn't accept the fact that once again Melthuron had escaped justice. She struggled to set herself free, yelling and screaming with anger as she attempted to free her arm from the alien's grip.

"You need to take me back to the ship right now!" Seleece screamed while being held back. She was so blinded by her rage that she couldn't even see straight. "We are going to go back there and—"

"Stand down now! That's an order!" Kalduron swiftly commanded. "I won't try to guess what the hell is going on right now, but making decisions out of anger can get us all killed! And I don't know about you, but I'm not ready to die just yet, Seleece. There's much work to be done!" he said, attempting to reason with her. It seemed his words got to her. Her demeanor quickly changed from agitated to reserved. "Please let go of me," Seleece said quietly to the alien.

The alien quickly released her, letting go of her hand before taking a step back.

"We must not fight among ourselves," Kalduron said. "Clearly this alien is our ally. We must show it the same respect we would to any other soldier of the Thespian army," Kalduron said.

Seleece remained quiet.

"Thank you for getting us out of that ship…what is your name?" Kalduron asked.

"I don't have one," the alien responded. "I have never had one before. There was no need for such a thing," the alien said.

Kalduron was surprised; but it didn't matter.

"Well, that takes care of that," Seleece said in a sarcastic tone. "Sir, what should we do now? What are your orders?"
"First, we are going to need the surviving leader's help," Kalduron said. "Aside from us, he's the only living witness to what Melthuron

has orchestrated. We will need him once we bring Melthuron to trial," Kalduron explained.

"I have teleported him back to his home planet. We can contact him when the time comes," the alien said.

"Yes. He needs to keep a low profile for now. It is best if he stays back on Earth. He would draw too much attention in Demora," Kalduron said.

"What Melthuron has done could start a war," Seleece said with a concerned voice.

"Yes, and we can't let that happen again. Our world is still healing from the civil war," Kalduron responded.

"Sir, perhaps we should take that leader with us to the Thespian council immediately and explain exactly what has happened. With him as a witness, we stand a chance of them actually believing our story," Seleece said.

"Your diplomacy won't solve this problem," the alien said, breaking its silence on the matter. "Melthuron seems to possess powerful allies back on planet Earth. Surely he must have an array of contingency plans ready for when we attempt to take an action as predictable as that one. He surely has agents working for him in this so-called council of yours."

Seleece's eyes suddenly grew heavy as she stared down at the alien. "So what do you suggest we do then? How can we fight Melthuron when he has so many advantages over us? Please enlighten us on your strategy," Seleece asked the alien angrily.

"The priority above all others remains the same. We must figure out a way to get my soul out of this body," the alien responded without hesitation.

Seleece suddenly broke out in laughter. "Was that a subtle attempt at joke?" Seleece said to the alien as her laughing quickly morphed into anger. "Do you even realize just what the hell you are saying?" she asked. "My species is being blamed for his disappearance. We are probably at the brink of war, and you want us to place all our collective efforts into figuring out how to get you out of that stupid body?"

"Yes," the alien responded. "That would be the best course of action we could take."

Seleece could not believe what she was hearing. The alien's audacity was too much for her to handle under these circumstances. "How can we even hope to fight Melthuron when he has so many advantages over us?" Seleece questioned. "He is still the Prime Consort of our planet. It won't be easy to get to him even if he resurfaces back on our home planet. Even if we manage to locate him, he still has those soldiers and who knows what else! There is no way we are going to waste our valuable time trying to help you get out of this so-called body of yours!" Seleece said.

"Neither of you understand the dangers this universe is in," the alien responded as its eyes began to glow.

"I am the only being in this world who can fix what Melthuron has done…all of it. Melthuron is only a symptom of the underlying problem," the alien said. The alien now had Kalduron's attention. "Can you explain what he might be planning and what he has done?" Kalduron asked, intrigued by the alien's response.

"I don't know what exactly he is planning to do, but it is irrelevant and of no concern to me. My only concern is figuring out how to reverse what Melthuron has done to me. Once I am able to do that, I can solve all of the current problems, or at the very least understand them."

Seleece was not pleased with that response. "You can do that on your own," Seleece said with a cold stare. "I will not waste any time on such a pointless task!"

The alien seemed quite indifferent. "We had an agreement," the alien responded calmly.

Despite their differences, the alien remained calm, composed.

"You will honor the agreement or pay the consequences. You will help me find Melthuron and get me out of this body. That is the only task we are going to undertake. Do we understand each other?" the alien asked as it stared at her with its piercing white eyes.

"I know these are rather dire circumstances we are facing, but let's not devolve into threats," Kalduron said with a smile as he tried to ease the situation. "I am sure we can all come to an agreement in—"

"I have already established an agreement with your subordinate; one it seems she does not want to uphold," the alien quickly said as it continued to stare her down. "I have saved both of your lives; now you will repay me by keeping your side of the agreement, Seleece," the alien said in calm voice.

Seleece did not take kindly to the alien's words. "Are you threatening us, Alien?" Seleece asked after taking out her blaster.

Even with a weapon raised against it, the alien remained calm.

"Even if you tried, there's nothing you could possibly do to me. It would be a futile attempt on your side to engage in a confrontation with me. You will gain nothing by initiating such a conflict. Let's keep our agreement in place so we can solve the problem at hand."

"Shut up!" Seleece said right after she fired at the alien. The alien quickly teleported above her and teleported her weapon away, only to appear behind her.

"Don't you understand there is nothing you can do against a being like me? It is in your best interest to be on my side," the alien said before appearing in front of her again.

Seleece seemed to be losing her cool quickly. "Damn you!" she screamed loudly. She rushed as fast as she could toward the alien, raising her hand as she attempted to punch it. She was expecting the alien to teleport behind her but she was wrong. The alien quickly blocked her attack with its left hand while simultaneously attempting to kick her in the back of her head. She ducked, avoiding what would have been a powerful blow to the head.

"That's enough, Seleece!" Kalduron screamed at her. "I am very sorry for her outburst. Please forgive her," Kalduron said to the alien as sincere as he could be.

The alien swiftly teleported closer to Kalduron.

"While I understand your agreement with her, you must also understand that the situation has surely changed since the agreement was made. Perhaps we can come up with new terms?"

"But sir, we must think about our—"

"That's enough, Seleece," Kalduron interrupted her. "It is painfully obvious that our friend here knows much more about what is going on than we do," Kalduron said. "Right now, you are bringing shame to the Thespian army with your behavior. I am very displeased. I will deal with you later," Kalduron said.

Those words reverberated down to her very core. Instantly, shame invaded every inch of her body as she thought about everything she had done to her supposed ally. "Sir, yes sir," Seleece said.

"Forgive me," she said to the alien with sincerity in her eyes.

"Our terms will remain the same," the alien responded, completely unshaken from its goal. "Both yourself and Seleece will keep that agreement. Our priority will be to figure out how to get me out of this body. While this goal is ongoing, you will have my assistance in whatever you may need. Do you personally agree to these new terms?" alien asked.

"How do you propose we figure that out?" Kalduron asked.

"It is simple. Once we capture Melthuron, I will just absorb all of his knowledge. If there is a way to reverse this, which I know there must be, I will gain this knowledge through this method. Once that is done, you are free to do with him whatever you please as long as you don't harm him."

Seleece was not in the least bit happy with the alien's demands. "Not harm him? What! Melthuron has committed too many crimes! That is simply outra—"

"We agree to your terms," Kalduron said without a moment's hesitation.

But Seleece did not seem to agree. Even though she didn't want to comply, her superior had made it very clear she had no say so in the matter. "Very well...I agree as well," the faithful soldier said grudgingly.

"So then," Seleece said while turning around to face the alien, "how do you propose we locate Melthuron? Since his soldiers seem to have the same abilities you possess, he could be anywhere right now."

"I may not know where he resides right now, but I may have an effective way to find him," the alien said. "Back when we had our encounter with Salvador, I was able to place some of my energy in his body without his knowledge. This at least gives us a chance to figure out where Salvador is. Even if he does not know where Melthuron is, he must know more about that human Ramos," the alien explained.

"And you are certain you can locate him?" Kalduron asked.

"Yes. But first we need to—"
"Then what the hell are we waiting for...let's go!" Seleece howled with anxiousness. The thought of capturing Melthuron brought her mind a new sense of peace.

"Let's not rush into battle so hastily, Seleece. We have the element of surprise on our side," Kalduron said.

"Kalduron is correct. We must control our basic impulses and take the more rational, calculating approach," the alien said.

"I know these are extremely stressful circumstances, but I need you to start acting more like yourself, Seleece. It's not like you to act so impulsively. I know well what is going through your mind, but right now I need you to be the soldier I know you are," Kalduron said sternly.

Seleece stayed silent.

"Well then, I propose we gather more soldiers regardless of where we go from here," Kalduron said.

"The greater our number, the better chance we stand if...no, when we collide with Melthuron and his forces."

Seleece seemed troubled by Kalduron's plan. Although she knew he was right, she no longer wanted to risk any other Thespian soldiers for this mission. Melthuron would be found and brought to justice without anyone else dying. She had made up her mind.

"With all due respect, sir, I think a large battalion is not needed for a reconnaissance mission such as this. Once we find Salvador we can quickly gather all the information we need from him. Adding more personnel seems a bit redundant for this mission."

"And if he doesn't know where Melthuron is? What then?" Kalduron asked.

Seleece didn't have an answer.

"We need to face the fact that we may have guerilla warfare in our near future. We need a battalion that is well trained for these situations. If we engage in battle with just the three of us, we will be slaughtered just like those poor bastards were moments ago. These are the deadliest soldiers I have ever had the displeasure of fighting in all of my years. They killed without mercy, without any remorse whatsoever. We will repay them a thousand fold, but we can't defeat them alone. Let's face it, we were completely outmatched. We will need the full force of an army behind us if we hope to defeat those three soldiers," Kalduron said without hesitation. He knew that if they waited too long to act, it would become much harder to defeat Melthuron. More than ever, time was of the essence. The longer they waited, the more time Melthuron had to plan.

The alien knew that as well. "Those soldiers will surely be by Melthuron's side at all times. What Kalduron has said is indeed correct," the alien said without hesitation. "I would have liked, if at all possible, to have avoided this situation altogether. However, I have no choice in the matter anymore. The time has come for us to go on the offensive," the alien said.

"Agreed! You and Seleece go find that traitor. I will gather the rest of our crew," Kalduron said with confidence. "Justice will be done," he said.

"Sir, yes sir!" Seleece responded without hesitation. "Can you feel where Salvador is now?" Seleece asked the alien.

The alien's eyes began to glow. "Yes," the alien said, with his usual calm. "I can take Seleece and myself there now," the alien responded.

"All right…let's go!" Seleece said with enthusiasm.

"Wait. Both of you take some of this first," Kalduron said to both of them. Kalduron then gently tossed two packed syringes at Seleece from his armor's pocket.

"Sir, yes sir!" Seleece said while taking one out of its package. She the punctured herself in the neck and quickly applied the serum.

"Here, take this one," Seleece said to the alien.

The alien looked at the serum for a brief second, appearing somewhat confused.

"I don't know if it will have any useful effects on you, but it's worth a shot," Kalduron said.

"There is no need for that," the alien responded with the usual monotone voice. "I don't require that type of nourishment, not even in this body. I am rapidly healing as we speak."

"OK, fine…let's go," Seleece said impatiently.

"Yes, but first I will take Kalduron to Demora," the alien said.

"Well, I thought that was obvious," Kalduron responded as the alien appeared next to him.

The alien quickly placed its hand on Kalduron's shoulder and they both disappeared. In what seemed like a second, the alien quickly appeared in front of Seleece.

"How come you didn't have to...you know, establish a connection or search memories or whatever before you took off?" she asked.

The alien seemed confused by her question. "Why would I do that? Your apartment is already quite familiar to me, I don't need to do any of that," the alien said calmly.

Seleece's face quickly turned red with embarrassment as she heard where the alien had taken her commander. She remembered how messy her apartment was. The thought of her commander seeing her home in such a state was very embarrassing. "You did

WHAT? Why would you do that, you moron?" Seleece said with complete embarrassment.

"Did I do my laundry? What about my underwear? Damn it!" she thought to herself. Her outburst seemed to catch the alien somewhat of guard; it did not seem to understand why she was upset.

"I do not understand the problem. Kalduron is back on Demora," the alien said.

"I know that!" she said while attempting to slap him out of frustration. The alien quickly teleported behind her avoiding the slap by a thread.

"Why are you attacking me?" the alien asked.

"Ugh! Just, never mind…let's go find Salvador now," Seleece said as she calmed down.

"I do not understand why you attacked me."

"I wasn't attacking you! I was trying to slap you for being such a moron! Never mind that…it's fine!" I'll get you back for it later. "Let's focus on the mission. Turn on your cloaking device," she said.

They both quickly turned on their cloaking devices.

"You couldn't defeat me even if you tried again at a later time," the alien said while appearing next to her.

Seleece let out a big laugh. "Ha, ha! That's not what I meant. We will see about that though; I am the best there is," she responded.

The alien quickly placed its hand on her shoulder and focused on Salvador's location.

"I...I feel him too!" Seleece thought.

"While we are linked, instances like that can happen. You may be able to sense what I am sensing...perhaps feel what I am feeling. The more we do it, the easier it will come to you," the alien said telepathically.

"I feel him...far away," Seleece said telepathically.

"Yes. I am not quite sure where he is, but I feel like I can still get us there," the alien said.

"So what you are saying is that you can teleport us to where he is but you don't need to know where that is?" Seleece asked.

"Well…I suppose it's a bit like walking," the alien responded while focusing on Salvador's location. The alien's eyes began to emit their strong, usual white light as it focused.

"A bit like walking? What do you mean by tha—"

Seleece's question was abruptly interrupted by the change of scenery. Her eyes shifted from the grassy planes of CB19 to a much louder, urban setting. There were tall buildings all around, for what seemed like miles. The sky was a dense, bright blue color with not a cloud in sight. They were now standing outside of what looked like a restaurant in a very busy street. They could see many alien species walking in and out of the establishment.

"I see lots of humans here. I guess we must be on Earth," Seleece said right after her helmet confirmed their location. "Earth, huh? Not surprising, not one damn bit," Seleece said telepathically to the alien. "So where the hell is Salvador? I don't see him anywhere."

"He just walked in there," the alien said while pointing at a sign. The Galactic Beer Garden, it said in Universal.

"What a crappy name," Seleece whispered to the alien.

"Yes, the place where life forms gather to consume matter," the alien responded with a calm tone.

"Right…let's go inside and see what he is up to. But be cautious; we are in public and we can't risk—"

The alien didn't let her finish what she was about to say. It did not seem to have heard what she said, or didn't seem to care much for her plan because suddenly, it disappeared.

"Damn it!" Seleece said to herself. She quickly rushed over to the restaurant, trying not to touch anybody as she sneaked through the front door.

"Where the hell did it run off to? Our cover might be blown if they find the alien here!" she thought.

Perhaps the alien went toward the back; it sure wasn't hanging out at the entrance. It was a rather crowded place for that time of the day. It was only 10:00 a.m. on Earth, on a Tuesday, yet the place was buzzing as if it were a Saturday night.

"It must be some sort of famous place. Perhaps that was why Salvador picked it or, rather, his superiors did. Easy to blend in if they are surrounded by so many civilians," she thought as she carefully scouted the place for any sign of the alien or Salvador.

As her search continued, her eyes suddenly caught a glimpse of one of her targets. Farther away, a familiar face could be seen standing next to what seemed like a VIP table, completely secluded from the rest of the restaurant. It was Salvador, looking serious and focused. He was still dressed in the same clothes they had seen him in before.

"Aha! I found you!" Seleece thought to herself as she stared straight at him.

"Wait…why is he standing like that?" she thought as quickly noticed that he was not there for his own pleasure. "That's…it's that human official Ramos! Salvador must be here on guard duty," she thought. Suddenly, the alien appeared right next to Seleece, startling her.

She took step back and almost tripped over an empty table. "Damn it! Don't do that!" She whispered to the alien, hoping no one noticed that the empty table had slightly moved. It seemed they were in the clear, no one noticed due to how busy and loud the restaurant was. She quickly signaled the alien to touch her shoulder to establish a connection between them. "What the hell is wrong with you? Are you stupid? Where the heck did you run off to like that?" Seleece communicated telepathically.

The alien could feel her anger, but that seemed to do nothing but confuse it. "You feel anger. Why? I don't understand," the alien responded.

"Ugh…never mind," Seleece said as she focused on her target. "Look over there. That is without a doubt Ramos. That's the human official who works with Melthuron. Finally, we got the break we needed!" Seleece communicated telepathically. "Yes, I know. I saw them when I first entered this place. They were walking toward the table they are now seated at," the alien responded.

"Damn it, we are so far away from Commander Kalduron. What should we do?" Seleece communicated with concern.

"We can't just kidnap a human official such as Ramos; not now. It would cause way too much commotion in a crowded place like this. But at the same time, he must have much more information on Melthuron and his plans than his lackey ever would," Seleece communicated while she pondered what their next move should be. She knew the risk of taking that course of action; she knew it well.

An anxious, uneasy feeling began to creep into the back of her mind as she thought about what they should do next. If they were to take Ramos, it could backfire quickly. He was, after all, a very important official. Not only that, but it looked like he was holding some sort of meeting with other elected officials. With no way to contact her commander, the decision fell solely on Seleece's shoulders.

She took a long, drawn out breath. "Let's do it. We can't miss this opportunity," Seleece said telepathically with her mind made up. "Whatever the consequences may be, his knowledge could trump them all. This is a risk we are just going to have to take." She was ready.

"All right, here's the plan. Take us closer so I can record what they are talking about. It looks like they haven't been here too long, so they are probably just starting their meeting. Once they leave this restaurant, we will take them back to Demora with us by force, understood?" Seleece commanded to the alien. "Move us over there," she said as she pointed to a small corner.

"We will not take him with us. We can't risk alerting the human authorities. I will just read his mind," the alien said defiantly. "We will only take him with us if he holds any information of value. It's not worth the risk." The alien could already feel Seleece's anger.

"Excuse me? What? He's right there. RIGHT THERE! To hell with the damn original plan! We have acquired a much more important target right in front of us, and that…that takes priority!"

"No," the alien communicated as it teleported both of them to the corner near the table.

"There won't be any more problems, I assure you," Ramos said as he looked at the person sitting across from him.

"We will talk about this later!" Seleece said telepathically as she focused on her target's conversation.

"We may have lost one of our weapons, but Melthuron reassures us that it won't be for long. It is only a matter of time before we get it back. We have planned for a scenario such as this," Ramos said with much confidence. "As long as Melthuron keeps his end of the bargain, you have my full support on this, Ramos. You have never let me down before," the unidentified person replied.

"They must be talking about you," Seleece communicated to the alien telepathically.

"I am inclined to agree," the alien said telepathically. Even after finding out about their plans to use it as a weapon, the alien seemed completely detached from what its captors were planning to do. The alien's lack of emotion confused Seleece.

"Doesn't it make you mad? The fact that they planned to use you doesn't make you the least bit angry? They were going to turn you into their slave. Don't you care at all?" she asked.

But her empathy seemed to fall on deaf ears. "Irrelevant," the alien responded without hesitation. "They would have never been able to fully control me, regardless of whatever they had planned."

"Have you witnessed the power of Melthuron's newly developed weapon first hand?" the unidentified person asked, eagerly hoping to hear more about it in detail.

"Only a brief glimpse," Ramos responded with enthusiasm. "But I assure you, what I was able to see before meeting you here was beyond my expectations. Melthuron assures me that as his research continues, new frontiers will be discovered. The possibilities are endless."

"Excellent!" the unidentified person responded with excitement before taking a sip of red wine. He was an old man, with white hair and light skin. "Let Melthuron know that the funding will continue for now. But I want a full demonstration, and I want it soon," the unidentified man said in a serious, demanding tone.

"But of course, sir. Melthuron has informed me that he only needs a few more days before he can present it to you. However, perhaps a small demonstration is in order. I hope it eases some of your concerns," Ramos said.

Hearing this seemed to please the unidentified man.

"But as I said before, this is only but a small glimpse of what Melthuron has achieved," Ramos said.

"I'll take that into account. I am quite anxious to see it," the unidentified voice said.

"Computer, take pictures of these two humans in front of me," Seleece communicated to her helmet. As fast as it could, the helmet's computer took a picture of them shaking hands together.

"Now then, would you come with us?" Ramos asked before snapping his fingers. Suddenly, one of Melthuron's soldiers appeared.

"No! We must stop them before they have a chance to escape. Stop them!" Seleece commanded from behind the shadows.

The alien, however, didn't move at all.

"What are you doing standing around for? They are going to get away," she said telepathically.

"Come, Salvador. We are leaving," Ramos said as he walked toward the unidentified man.

"No you don't! I won't let you!" she thought as she raised her weapon in their direction.

Seleece didn't have much of a choice; it was risky, but she had to take the shot. But it was too late. She missed; they had disappeared from her sight. Instead, the blast blew a table into pieces, scattering it all over as customers began to run out in horror.

Screams could be heard throughout the restaurant as other customers heard what had just happened.

"No! Damn it!" she screamed out in anger. "Why didn't you stop them? Why?"

"Not here," the alien responded telepathically.

Suddenly, they were no longer standing inside the restaurant. Seleece's eyes quickly adjusted to the blue sky in front her. Hundreds of sky scrapers stood ahead; the whole city was now in plain view.

"Damn it! Where are we?" Seleece shouted as she took off her helmet.

"I have taken us to the top of the building. This was the right course of action," the alien responded.

"No it wasn't! Why did you do this? We could have stopped them!"

"Because if I am captured, it will all be over. I won't risk engaging in battle when Melthuron is not present. It is not worth the risk, especially when one of his soldiers is present. We should head back and discuss what we have found with Kalduron," the alien responded. Seleece had no intention of letting it go.

"I know keeping you safe is important, but the information we could have obtained was well worth the risk!" she said. Seleece was absolutely furious for the lost opportunity.

"Do you realize what you have just done? We should have taken both Salvador and Ramos when we had the chance. We may never get another one again," Seleece raged as she pounded the roof of the building with her fist. The force of the punch completely crushed the floor, leaving a small hole underneath her fist.

"You…you can still feel him, can't you? You know where Salvador is?" she asked the alien as she stood up.

"Correct. I can feel him, but we shouldn't jump into a battle like this so unprepared. This body is still somewhat injured from our last encounter with Melthuron. It should regress to the original state in a couple of hours," the alien concluded as it stared at Seleece.

"I don't care. You and I have a job to do. We have the element of surprise on our side," Seleece responded. She knew all too well what could happen if they were to face Melthuron's soldiers head on again, but she didn't care. She wanted revenge. And she was willing to risk her own life for it.

"Is Salvador close?" she asked as she picked up her helmet.

"That question is relative to what you define as close," the alien responded.

"Are they still here on Earth," she asked before double-checking her inventory.

"That appears to be the case," the alien responded.

"Then we must go after him now. Let's not waste any more time here," she said as she grabbed the C1 blaster from the back of her armor.

The alien didn't respond.

"What are you waiting for? Take me there now!" she demanded. "No," the alien replied. "We should wait until Kalduron gathers the rest of our allies before we attempt to do this. The more

soldiers we have, the better our chances will be. If something

happens to you or me while we are out here, it will leave us at a huge

disadvan—"

"We need to go...NOW! They won't see us coming!"

Seleece screamed.

The alien just stared back blankly. "No, we won't do that. No

matter how much louder your voice becomes, it will not change the

course of action we will take. We will regroup with Kalduron for

now," the alien said as it began to walk toward Seleece.

"The hell we are!" Seleece said as her postured changed to a

defensive stance. She turned her electroglove on as she got in a

fighting position. "I want you to take me to where Salvador and

Ramos have gone. Don't you DARE try to take me anywhere else,"

she said menacingly. The alien suddenly came to a stop. It seemed

unamused by her behavior.

"Let's make something clear," Seleece said as she paid close

attention to the alien's position, trying to make sure it didn't disappear and try to take her with it. "I am the one giving the orders here, not you," she said. "I'm not asking you to come with me. But don't force me to do what you want when we have been given clear orders to retrieve Salvador. I will not fail this mission. You can either take me there willingly or try to take me back to Demora by force," she said without taking her eyes off of the alien.

Her threats seemed to fly right past the alien; it was completely unmoved by her words. "Very well, I chose the second option," the alien said as it disappeared from Seleece's gaze.

"Shit! Where did it—"

Immediately, Seleece felt a light touch on the back of her head before her eyes adjusted to the bed that was now standing before her.

Chapter 8

"Damn it!" she said as she realized that the alien had taken them back to her apartment. "How dare you do this to me," she screamed out loud, furious by the alien's actions.

But she knew there was nothing she could do about it. Even if she left now, it would take her way too long to get back to Earth. Even if she took the fastest ship available, she would never make it back in time.

"You gave me two options, and I chose the second one," the alien said. "Now contact your leader. It is time to regroup with the rest of our forces. That's when we will decide which course of action to take," the alien concluded before teleporting away, leaving Seleece completely alone in her apartment.

"Ugh! That smug bastard," Seleece said as she put on her helmet. She quickly turned it on, making the interface visible. The helmet lit up inside, showing all sorts of data from her vital signs to the helmet's battery life. "Elevated heart rate detected," the helmet said.

"Shut up and contact Kalduron!" Seleece said telepathically.

"Status report," Kalduron said as he picked up her call.

"Sir, Salvador's whereabouts are currently unknown," Seleece responded with a hint of shame in her voice. She couldn't believe that she had failed Kalduron again.

"Unknown? Were you not able to locate him with the alien's assistance?" Kalduron asked via the voice transmission.

"Yes sir. We had him on our sights, sir, but he was teleported away by one of Melthuron's soldiers. The soldier showed up out of nowhere and took both Ramos and Salvador to an unknown location before we could engage."

Kalduron's tone quickly changed. "What have you got for me then?" Kalduron asked with impatience.

"Well, sir, I was able to gather audio and photo intelligence. The human official Ramos was in a meeting with a high-class human. They were discussing Melthuron's experiments, although not in great detail. The unidentified human mentioned Melthuron's newly developed weapons but nothing substantial was shared about them. I'm transferring the data to you now," she said as the helmet transmitted the data she had gathered.

Kalduron quickly received all of the intelligence and noticed that the person Ramos had a meeting with seemed familiar. He couldn't quite put his finger on it, but he had seen that person somewhere before. "The picture isn't very clear, but I believe I've seen this human somewhere before. Have you run his face against the universal database?" Kalduron asked.

"No sir. I will do it right now," Seleece responded without hesitation.

The universal database had been established long ago as a means to identify possible criminals across the galaxy. All foreign governments had full access to this vast collection of perhaps trillions of civilians. It had an array of information, everything from facial recognition to fingerprints to genetic makeup. But it didn't work. Whoever this human was, the database was unable to recognize him via facial recognition alone.

"Sir, it seems the program was unable to recognize him using just facial recognition," Seleece said.

"It doesn't surprise me in the least bit," Kalduron said as he let out a sigh of frustration. "If this human is as rich and powerful as I think he is, there's no way he would be in that database. Rich and powerful people have been above the law ever since I can remember. They play by different rules. "We will figure out who this human is in due time. For now, I want you and the alien to join me at this location," Kalduron quickly sent Seleece some coordinates she had not seen in a long time, not since the war.

"Yes sir, but there's one problem. After the alien brought me back to Demora, it disappeared. Its whereabouts are unknown to me at the moment."

This news infuriated Kalduron. "You let it go out on its own?" Kalduron said angrily.

"Sir, there was nothing I could do. This alien is proving to be too difficult for me to control. It brought me back to Demora by force and then disappeared before I could even speak to it," she responded.

Kalduron took a second to relax. The alien was proving to be hard to control, just like Kalduron anticipated.

"In due time. We will figure out a way to control it and make it our best asset. For now, we need to gain its trust so that it does not run around doing who knows what without our knowledge," Kalduron said calmly. "Knowing you, you two have probably been butting heads the whole time. I need that to stop. I want you, until otherwise ordered, to follow all of the alien's commands without question. We need it to think we are working toward its goal and nothing else," Kalduron said.

"Sir, yes sir!" Seleece responded without hesitation. "What should we do about the alien's disappearance? Would you like me to go search for it, sir?" Seleece asked.

"No, that will not be necessary. I'm sure the alien will come to us in due time. Be at this location within the hour," Kalduron said as he ended the call.

"Follow the alien's every command, huh?" Seleece thought to herself as she walked toward the other end of her bedroom.

It had been over a hundred years since she undertook such a covert mission. She had to make sure she never consciously thought about this new mission. If she did, the alien would figure out what they were planning, and that was something she couldn't risk. Seleece knew it would be difficult to gain the alien's trust, but the alien was vital to their struggle against Melthuron.

"Guess I will have to suck it up for now," Seleece thought as she laughed. She needed to laugh. In fact, she had to. She needed to clear her head and relax a little.

"Perhaps a shower could do the trick," she thought. She walked over to the bathroom which was on the other side of her bedroom. For a bathroom, it was quite big. The walls and tiles were made out of reinforced glass, which could never get dirty. The whole bathroom sparkled with cleanliness; a complete opposite to her untidy bedroom.

There was a standard shower to the far left. To the far right there was a big circular tub extending upward from the floor. She walked over to the shower, stripping down step by step as she got closer. She was still mentally exhausted from everything that had been going on. As she turned on the shower, she hoped the hot water would wash away all her troubles, or at least help alleviate some of the pain she had been trying so hard to avoid, but it didn't.

All her mind could do was obsess about Melthuron, the Thespian she had grown to hate more than anyone or anything else in her entire life. As the hot water began to flow down her short, black hair, she clenched her fists as she thought about her fellow soldiers; the friends she had unknowingly led to their deaths.

"Melthuron! I will kill you for what you've done!" she screamed as more than just water began to drip down her face. She pounded the wall in front of her, breaking the reinforced glass with ease. She took a deep breath.

"I have work to do," Seleece said to herself as she calmed down. "Servebot!" Seleece screamed as she stepped out of the hot shower before covering herself with a long, silver towel.

The robot's voice recognition software recognized Seleece's voice. It wasn't long before it appeared.

"Welcome home, master Seleece. How may I serve you?" the Serverbot replied as it rolled toward the bathroom.

"Fix the hole in the bathroom wall," Seleece commanded as she walked past her robot, picking up some loose-fitting clothes to wear underneath her armor.

"Yes, master Seleece," the robot said as it rolled toward the bathroom to assess the damage.

"This will do," Seleece said as she picked out some clothes from the closet. She quickly got dressed before putting on her armor and helmet.

"Computer, show coordinates 60'45'34 S '23'15'7 E on the map," she communicated telepathically to the helmet's interface.

"I see, we are meeting at the old base," she thought.

Those coordinates marked the location of an old Thespian military base used by Seleece's species during the Thespian civil war. One of the last, deciding battles had taken place in that area over one hundred years ago. Although most of it had been destroyed, an underground bunker was mostly intact. That must be where Kalduron is holding the meeting.

"I'll make it with time to spare," she thought as she made sure all of her weapons were accounted for. She quickly wrote down the coordinates and left them on the table in her living room.

"Make sure our guest receives these coordinates if it happens to stop by," Seleece said.

"Yes, master Seleece. I will have that hole fixed by the time you come back," the Serverbot answered as Seleece made her way toward the door front door.

"Oh, and tidy up the place! I don't want to see a mess when I come back," Seleece shouted as the door slammed shut behind her.

"Let's see, I think that base is about thirty minutes from here if I take my hoverbike," Seleece thought.

She didn't have just any hoverbike. Seleece, along with all other soldiers of her unit, had personalized military grade vehicles, but the hoverbike was her favorite. It could fly up to seven hundred miles per hour. It was a slim, well-designed vehicle that, compared to civilian hoverbike, had up to 50 percent more air resistance and speed than its civilian counterpart

She turned on her cloaking device as she walked down the building's chrome corridor toward the stairs. She ran up the stairs quickly, reaching the roof of the building in mere seconds. As the door of the roof slid open in front of her, the outside of Demora became visible. It was later in the evening now.

The sky was slowly turning into fiery orange as the star Demora circulated began to set on Demora's horizon. Her eyes caught a small glimpse of the huge skyline as she walked up to the roof. In just about every direction, huge skyscrapers filled the land. Buildings could be seen extending far beyond what Seleece's bright violet eyes could see. The entire population of Demora lived inside the capital, which had been renamed New Jermaxus. Most of the planet had been laid to waste during the war. New Jermaxus was the only place that was free from the pollution than ran rampant across the once fruitful planet.

The city itself was engulfed by a powerful magnetic field that kept the radiation at bay. Leaving the city was forbidden to all civilians.

"I will protect with my life the peace my species fought so hard for. I won't let war happen again on Demora's soil as long as I am still breathing," she thought as she stared straight into the city in front of her.

Just the possibility of war turned her stomach. She had enough of that for a hundred lifetimes. Every Thespian did.

"If that bastard thinks he can start another war, he has another thing coming. I won't let that happen. Never again," She thought as she stared straight ahead into the orange sky.

"Computer, activate hoverbike," Seleece said telepathically to her helmet's computer as her mind drifted back to the mission.

Within seconds, her helmet's interface lit up, indicating that the hoverbike was homing in on her location. She took a deep breath and began to run full speed toward the end of the roof.

She jumped. The ground began to grow closer as she fell with increasing speed until her hoverbike caught her, magnetically attaching itself to her armor with ease.

"That never grows old," she thought as she reminisced about the times she had jumped off onto her hoverbike with her fellow soldiers; too many for her to count. It was almost like a tradition, to ride off into a mission with the possibility of never coming back. Now it was just her, riding off alone for the very first time.

"Engage autopilot," Seleece commanded through her helmet's computer. Her hoverbike quickly began to accelerate forward, speeding up to full speed in just five seconds as it began to set course for her destination. Seleece's eyes could barely keep up with the fast-moving buildings as she flew past them. As her gaze shifted away from the city, a grimmer picture began to set on the horizon. Just outside the outskirts of the city, the rubble of Old Jermaxus was visible for anyone who dared to step outside the sanctuary that New Jermaxus had become. Seleece didn't want to look; in fact, she couldn't. It had been over ten years since she laid eyes on that part of her world.

Over one eighty years ago, Seleece had been part the battalion that had laid siege to the city. It only took her and her army a couple of hours to reduce that once thriving city into the wasteland that it is today. That was her darkest, most shameful moment. Something she could never forget.

"No, I don't want to remember," she thought as she closed her eyes and ignored the destruction she had caused so long ago. She kept her eyes shut for over twenty minutes as her hoverbike continued at full speed, painfully trying to ignore what had happened so long ago.

"Estimated time of arrival is ten minutes," her helmet said.

"That's long enough," she thought as she opened her eyes.

The scenery had changed. She could now see a big, snowy mountain range that extended for what seemed like miles. But it wasn't just snow that covered those mountains. Everywhere she looked was covered in ash and debris; the one painful reminder of how far destruction had spread. The debris from the war had slowly taken over most of her planet.

"I wonder who Kalduron is assembling for this meeting," she pondered as she tried to shift her mind away from those old thoughts. She had a couple of ideas as to who could ally themselves with Kalduron, but she wasn't quite sure if she could trust them. Suddenly, she was interrupted by the sound of her hoverbike stopping.

"You have arrived," her helmet announced.

"Good!" she said as she jumped off her hoverbike onto the ground below. Her body instantly sank into the ash-covered snow, completely covering one-third of her body. There was nothing but mountains for miles.

"Activate cloaking device and power down," she said. The

hoverbike slowly descended into the snow covered ground before turning invisible.

"Let's see here, where is that damn entrance?" she said as she looked around, shifting some the black snow around as she looked for a switch.

"Extreme temperature detected. Activating temperature control measures," her helmet said to Seleece. Her suit started to warm up her body, which had started to feel the effects of the cold environment around her.

"Ah, that's better!" she said as she started to feel the effects of the suit. The Thespian battle suit had been designed to take stimuli from the environment and change itself accordingly to make sure the wearer would not be harmed or slowed down due to environmental conditions. It could take such measures as changing its density and temperature. Seleece was sure feeling glad about that, she hated the cold.

"There it is!" she said before pressing the big red button. A hologram quickly scanned Seleece's battle armor, identifying

Seleece by her identification code.

"Welcome back, soldier one one zero one," the interface said.

An underground entrance opened up, revealing a deep underground

tunnel. The lights inside the tunnel began to switch on one by one,

displaying a long, underground tunnel that descended vertically into

the underground base. The walls of the tunnel were made out

stainless steel, giving it a clean, silvery look. Seleece swiftly hopped

onto the platform under her, magnetically latching onto it with her

suit.

The platform began to descend at an increasing rate. Seleece

closed her eyes. She began to mentally prepare herself for the

meeting that was about to take place. Kalduron was probably

furious; she didn't have Melthuron's location and had lost both

Salvador and Ramos when they were right in front of her. Not only

that, but their new weapon was running around, unchecked. She had

been a complete failure; that was something she was not used to at

all.

"It's gonna be fine," she said to herself as she inhaled deeply in an attempt to relax. "Kalduron will know what to do. He always does," she thought.

After all, Kalduron had been her superior for over one hundred and fifty years. In Seleece's eyes, there had never been someone more capable than her commander. It was his swift, uncompromising leadership alone that had kept her species out of extinction during the civil war. After a few minutes, the platform had come to a complete stop at the very bottom of the tunnel right in front of a large metal door.

"This sure brings back memories," she thought as she walked forward into the room ahead, remembering all the times she and her soldiers had done so together during the war. She walked through the sliding door into the room ahead, appearing a few yards away from where Kalduron was standing. In the middle of the room stood what seemed like an outdated, old control room with a circular hologram display, which was currently offline. The walls were a dirty, stained mess. It was safe to assume no one had been there to clean in a long time.

"Sir! Reporting for duty!" Seleece said as she greeted her commander.

"Well, would you look at that! But if it isn't the famous Seleece! The decorated war hero. It's so great to be in your presence," a voice said in a sarcastic tone, coming from the far left of the room. Seleece recognized that voice almost immediately; she was quite annoyed hear it.

"There were no heroes in that war. You of all people should know that," Seleece responded angrily.

"Well... good to see you too," the voice replied in an annoyed tone before taking off his helmet. It was Lieutenant Greynor. This Thespian soldier had fought alongside Seleece back in the Thespian civil war, but their history dated back much further than that. They had been bitter rivals since the academy; both praised for their above-average performance in all of the academy's exams. He had been her superior for much of the war until one mission changed it all.

She disobeyed his orders and decided to follow her own instinct instead. Her disobedience ended up saving millions of lives and earned her the title of war hero. Greynor, on the other hand, ended up being demoted for his lack of judgment, losing his rank to Seleece. This did nothing but fuel their bitter rivalry further.

"I heard you led our brothers to their de—"

"That's enough!" Kalduron screamed at Greynor viciously. "Both of you will be quiet until the rest of our members join us. I don't want to hear a word out of you two until then!" Kalduron commanded.

The room went completely quiet. Both of them could feel the anger and frustration coming out of Kalduron's every word. A few, silent minutes went by before the gate behind Seleece opened, revealing the last two members of the group.

"Kalduron, you better have a damn good reason for calling me all the way here. It's damn near freezing cold on this part of your planet!" one of the members said as he walked in. The human was Thomas Johnson III, one of Earth's most powerful and influential figures. Although recently retired, he had served as chief commander

of Earth's army for thirty years before joining the Intergalactic

Alliance as an advisor

"I guess we are about to find out," the other member said as

he walked in. "I don't think Kalduron would waste our valuable time

unless it was the direst of situations." It was Jamos, a Thespian

leader and a member of Melthuron's species. Jamos and Kalduron

were almost the same age and had known each other for hundreds of

years. They had sadly fought against each other during the war, but

both survived and so had their friendship. Back then, it was not rare

for Thespians of both species to befriend one another, but that had

all changed since the seeds of war were first sewn long ago.

"Kalduron, it's good to see you old friend," Jamos said as he

warmly greeted his childhood friend.

"Likewise, Jamos," Kalduron said warmly. "I am sorry to

have called you two here on such short notice, but Jamos is sadly

correct. The fate of this side of the galaxy may be at stake,"

Kalduron said as he walked closer to the center of the room.

"What I am about to tell you is difficult to hear, but nonetheless you must believe me. There's no easy way to say this, so I'm just going to come out and say it. Melthuron has committed high treason against the Intergalactic Alliance by murdering all but one of the officials. We must find him and bring him to justice."

There was only silence for a moment. They both knew something bad had happened, but they would have never guessed it would be that bad. They were shocked.

"It's true," Seleece said, breaking the awkward silence that had filled the room. "I fought against Melthuron back at headquarters and barely escaped with my life."

"If that's the case, where is the proof?" Jamos asked with an almost pale face. He knew Kalduron would never lie to him, but these revelations were a lot to take in.

"These are serious accusations. Where is the proof, Kalduron? Stop wasting my time," Thomas said concerned. "Melthuron has been one step ahead of us the entire time. He not only killed every single one of the intergalactic soldiers stationed there, but he managed to get rid of almost all evidence as well," Seleece said nervously.

They were again silent.

"It is all true. I was there," Kalduron said as he walked over to Seleece. "Soldier, please share with us the few bits of evidence you have gathered," Kalduron said as he placed his hand on her shoulder to comfort her.

Seleece quickly put on her helmet and turned it on. "Transfer all data to main computer," Seleece said to her helmet telepathically.

"Transferring…transferring…complete," the helmet's interface said.

As soon as it was completed, the display in the center of the room turned on. Everyone in the room could see the various pictures and audio files gathered by Seleece from her previous encounter with Salvador and Ramos.

"Play audio file BC7894," Seleece said. Soon after, the audio file began playing loudly in the room. Their faces paled as they heard everything Ramos had discussed with that unknown human not even two hours ago.

The room grew even more silent after the file ended; both Jamos and Thomas appeared to be beyond shocked by what they had heard.

"This can't be happening…this…this is one of the worst situations I have seen in a long time," Jamos said with great concern. "Do we know what type of weapon Melthuron has or is developing?"

"Negative," Kalduron responded. "I realize this is a lot to take in. Take your time to process this," Kalduron said as he walked toward the display.

"Gentlemen, we have seen this happen before. I can say without a shadow of a doubt that if these weapons are being developed to be sold to a third party, or if they fall in the wrong hands, there will be war," Kalduron said. "History has taught me a painful lesson. When societies develop new weapons, it is certain that war will follow to test them. If this happens…when this happens, I need to know that both of you will stand with me," Kalduron said as serious as ever.

"Kalduron, what you are talking about is borderline treason," Jamos said.

"There's more," Seleece said. "As my team led the rescue mission aboard the unidentified ship, where we believed Melthuron was being held, I stumbled on one of Melthuron's experiments. It was some sort of alie—"

"I guarantee you I am no alien life form, at least not in the sense you are referring to," the alien said as it appeared in the center of the room.

"What is that?" Jamos screamed as the alien's naked and sudden appearance startled him.

Thomas was perhaps even more shocked since the alien appeared much closer to him. He fell backward, completely startled by the alien's sudden appearance

"What on earth is that? How the did that thing get in here?" Thomas screamed as he reached for his weapon inside his jacket.

"Stop, Thomas! This alien is an ally," Kalduron screamed.

"You there, soldier of Kalduron, your leader is telling the truth. Lower your weapon. You don't want me to take them all away from you," the alien said calmly. Greynor just stared back at the alien with a disturbed look, unseen from behind his helmet. He took his hand off the trigger and placed his weapon away.

"Who…who are you?" Jamos asked, intrigued.

"Who I am is of no importance; what I am is important. I am your ally," the alien staring into Jamos's blue eyes.

Jamos doubted the alien, but he trusted his old friend. "A friend of Kalduron's is a friend of mine," Jamos said.

"This friend has saved not only my life, but that of Seleece and Councilman Peter Jiggs. This alien will be vital in our efforts to stop Melthuron," Kalduron said, somewhat relived to see the alien again. At least now he knew where the alien was.

"But why are you naked? Put some damn clothes on!" Thomas said as he looked away from the alien.

"Clothes? I have no need for them, nor do I have any to use," the alien responded calmly.

"Yeah really, though…we need to get you some clothes. Anyway, this alien has very powerful and useful abilities that will greatly aid us in our efforts. I have witnessed them first hand," Seleece added.

"Melthuron has developed soldiers with similar abilities to this alien. They have proven extremely difficult to fight against. If Melthuron develops more soldiers like them, we will be at a great disadvantage," Kalduron said as he stared at Thomas.

Thomas looked uneasy, concerned by what he had just heard. "You mean to tell me Melthuron created this…this alien thing?" Thomas asked as he stared at the alien, both scared and shocked by it. He had never seen anything like it. The alien quickly teleported in front of Thomas, appearing just four feet away from him. He completely towered over the six-foot human, almost twice his height and probably four times his weight.

"I am no experiment of Melthuron. Please don't call me that again," the alien said.

"All…all right, sorry," Thomas said in a shaky voice.

The alien did not seem to know it was scaring Thomas. It probably still didn't understand facial expressions. "Are these all the allies you can muster? Or will others be joining us?" the alien asked Kalduron.

"Thomas and Jamos are both trustworthy allies with powerful connections. They will be on our side if a struggle against Melthuron ensues. They are all that we need and, more importantly, I know I can trust them," Kalduron said. "Moreover, they have the power to help gather much-needed muscle that we will desperately need if the moment arises," Kalduron concluded.

The alien seemed pleased, although it was hard to tell from its expressionless face.

"I will proceed then," the alien said as it walked toward the display in the center of the room.

Kalduron seemed somewhat nervous to let the alien take over the meeting, but decided not to intervene. "Perhaps it's best if I let it say what it wants to say. I don't want that thing to realize we are really just planning to use him," Kalduron thought to himself.

Seleece saw Kalduron's expression and realized what he was thinking, but she felt somewhat guilty. Even though the alien had been causing her much trouble lately, Seleece was starting to have second thoughts about using the alien for their own agenda. The idea of using it as their own weapon was starting to feel wrong. If they were successful, they would be no better than Melthuron, and that was something that was starting to eat away at her.

"It is unknown to me what Melthuron's goal is, but it does not matter," the alien said out loud to everyone in the room. "He will have no chance to enact what he desires. I presume our agreement is still in place, Kalduron?" the alien asked Kalduron.

"But of course," Kalduron said. "Melthuron is yours once we find him. When you are done extracting the information you seek, we will bring him to justice and, as promised, he won't be harmed in any way," Kalduron responded.

"In return, you have my abilities at your disposal for whatever you need," the alien said. The alien then turned to face them. "Now you must all agree to these terms," the alien said as it stared down at Jamos and Thomas.

Although Jamos appeared quite calm, Thomas was anything but. "These are absurd terms! Who are you to dictate a deal such as this? I do not agree at all. We will have to renegotiate."

"There is nothing needs renegotiation," the alien said. "You either accept this deal or force me to complete this mission on my own."

"Oh crap…here we go," Seleece thought as she remained silent.

"There's no need for that. We will all agree to these terms, won't we, Thomas?" Jamos said in an attempt to calm everyone.

"I agree to your terms, my new ally," Jamos said with sincerity. "If Kalduron trusts you, so do I," he concluded, waiting to see how Thomas would react.

"Have you both gone mad? Or perhaps you both have lost your judgment with old age? We can't let this...this thing do whatever it wants!" Thomas said loudly, staring at the strange alien in front of him.

"How dare you speak to Kalduron like tha—"

"Mind your tongue, Seleece!" Kalduron yelled, swiftly interrupting her. "Thomas has been a great ally to our kind for many years. You will show him the respect he deserves," Kalduron screamed.

"Yes sir! My sincerest of apologies, Councilman Thomas," Seleece said quickly.

"I understand your concerns, Thomas, but we have little to no choice," Kalduron told him. "Melthuron's soldiers killed every single soldier aboard the headquarters ship, all twenty, without getting as much as a scratch on them. If we were to ever engage in a confrontation without this alien's help, we would be killed without as much as laying a hand on them. They are ruthless, precise killers. I have never seen anything like it," Kalduron replied with honesty.

"If you want the human race to help you, I want to know more about you first. It's either that, or you have no deal at all. I will not just agree to a deal without being properly informed. Now tell me, who are you? What planet do you come from?" Thomas asked the alien.

The alien ignored his question.

"Do you accept my terms?" the alien asked.

"I know you are not deaf! Answer the questions or you have no deal! Who are you? What has Melthuron done to you?" Thomas asked the alien in a threatening tone, his patience running thin.

"Melthuron has placed me in this body. The reason as to why or how he has done so still eludes me," the alien responded softly. "Now do you agree to my terms, Mr. Thomas?" the alien asked.

"Absolutely not! I would be crazy to trust a thing like you. I don't even know what you are! And what on earth do you mean by 'placed in that body'?" Thomas yelled back.

"None of those answers concern you. You do not need to know anything else other than the information I have already provided," the alien responded. "Are you satisfied now? Do you accept my terms, Mr. Thomas," the alien asked in its monotone voice.

"Thomas, I implore you to accept. There are bigger concerns right now than your ego," Kalduron said with an emphasis on "implore you." His efforts to enlighten Thomas on his plan paid off. Thomas understood Kalduron's expression and what he had been trying to imply.

"Very well, I accept all of your terms," Thomas said.

The alien stared back at him blankly.

"Now then, let's shift our efforts to figuring out how to best find Melthuron," Jamos said, trying to get everyone back to the task at hand.

"Yes. Our new ally has a very useful ability. It can track anyone it touches no matter where they are," Kalduron informed his allies while looking straight at Thomas.

"Is that the case?" Thomas asked with a curious tone.

"That is only but a small fraction of what I can accomplish," the alien added.

"Well that will prove most useful," Thomas responded. He was now beginning to understand exactly what Kalduron had silently tried to tell him. If they were able to somehow control this alien, study it, reproduce it, it could bring them a giant advantage militarily for centuries to come. Thomas now knew that keeping tabs on the alien was very important; he would not pass on that opportunity. "Kalduron…you sneaky bastard," Thomas thought as he smirked.

"Well, I have to say I am very impressed. What else can you do Mr.…what is your name?" Thomas asked, trying to get as much information as possible out of the alien. The more he learned about it, the more uses he planned to find for it once they could control it.

"I have no name. I've had no need for one. Also 'mister' implies a gender, and I have no such thing," the alien replied. "I digress. Anything else is of no concern to you," the alien said as it walked toward the display.

"Well, I just think that knowing what you can do would prove beneficial when plan—"

"This human here," the alien said as it pointed to the unknown man in the picture, "does anyone know who he is?"

"Damn that alien," Thomas thought as he stared at the picture, trying to ignore the fact that he had been completely cut off.

"It's hard to tell from this picture, but I believe I know who that is," Thomas said as he stared at the picture. "That man there looks like Charles Locke, the founder and CEO of Deon Corp. That is the largest armament manufacturing company of Earth," Thomas explained.

"I've heard of him!" Jamos said as he looked at the display. "But he has been out of the public eye for many years. He sure looks different now," Jamos said.

"You humans do age rather horribly, don't you," he said as he laughed a bit. He was right. Thespians, unlike humans, did not age the same way. They stayed looking younger much longer than humans did; it was how they had evolved. Even Kalduron, who was one of the oldest Thespians alive, did not look that much older than Seleece who, by comparison, was more than one hundred years younger.

"I don't understand this exchange. Let's stay focused on what is important," the alien responded.

"Indeed. So, Melthuron is working with Deon Corp. This…this is quite troubling," Kalduron said with concern.

"It seems that way. Whatever they are planning can't be good for either of our planets," Thomas agreed.

"We must mobilize quickly," the alien said as it turned to face Jamos and Thomas. "How long would it take both of you to gather your forces?" the alien asked both of them at once.

"Let's hope we never have to do that," Jamos responded.

"From my end, it would take some time. I am no longer the commander of Earth's military. However, I still have considerable political muscle. I should be able to convince my colleagues in a matter of days, provided I present the right evidence. I guarantee results…the human race will be on your side," Thomas responded to the alien.

"Excellent. What about you, Jamos. You have not answered my question," the alien said.

"Unlike Thomas here, I have no hold over our military. That is Kalduron's job," Jamos replied. "Kalduron probably wants me to use the senate to thwart Melthuron's political power. After all, I am the head of the senate. I will wield the full power of the senate to fight him," Jamos concluded.

"I see. You have chosen strategic allies, Kalduron," said the alien. "How many soldiers can you provide right now? The more you provide me, the better our chances once will be once we go on the offensive." The alien asked.

"Seleece and Greynor are my best soldiers. They will accompany you at all times and be under your command. I can also provide you with all of the robot soldiers still hidden under this base. Seleece and Greynor can control them effortlessly. It would be suspicious if I mobilized a battalion at this time. I believe it is in our best interests to remain as hidden as possible. We must try to avoid war at all costs."

"Under the alien's command? Well, that blows. I'll be killed for sure," Seleece thought to herself.

"I will repeat my question once more," the alien said. "If the need arises, how quickly can you mobilize the Thespian army?"

"He can't do that, at least not by himself," Jamos responded swiftly.

"After the civil war, we came up with two ways to mobilize the Thespian army. One way is for every single member of the senate to vote yes on a resolution. The other is for the prime consort and half of the senate to vote on the resolution. Once either one of them gets passed, both Kalduron and Melthuron would have control over the military," Jamos replied.

It was hard to tell how the alien felt about this answer. The alien just stared at Jamos after hearing his explanation. While the alien's face was as expressionless as usual, Seleece knew that its silence meant something.

"I understand," the alien suddenly responded.

"What is it thinking?" Seleece wondered, knowing the alien had not taken that pause to catch its breath.

"So then...do you know where Melthuron is right now?" Jamos asked the alien.

"I don't know his location at this moment," the alien responded. "His soldiers are well adapted to fighting even a being like me. I didn't have the chance to place my energy on his body."

"And what power would that be?" Thomas asked, hoping this time he could gain some sort of knowledge about the alien's abilities.

"I do know where Ramos's bodyguard is located at this moment. It is in our best interests to find him," the alien said, completely ignoring Thomas.

This infuriated Thomas. He was not used to being treated in this way. Kalduron, however, was quick to intervene in an attempt to diffuse the situation.

"Seleece and Greynor will accompany you on this mission. Bring him back to us alive," Kalduron said.

"I will bring both Ramos and Salvador back this time, if possible. They will be useful," the alien responded.

It was a futile attempt. Thomas had been ignored for the last time. "That's it! I will not stand for this. You will answer my questions and you will answer them now!" Thomas screamed at the alien, clearly irritated by the way he was being treated.

"The questions have not been answered because there is no need to answer them. They are irrelevant to the matter at hand," the alien responded in a calm tone

The blank expression Thomas received from the alien only served to upset him further. "Kalduron, how do you expect us to work with such an alien? It shares nothing about its strategies, its abilities. How are we supposed to trust someone who doesn't trust us in return?" he asked as he stared at the alien angrily.

"I know these are stressful times, please forgive him for his outburst," Kalduron said.

"I'm sure the stress from these events is causing you to act uncharacteristically, Thomas. Just try to calm down," Kalduron said. Upsetting the alien was not an option for Kalduron. He knew what they would lose if the alien disappeared once again.

"No, Kalduron. I've had enough of this blatant disrespect! Don't forget that it was you who called me here! You want my help, not the other way around. I will be shown the respect a man of my stature deserves. Do not forget who you are talking to," Thomas responded.

"Don't be a fool, Thomas. The human race could also be in danger," Jamos responded.

The alien did not seem to care, or perhaps it didn't understand, but it suddenly teleported in front of Thomas. It was looking down at with its usual blank expression. "I do know how you creatures define disrespect, but I do not know what causes it or what it consists of," the alien said as monotone as always. "I don't want to waste any more time with these questions," the alien said calmly.

"Then stop ignoring me and answer them!" Thomas quickly replied, refusing to back down.

"How about I just show you what you want to so desperately see, although it is of little point to our mission?" the alien asked as it grabbed him by the throat and lifted him off the ground with ease, slowly choking Thomas. "I hope you will be satisfied with this performance," the alien said.

Thomas began to gasp for air. He grabbed the alien's arm and tried to shake him off, but the alien's brute strength was overwhelming.

"Stop, don't hurt him!" Seleece screamed, hoping the alien would listen. She knew there was nothing she could do. The alien was simply too strong and fast for them to stop.

As the alien turned to look at Seleece, it noticed that Greynor was reaching for his weapon. In what seemed like an instant, the alien teleported in front of Greynor and kicked the weapon out of his hands.

"Do not interfere" the alien told Greynor calmly. The alien's face was expressionless, but for some reason this time it struck fear into Greynor's very core. The alien wasn't messing around; it meant business. The room grew tense as the alien teleported back to where it was before, appearing in the middle of the room with Thomas still firmly held in the air. Everyone just stared as this was taking place. No one was going to lift a finger to help Thomas. At that point, they all knew there wasn't much they could do; the alien wouldn't allow it.

"Are you satisfied with my performance? Have you learned whatever information you were hoping to acquire?" the alien asked Thomas loudly, so everyone could hear. "You will serve your purpose in this group. There will be no more interruptions. Give me a thumbs-up if you are going to comply with my request," the alien said, waiting for his response.

Thomas immediately extended his arm out and gave the alien a thumbs-up as he struggled to breathe.

"Thank you," the alien said as it set Thomas down slowly. "I do apologize. No one deserves to be treated like that, but this was the quickest way to get you to move on from such pointless questions," the alien said as it touched Thomas's shoulder.

"It's…fine," Thomas said in a low tone as he gasped for air.

It seemed Seleece was the only one who was not shocked to see this. She knew the alien better than anyone else at that point. It seemed the alien was capable of both kindness and ruthlessness. It was better not to push it in the ruthless direction. To Seleece, it didn't seem as though the alien was evil, but it didn't seem like it was benevolent either.

"Well, when it gets serious, I guess it gets really serious," Seleece thought as she laughed a little bit.

"Are you satisfied, Thomas?" Kalduron asked condescendingly.

There was an awkward silence for a brief second. Thomas did not respond. He just stood there, still a bit shaken up by what the alien had done to him.

"Kalduron, I'll be taking Seleece and Greynor with me now. We will return with Ramos and Salvador, whatever the cost," the alien said.

"Very well. I will go back to the senate and assess the situation there. Melthuron must have people working for him in there. I'll try to root them out," Jamos responded quickly before exiting the room.

"I…I will go back to Earth and begin preparations…just in case. There is a lot I must do before I can proceed from my end," Thomas said, still a bit shaken up.

"I will take you to Earth now," the alien said as it teleported next to Thomas.

"No…that's not—" Thomas didn't get to finish. As quickly as the alien appeared, it disappeared, taking Thomas along with it.

A few seconds later, the alien appeared right back where it was standing moments ago, ready to begin the next phase of their mission.

"Welcome back," Seleece said as she walked toward the alien, eager to start.

"These robots…where are they, Kalduron?" the alien asked.

"I believe we have about one hundred units in the bunker bellow us," Kalduron responded.

"Very well," the alien said as it disappeared.

"It wastes no time, huh," Greynor said nervously.

"You have no idea," Seleece responded.

The alien appeared back in the meeting room after a few seconds later.

"Will you be taking the robots with you?" Kalduron asked the alien.

"They are an older model but can still pack quite a punch. Not to worry, no one will know you used them. After all, this facility has been out of operation for decades. Most Thespians don't even know it even exists," Kalduron said.

"I will bring them with us only if necessary. For now, they can stay here," the alien responded.

"We are late to the party. Let's get a move on," Seleece said.

"There is no time for festivities. Have you forgotten what we have to do?" the alien responded, not understanding what Seleece was trying to say.

"No...ugh, never mind. Let's go. Greynor, get over here," Seleece commanded.

"Since when am I under your command?" Greynor responded as he walked closer to the alien.

"Just go," Kalduron ordered.

"Yes sir!" Greynor responded quickly as he rushed over to the alien's side.

"Don't forget, I am placing both of you under our friend's command. You are to follow all orders as if they were my own," Kalduron said.

"Yes, Commander!" both chanted as the alien placed its hands on their shoulders, establishing a link between all three of them.

Suddenly, Greynor could hear both Seleece's and the alien's thoughts. He could feel their feelings; everything that was going through their minds was going simultaneously through his.

"Whoa! What the—" he said as he stepped away from the alien's shoulder.

"What's wrong?" Seleece asked Greynor.

"What the hell was that?" Greynor asked.

"Our minds…our very souls were connected together," the alien responded.

"While we are connected, we can communicate telepathically and share information such as memories and feelings, among other things. You will see that it is a very useful tool," Seleece explained.

"Well, whatever it was, I don't like it. I almost felt sick. Can we just skip holding hands and get a move on?" Greynor asked, directing his question to the alien.

"Yes," the alien said as it concentrated on Salvador's location.

The alien quickly placed its hand back on Greynor's shoulder and continued to focus.

"Why did it make him feel that way?" Seleece asked the alien telepathically out of curiosity. After all, it had never happened to her before.

"I do not have the answer to that question," the alien responded telepathically as its eyes began to emit its usual white light. "This is as new to me as it is to you," the alien said.

"Do you feel him? Do you feel Salvador?" the alien asked Seleece, diverting their attention back to the mission at hand.

"Yes...I do, but I can't quite understand where he is...he feels far away," Seleece responded as she concentrated on everything she was feeling. It was beginning to feel more natural, almost as if she were the one doing it.

"His location is clear to me. He's still back on Earth. Not in the same location, but still on Earth," the alien responded.

"Let's go," Seleece said without a moment's hesitation.

"All right, now we are talking," Greynor said as he turned on his cloaking device.

Seleece and the alien quickly followed, rendering themselves invisible before taking off.

"We will be back soon with results, sir. We will not fail you," Seleece said with confidence in her voice, right before disappearing from Kalduron's sight.

Chapter 9

Greynor's eyes suddenly adjusted to his new surroundings. They were now somewhere on Earth, staring down a yellow hallway that seemed to stretch for hundreds of yards. There were many small, circular lights scattered down the walls, unevenly illumining the decaying hallway. It was perhaps a hotel, or maybe a cheap apartment building.

"Whoa!" Greynor whispered as he discovered himself at a completely different location. "This is unreal! I knew the alien could do it but experiencing it for myself…what a rush!" he thought as he shifted his gaze around the new surroundings, completely amazed by what the alien was capable of.

"Focus, Greynor! We have work to do," Seleece communicated through her helmet.

"Don't tell me what to do. You're not the commanding officer on this mission," Greynor responded.

"That would be correct. I am in control here. And Seleece is right. Put your amusement aside," the alien communicated telepathically.

"How did you do that?" Greynor asked in complete surprise.

The alien wasn't wearing a helmet. It didn't establish a connection between them, yet it was somehow speaking telepathically with him.

"Your questions are of no concern to me at this moment. Salvador lies ahead through that door," the alien said telepathically while pointing to the door right next to Seleece. "We are going inside now," it said as it touched both of them and teleported them to the other side of the door.

There was now no doubt now that they were in a hotel. On the other side of the door stood a small sized-hotel room. There was one bed, one small refrigerator, and a small table. The room was quite dirty. Stains covered both the rug and the walls. The bathroom was located directly next to the entrance, and it was also a mess. The whole room looked like it had not been cleaned in months.

"What a crappy place. I'm starting to feel bad for the guy," Seleece thought as she looked around the room. But it didn't make any sense. "Why would Salvador stay at such a cheap place?" she thought as she slowly moved forward.

She then noticed a glass door toward the back end of the room, which probably led to a balcony. "I think Salvador is outside on the balcony," Seleece said through the helmet's interface. But before she even started to walk toward the balcony, the door slid open and Salvador walked in. He was wearing the same clothes he had on earlier.

"Both of you stay invisible. I will talk to him," the alien said.

"Wait, what? Talk?" Greynor thought.

The alien turned off the cloaking device.

Salvador suddenly spotted the alien in front of him. "No! Not again!" Salvador screamed as he reached for his blaster from inside his brown jacket. "We will be doing none of that. I just want to talk," the alien said as it teleported in front of him, pushing Salvador against the wall with ease.

It all happened so quickly that Salvador had no time to react. The force of the push caused him to drop his weapon, which the alien quickly picked up.

"We don't need to have this around," the alien said as the weapon disappeared from his hand. Salvador was stunned by the alien's sudden appearance.

"How…how did you find me?" Salvador asked as he pushed himself off of the floor.

"That is of no importance right now. I have some questions for you," the alien replied calmly.

"Questions? As if I would give you any answers, you freak!" Salvador howled back while keeping his eye fixed on the alien's location.

"I am not here to harm you. I just want information, nothing else. Will you comply with my request this time?" the alien asked

Salvador. Seleece and Greynor only stared as this was taking place; the alien seemed to have everything under control.

"You are wasting your time with me. I'm just a soldier. And even if I knew something, there's no way I would tell you!" Salvador screamed as he charged toward the alien.

"Futile," the alien responded as it appeared behind him. Salvador couldn't even react. The alien now had him by the neck. It then lifted him off the ground and began to apply pressure around Salvador's neck, slowly choking him once again. He placed his hands around the alien's fingers and tried to free himself, but the alien's grip was too strong. Salvador couldn't even shift one finger off of his neck.

"Da…Damn it," Salvador whispered as the alien held him up off the ground.

"I'm quite aware of that fact," the alien said as it placed its other hand on Salvador's head. "I'm not here to ask you about Melthuron," the alien said as it slowly applied more pressure on Salvador's throat. "I'm here for Ramos. Where is he now?

Salvador did not respond. The alien's eyes began to glow white as it searched Salvador's mind.

"What's that thing doing?" Greynor asked Seleece via his helmet.

"The alien is gathering information from Salvador's mind," Seleece responded while keeping her gazed fix on the alien.

"Really? That thing can also read minds?" Greynor thought.

"It seems you are telling the truth this time. You don't know anything about their locations. We will have to find another way to locate them," the alien said as it removed its hand from Salvador's head.

"What…what are you rambling on about?" Salvador asked as he gasped for air, unaware that Seleece and Greynor were with the alien.

"You'll never learn, will you," Seleece said in taunting tone as she became visible.

"Oh great," Salvador said sarcastically.

"So are we taking him back with us or what?" Greynor asked as he also turned off his cloaking device.

"Yes…he is not our enemy," the alien responded.

"All right, you know the drill. Come along quietly," Seleece said while she restrained him. "Don't even think about removing those cuffs; they have a very nasty shock mechanism. Now, let's search this room for anything that could be of use to us," Seleece said.

"Let's search him first," Greynor responded as he patted down Salvador.

"He doesn't have anything on him at the moment. There is no need to search this room," the alien said as it walked up to a small, wooden nightstand next to the bed.

"And how do you know that?" Greynor asked as the alien kneeled down to open the drawer.

"I searched his most recent memories. He only has four items in his possession: a government ID, a glucose meter, a cellular device, and…well, that item shall remain private. But please feel free to search him if you don't trust me," the alien said as it reached inside the drawer.

"A glucose meter? What is that?" Greynor asked as he searched Salvador's pockets.

"It measures what humans call a sugar, the basic molecule their bodies use for fuel. A glucose meter measures the amount of glucose contained in the blood," the alien responded as it pulled out a device from inside the nightstand.

Greynor was amazed by the alien's power. It was absolutely right. The only things he found on him where the ones the alien had mentioned.

"Oh? What's this?" Greynor said as he grabbed a small, circular piece of metal from one of Salvador's pockets.

"No! Give it back!" Salvador screamed.

"Oh, it must be very important. Let's see," Greynor responded. It didn't look like any weapon he had ever seen. It had a small, red button in the middle.

"Give it back to him. It is of no use to us," the alien commanded before Greynor had a chance to press the button.

"Oh! I know what this is…it's a—"

"I said give it back to him!" the alien commanded once more.

"All right, all right…I got it," Greynor responded before placing the small device back in Salvador's pocket.

"That's odd," she thought to herself. She didn't get a chance to see what it was, but the alien was quite adamant about not taking it away.

"Anyway," Seleece said as she turned to face the alien. "What do you have there? Is that his phone?" she asked the alien.

"Yes. I saw that Salvador had Ramos's personal phone number saved on this device," the alien responded as it contemplated what to do.

"Well, what are we going to do? Call him up on his phone and have ourselves a little chat?" Greynor said as he laughed at that ridiculous notion.

The only way Ramos would provide them any information is if they used Salvador to talk on their behalf, but they knew Salvador would never go for that. He would never willingly betray his employer. The alien was silent for a moment.

"Yes, perhaps that's not such a bad idea," the alien responded as it teleported next to Salvador.

"You can't be serious. Ramos would never tell us anything." Seleece said as she wondered just what the heck the alien was trying to accomplish.

"He may not tell us anything, but perhaps Salvador would yield better results," the alien said as it stared at Salvador.

"Don't resist me," the alien said as it placed its hand on Salvador's head, completely engulfing it with its big palm.

"What…what are you doing now? I told you I don't know where they are!" Salvador said with a shaky voice.

The alien now looked completely focused. Its eyes slowly began to lit up. "Don't resist me; it will only hurt you more," the alien said as it continued to focus on whatever it was trying to do.

"No…please! Don't do this!" Salvador screamed in pain as the alien's eyes continued to glow an almost blinding white, brightening the entire room.

When the alien was done, it quickly teleported the handcuffs off of Salvador and handed him the cell phone.

"Hey, what the hell are you doing?" Seleece asked angrily as she noticed that the handcuffs had disappeared.

"Both of you stay silent. Salvador will be calling Ramos now," the alien ordered calmly.

Before either one of them could respond, a calm "Hello" was uttered by Salvador. He was now on speaker phone with Ramos.

"Calling me at this hour? This better be good, Salvador. You know I haven't slept in days," Ramos said with a confused voice.

"Sir, I just had a bad feeling. I wanted to make sure you were still at the same location and were there safely, sir," Salvador said.

"You are waking me up for a 'bad feeling'? And what the hell is wrong with your voice?" Ramos asked, sounding annoyed.

"Perhaps it's the phone, sir," Salvador responded

"The phone?" Ramos asked.

Salvador didn't reply.

"Anyway, why wouldn't I be fine? I'm being looked after by some of Melthuron's guards like we arranged. If you don't have any useful information for me, then get back to work and stop wasting my damn time. Do you have any leads on where that alien is hiding?" Ramos asked.

"Not yet, sir," Salvador responded.

Ramos was not pleased to hear this at all. "You better figure it out soon! Melthuron is growing impatient," Ramos said.

"Working hard on it, sir," Salvador responded.

"What was that? Working hard? I don't care how hard you are bloody working! Just do your damn job like everyone else! We will meet tomorrow at the prearranged location. You better find them by then! Melthuron has given us two days to find out where the alien, Seleece, and Kalduron are hiding. Don't fail me, or you will be as good as dead. Do you understand? Don't forget, you won't get what you so desperately need if you fail me," Ramos said as he hung up.

"He's...going to kill him?" Seleece thought.

"That's enough, Salvador," the alien said and placed its hand on Salvador's head again. Salvador suddenly fell to the floor. He now appeared to be unconscious.

"What did you do? Did you just mind control him or something?" Seleece asked with a hint of anger.

It was now clear that Salvador wasn't just some regular soldier. Ramos seemed to be blackmailing him somehow. Not only that, but he was willing to kill Salvador if he failed. And that bothered Seleece the most. As a Thespian soldier, Seleece was taught to always follow her orders. However, no one in the Thespian army had the right to do execute another soldier. To Seleece, he was no longer an enemy soldier. He was just a slave.

"What can't you do?" Greynor asked as he praised the alien's abilities.

"We are bringing Salvador with us, right?" Seleece asked as she picked him up off the floor with ease, placing him on her left shoulder.

"Well, he has no useful Intel for us anymore, but maybe we can still use him to our advantage," Greynor replied. "If we wait until the next time they meet, we can—"

"Use him to our advantage? I think he's been through enough already," Seleece replied, growing angrier by the second.

The mere thought of punishing a soldier for just doing his job, one who was just following orders while afraid for his life really pissed Seleece off.

"Who cares what he's been through? He's our enemy, or did you forget that?" Greynor replied.

"That will be enough arguing for now," the alien interrupted calmly. "Yes, we will take him with us. That was part of our mission. It is better to have him under our surveillance. We don't want him to give Melthuron any intelligence regarding our whereabouts," the alien concluded.

"Yes, we can't let any intel he may have gathered to fall into Ramos's hands," Greynor agreed.

"That is correct," the alien said. "I was not able to gather any information regarding their next meeting. I will have to wait until he wakes up before reading his mind again. If I were to do it now, I could harm him even more than I already have. So, Salvador must come with us regardless," the alien concluded.

"It's clear from the phone call that we will have a fight on our hands once we find Ramos," Seleece said as she tried to brush off her anger. Both of them were talking about Salvador as if he were disposable, as if his life didn't matter at all. That was starting to get on her nerves.

"Seleece, I want you to go into the bathroom and take the Duffle bag that sits inside the bathroom's cupboard. The rest of his possessions are stashed in there," the alien ordered as it took Salvador off of Seleece's shoulder.

"All right," Seleece said as she walked off, slamming her shoulder against Greynor before entering the bathroom.

"What was that for? What's your problem?" Greynor exclaimed as Seleece walked away from him. He was angry and confused by her attitude.

"It was clearly a mistake," the alien responded.

Within seconds Seleece walked back into the room with the reinforced metal Duffle bag in her hands.

"Here, take it," she said as she threw the bag down at the alien's feet.

"All of the Intel gathered by Salvador is stored on his computer, inside this bag," the alien said.

It was a military grade Duffle bag. The Intel was being held inside it with some sort of locking mechanism they had not seen before.

"What the…I've never seen a bag like this before," Greynor said as he examined it. It was a black bag coated with some sort of metal alloy.

It had two handles like a regular bag, but at the top stood some sort of rectangular locking mechanism with a display attached to it.

"Yes, Melthuron himself developed this locking mechanism. I felt it as I was searching through Salvador's mind," the alien said.

"Well…can you open it or what?" Seleece asked.

"I cannot. The bag was designed in such a way that only Salvador can open it," the alien replied.

"I guess we'll have to wait until he wakes up," Seleece responded with a hint of impatience.

"I may not be able to open it, but perhaps there is another way to get the contents out of this bag," the alien said as it kneeled down to look at the bag. It placed its hand on the side of the bag, trying to get a feel for it and what was inside. The alien's eyes then began to shine their white light as it began to concentrate.

"What's it doing?" Greynor whispered to Seleece as they both watched the alien.

"I have no idea," Seleece whispered back while watching the alien.

Suddenly, the bag disappeared before their eyes, leaving its content scattered on the floor.

"Nice! Good idea, there…useful as always," Seleece said as she walked over to examine the items on the floor.

"Brilliant!" Greynor responded as the alien kneeled down. "Let's see here, a blaster, a set of keys…ah, there it is!" Seleece said as she picked up Salvador's personal computer. It was a small, three-inch rectangular computer with holographic display capabilities.

"I wonder what they keys are for," Seleece said.

"To open something, I bet," Greynor responded in a condescending tone as he stared down at her.

"How mature," she replied.

"They aren't of any value to us. They are not part of his intel," the alien responded, unknowingly interrupting their childish bickering.

"How do you know what these keys are for and where that bag was, but you didn't find out any information regarding their meeting?" Seleece asked, curious about how the alien was learning information. "For that matter, how come you didn't use your mind control ability on Salvador the first time we had him instead of beating him senseless like you did?"

"That's not relevant to the mission," the alien responded calmly. "But to answer your question, I simply couldn't do it back then. I'm still quite inexperienced with this body. The longer I reside in it, the more I train, the more my abilities develop. Even now, I wasn't quite sure mind control would even work. I have never done it before. For that matter, I haven't done any of this before," the alien responded.

"The alien's powers must still be growing then. Just as Kalduron said, it's going to be important to keep it on our side," she thought. But she no longer felt comfortable with betraying the alien…it just didn't sit right with her.

"The second question is also useless in regard to our mission, but I will answer it anyway," the alien said, interrupting her thoughts

"When I search through thoughts and feelings, I am looking for specific information. Given the limit this body places on my abilities, it would take me longer to search through every thought and memory that Salvador possesses if I don't have something in particular I am searching for. In this case, I was searching for Ramos's location, which was shrouded in a web of millions upon millions of thoughts and memories. I would have never found that piece of information unless I had known ahead of time that it existed. Theoretically I could have, although even I'm not sure how long it would have taken me given the fact that he fights me every step of the way," the alien said.

"Well, you sure make it look easy!" Greynor responded with a grin, unseen from behind his helmet.

"It certainly is not," the alien responded. "Seleece, Gather up Salvador's personal belongings. We are leaving," the alien said as it walked toward her with Salvador still on its shoulder.

"All right, let's go," Seleece said as she gathered all of the items from the floor and placed them inside her armor's back compartment.

"Roger that," Greynor said as he walked up to Seleece and the alien, eager to report back to Kalduron.

The alien placed its hands on their shoulders and began to focus, emitting white light from its eyes before disappearing from the hotel.

Chapter 10

"And just like that, we are back on Demora," Greynor said as his eyes readjusted to the wall in front of him.

"Report," Kalduron said as he noticed their sudden appearance.

"We have apprehended Salvador, sir," Greynor responded swiftly.

"Salvador had been ordered to collect Intel on us, but not to worry. We have collected all of his data. It is safely stored on his personal computer, which we are also in possession of. He won't be reporting to Ramos anytime soon," Seleece added.

Greynor was not happy with the sudden interruption.

"Ramos and Salvador have a scheduled meeting sometime within the next Earth day to discuss this Intel," the alien said as it walked forward, resting the unconscious Salvador against the circular holographic display in the middle of the room.

"As soon as he wakes up, I'll read his mind and find out when and where this meeting will take place. That is when we will take on Ramos and his soldiers," the alien concluded.

"And what exactly has Salvador been able to find out about us?" Kalduron asked. He didn't seem very worried, probably because they had come back with both Salvador and his Intel.

"We don't know yet, sir, we haven't gotten the chance to—"

"We will know when he wakes up; I will take care of that," the alien responded, cutting Greynor off midsentence.

"I see. You have done well. We will take the fight to Ramos tomorrow. If we are lucky, he will know where Melthuron is hiding," Kalduron responded as he turned to stare at Seleece. "For the time being, I suggest you get some rest, soldier," Kalduron said.

Although she would hate to admit it, Kalduron was right. Seleece was tired. She had been on duty for over twenty hours already. But she had no intention of resting. There was still much she could do.

"With all due respect sir, I feel fine. I don't need to rest," Seleece lied from behind her helmet.

"I need you at one hundred percent for tomorrow. I can't have you distracted. That's an order, soldier. Go home and get some sleep," Kalduron responded swiftly.

"Actually, I would like to take some of this time to train Greynor and Seleece in combat. Melthuron's soldiers clearly outmatched your soldiers before, and it's imperative that we train them in how to more efficiently battle Melthuron's soldiers," the alien said calmly.

Kalduron's face turned a curious hue as he heard this information.

"Training?" Seleece thought curiously.

"Yes!" Greynor exclaimed as he heard the alien's plan. "Count me in. I'm ready," Greynor said, eager to learn any secrets about the alien and its powers.

"We don't have much time. Are you sure you will be able to teach such skills in a matter of hours?" Kalduron asked as he questioned what the alien was hoping to accomplish in such a short amount of time.

"I am quite sure. My training methods are very effective," the alien replied.

"Very well then, follow our friend's instructions with the same diligence and respect you would give if I were your instructor," Kalduron said.

"Sir, yes sir!" both chanted in unison.

"Kalduron, it would greatly benefit you as well. You must come with us," the alien said as both Seleece and Greynor walked over.

"Negative. There are many things I must do. I will be meeting with Thomas and Councilman Jiggs soon to discuss everything that has taken place. I leave this mission in your hands for now," Kalduron said as he walked out of the room.

"What are we going to do about Salvador? We can't just leave him here alone and risk an escape," Seleece said.

"That is not a valid concern. We will train right here. There is no need to go anywhere," the alien responded.

The Thespians did not agree.

"But we have very limited room here. How are we going to train? Everything is going to get in the way," Greynor said, wondering what type of training he was about to receive.

"It won't be that kind of training," the alien responded. "You will see. I need both of you to take off your helmets and sit facing each other," the alien said with its monotone voice.

They both took off their helmets and sat down on the floor facing each other, only inches away.

Quickly, the alien teleported itself right in front of them and sat down. It placed one hand on each of their heads, getting ready to establish a link between them.

"I need both of you to close your eyes and empty your minds of all thoughts. I will take care of rest," the alien said as its eyes lit up. They tried their best, but this was a task they had never undertaken before.

"It won't work unless both of you clear your minds. Only when you do, will I have full access to your minds and souls. You need to let me in," the alien commanded telepathically. "Yes, that's better," the alien responded as both Seleece and Greynor successfully emptied their minds, slowly allowing the alien to do whatever it was trying to do. "Open your eyes," the alien said out loud.

"This place…what is this?" Seleece asked as her eyes adjusted to her new surroundings.

"I thought you said we were going to train back at base…where the hell did you take us?" Greynor asked as he looked around.

They were no longer sitting down at base. All three of them were now standing in what seemed like a white void. There were no walls, no buildings, no plants or animals anywhere. All they could see was an empty, white void that seemed to stretch out forever. They couldn't even see what they were standing on, there was absolutely nothing as far as their eyes could see.

"I don't even remember getting up, and why do I feel so different? What did you do to us? Where are we?" Seleece asked, confused and somewhat concerned. She was no longer tired. She felt completely rejuvenated as if she had woken up from a long nap.

"Do not be concerned. We are still all physically located back at base. Your minds, however, are now part of my own. You are inside my mind; in a world I have created with the sole purpose of training you," the alien responded as monotone as always.

"So, basically we are asleep in a dream?" Greynor asked.

"That would not be correct, but you may look at it that way if you wish. I have complete control of time and space in this world. Anything your mind learns here will be translated into your muscle memory, as if it were real, physical training. When our training ends, it will be as if you had trained in the real world. You will retain all the knowledge," the alien responded.

"You just keep surprising me," Seleece responded with a smile. "So, since you control both time and space here, that must mean that we can train here for a much longer period than we would if we were to train in the real world?" she asked as she moved her shoulders and arms around, trying to get a feel for this new reality.

"That is correct," the alien said.

"Great. Let's get to it," Seleece said with a more serious, determined tone as she took out a blaster from the back compartment of her armor.

"Yeah, let's go," Greynor agreed as he clenched his fists with excitement.

"First, I must explain how my power, and most probably their power, actually works," the alien said. "While it is true that their teleporting is indeed instant, they will not be able to instantly strike you in combat. That is because they must materialize again before striking you," the alien said.

"Uh…what?" Greynor asked.

"What I mean is that they can't teleport a direct physical blow to you. Rather, they must teleport and then attack. That gives you a small window of opportunity to react," the alien explained.

Seleece already knew this, but she still felt hopeless.

"So what if they don't strike as fast as they teleport? Their attacks are way faster than anything we could ever hope to counter. On top of that, we don't have any way of knowing where they will appear. How can we counterattack effectively?" Seleece asked with frustration in her voice. They were just too strong.

"You sound like a coward, Seleece. We can take them on if we work together," Greynor responded.

"You have no idea what you are talking about. You were not present back at the headquarters. They are fast, strong, and ruthless killers. You wouldn't last five seconds against them on your own, you dumb fool," She growled back.

"Ha! That's rich coming from you! The only thing you have managed to do since your mission began has been to bring shame to the Thespian army, you coward! There is nothing I can't handle, unlike you who failed to protect—"

His words struck a dangerous nerve. "You better choose those next words carefully, or I swear they will be your last," Seleece said in a low tone.

"We are here to train, not to fight among ourselves," the alien said calmly. "Since you are so sure of your abilities, I will now show you what you are up against. Let's see how well you perform," the alien said as it appeared in front of Greynor, knocking him almost twenty feet into the air with a swift kick to his chin.

"Shit!" Greynor exclaimed as he quickly pulled out a blaster from his armor. He fired several shots at the alien while in midair, but all missed the mark as he fell down onto the white floor, landing on his feet. The alien had disappeared. Greynor's armor didn't pick up any movements.

"Where did that bastard go?" Greynor said as he looked around.

"Behind you," the alien said as it appeared behind him.

As Greynor turned to shoot, he felt a powerful blow land on his back, sending him flying several feet forward.

"Ouch, he felt that for sure," Seleece said as she carefully observed their battle, enjoying every second of it. "Get your ass up! I though you weren't going to have any problems!" Seleece yelled as Greynor struggled to compose himself.

As he tried to stand up, the alien appeared in front of him, stepping on his back. This immobilized Greynor, who was completely unable to push back against the alien's almost monstrous strength.

"A mere ten seconds have passed, and you are already defeated," the alien said as it stepped back, letting Greynor stand.

"If it had been one of Melthuron's soldiers, you would have been dead the second that first strike landed. Do you understand now what you will be facing? They are not to be taken lightly," the alien asked.

"I guess I was wrong. You wouldn't even last a full five seconds," Seleece said before she laughed.

"Oh yeah? You wouldn't even to last one," Greynor responded as he struggled to catch his breath.

"Actually, Seleece was able to last much longer than that. Seleece and I have fought them before," the alien responded quickly.

Greynor's pride had suddenly been reduced to nothing. "What? How can that be?" Greynor thought to himself.

"Because I'm better than you," Seleece responded.

"What? How did you know what I was thin—"

"We are all connected right now, remember?" the alien interrupted, knowing exactly what Greynor was going to say almost before he even knew it himself.

Greynor had enough. "Can we just start the damn training already?" Greynor snapped as he tried to ignore what he had just heard.

The mere thought of Seleece being better only infuriated him more.

"What's the plan then?" Seleece asked, shifting her mindset back into training mode.

"I don't see how any sort of normal training will benefit us in any way," Greynor added.

Seleece knew Greynor was right. Melthuron's soldiers just too fast for them to catch off guard. Even their weapons couldn't fire fast enough to hit them.

"You are correct. Just training your body would be a waste of time. We are not here for that type of training," the alien responded. "In order for you to stand even the smallest of chances, you will need my power," the alien concluded.

"Go on," Greynor responded. There mere thought of receiving some of the alien's power filled Greynor with excitement. He felt a rush of emotion as he contemplated what it would be like.

"Let's try this again. But this time I will give you some of my energy," the alien responded as it disappeared.

As fast as ever, the alien appeared above Greynor, attempting to grab him by the throat. This time, however, Greynor ducked as quickly as the alien appeared, dodging the alien's move by just a thread.

"Whoa...I don't believe it! How the hell did it manage to do that?" Seleece said.

The alien quickly teleported back to where it was standing earlier, moving itself about ten feet away from Greynor.

"I knew where you were going to appear. I felt you behind me somehow..." Greynor said in surprise, looking just as confused as Seleece was.

"That's correct. You felt it. That is the kind of training we will be doing here," the alien responded. "Your turn, Seleece. Let's see how well you do," the alien said as it teleported in front of her, appearing just inches away.

Before the alien even appeared, her hand instinctively turned on the electroglove, throwing an electro-packed punch at the alien as it appeared in front of her. The alien quickly dodged it before retaliating with a kick, which she quite easily dodged by jumping up. Faster than ever before, she took aim at the alien, firing several blasts in his general direction. The alien quickly appeared behind her. A grenade was already waiting for the alien. Its blast caught the alien by complete surprise. The alien could now be seen about twenty feet away. It looked as if it had been gravely wounded from the blast. The right side of its body looked completely burned, and it was even having trouble standing up.

"Well done, Seleece. You exceeded my expectations," the alien said in its calm, monotone voice. It was as if the alien couldn't feel any pain at all.

Greynor couldn't stand it. "You went easy on her!" Greynor screamed out with jealousy. While he had a hard time keeping up with the alien, she was easily able to not only keep herself out of harm's way, but she was actually able to cause significant damage to it. This only angered Greynor further.

"I didn't take you for such a petty whiner, Greynor. How about you just do better instead of complaining like a child?" Seleece responded calmly, unimpressed by his behavior.

"I will show you!" Greynor said as it charged at the wounded alien, pulling his blaster out of his armor.

"Stop," the alien commanded.

Greynor refused. He kept running toward the alien before taking aim at the alien's burned body. But before he could open fire, Greynor collapsed. He was now completely unable to move.

"What is this? I can't move a single muscle!" Greynor said while being completely immobilized.

"I told you to stop," the alien said as it appeared in front of Greynor, completely healed from its wounds as if it had never been burned at all.

"What have you done to me?" Greynor asked, still unable to move.

"I took away your muscle memory. You can't move a single muscle or ligament in your body; well, other than the ones in your face, of course. I didn't restrict those," the alien said.

"You also healed. Can you do that in the real world?" Seleece asked.

"You are both forgetting that this place is my creation. I am in complete control of everything while we are in here," the alien responded. "From the emotions I am sensing, it seems you both think I brought you here to compete, to try to prove yourselves. I brought you here to train. You better focus on that goal," the alien said with a cold, unforgiving stare.

For the first time, both Greynor and Seleece could feel the alien's true emotions. The sheer strength of the alien's anger toward them made the whole world it had created feel heavy. It was as if at any moment, the pressure they felt around them would crush their bodies into mush.

"I'm sorry. Let's focus on our goal," Greynor struggled to say under the weight of the alien's anger.

"Yeah," Seleece said as she felt the same fear almost take over her entire body.

They both began to tremble under the alien's power; they had never felt anything so strong in their entire lives.

"Good," the alien said as it calmed down a bit, shifting the atmosphere of the world back to normal. "I still don't have good control or understanding of emotions. I have never had a body that let me experience them before. I'm confident I will get better at it," the alien said.

"Ha, ha, let's hope so," Seleece responded nervously.

"Could you let me get up now?" Greynor asked softly, still unable to move.

"Yes," the alien said as it gave Greynor full control of his body again.

"Now that you both have experienced fighting using my energy to guide you, I must explain the course of action we will take when the battle ensues," the alien said as it watched Greynor stand up. "The reason you are able to feel me, to sense my location is because once my energy is inside you it creates a connection between our bodies. You don't feel the location of my body, you feel the location of the energy inside my body, as if it were an extension of yourself," the alien explained.

"But why would this be useful in a battle against Melthuron's soldiers? It's not like they will willingly give us their energy to track them," Seleece said.

"You are not thinking," the alien responded.

"We will be sensing your energy, right?" Greynor asked. It was then that the alien's plan began to make sense.

"That's correct," the alien responded softly. "All I must do is land a physical blow on them to place my energy inside their bodies. Once that happens, you will be able to sense their location. I will take them on at first until the energy link has been established. Only then will you jump into the battle and help take them out," the alien concluded.

That plan, however, was far from what Seleece and Greynor had expected to hear.

"Wait…are you saying you want us to do nothing until then?" Seleece asked.

"That is correct. You are to stay invisible until then. I can't take any chances. If they find your location, you will both be taken out of the battle in mere seconds," the alien responded.

But Seleece was unsatisfied with such a risky plan. "But that's suicide! You can't take them on all at once by yourself! We barely managed to escape the last time we faced them!" Seleece vehemently protested.

The alien nodded. "I am aware of that. However, this course of action has the highest probability of success. If you think differently, what is your preferred plan of action? One in which you are actually of use to the mission and manage to stay alive," the alien responded. The alien was well aware of the risks involved with that plan, but it didn't matter.

Neither of them had an answer for such a question. They both knew the truth: without the alien, they would be anything but useful in battle.

"What makes you so sure you will even be able to land a physical blow on any of them?" Seleece asked while trying to remain respectful. She couldn't risk upsetting the alien again.

"Even I don't know how the battle will go ensue. The best-case scenario is that I manage to catch Ramos and his soldiers off guard. If I manage to do that, I can teleport him back to base before they are able to react. The battle could be over in a fraction of a second, but there really is no way of knowing. Again, this is the best course of action we can take," the alien responded calmly as it looked at Greynor.

Greynor had a look on his face as if he wanted to say something, but he wouldn't dare open his mouth again.

"What I know for certain is that if you engage in battle alongside me from the start, you will be taken out first. I want both of you to stay invisible and engage only if they manage to damage this body or after I manage to link us. If you get yourself killed at the start of the battle, you will be completely useless to the mission. I would rather use something for its intended purpose rather than throw it out," the alien responded.

The alien didn't seem to care about their safety. That wasn't the reasoning behind such a plan. It was only to make the best use out of them; it was all about successfully completing the mission.

Seleece could feel this, in fact they both could. The entire time they had been connected in this world, they had felt absolutely nothing at all from the alien. While both Seleece and Greynor could feel each other's emotions, hear each other's thoughts, when it came to the alien there was nothing but a sort of emotional silence, like a void. The alien felt completely empty to them.

"Very well, we will do as you command," Seleece responded as nicely as she could.

"I will follow your orders," Greynor responded, following Seleece's lead without hesitating.

"I won't just engage without any backup. I will be taking all of these with me," the alien said as hundreds of robots appeared in front of them. Some were carrying weapons while others were not. They looked just like the robots they had encountered back at Melthuron's ship.

"Those are old Thespian battle bots! You have those back in the real world?" Greynor asked with a confused look on his face.

"That's right. These are the ones located back at base. Before we left to find Salvador, I went down to where they were stored and placed my energy in all of them. I now have complete control over all of these units. I'll be bringing them with us to battle," the alien responded.

"It seems you really thought this plan through," Seleece said with a smile on her face. She was now a bit relieved to hear that the alien wouldn't be fighting alone in the beginning.

"I believe they will provide sufficient backup until it is your turn to engage. Hopefully, with the training I am providing both of you today, we can take all of the soldiers down and bring Ramos with us if a sneak attack fails," the alien said.

"Can you really control all of them telepathically?" Greynor asked with the same curious look on his face.

"Yes. Now that we have all of this out of the way, let's go back to the training," the alien responded as the world it had created suddenly changed.

They were no longer standing in that white, empty void. The alien had created a new setting in the blink of eye. There were buildings all around them, with humans walking around everywhere they looked. Overhead was a clear, blue sky. Light from the Earth's sun beamed down on them. It felt as if they were no longer in the alien's world, but out in the real one.

"It all feels so…real," Seleece said as she felt a light breeze hit her armor. It was an uncanny replica of the real world. The weather, the sounds of the city, the movement of its citizens; there was no visible difference.

"Since we will be fighting in the real world, it is only proper that we train in conditions that will be similar to that of the real world," the alien responded as it appeared behind them.

Both Seleece and Greynor were now wearing their helmets and had their cloaking devices turned on.

"The battle starts now," the alien said.

Suddenly, in a crowd of humans waiting for a traffic light to turn green, about eighty feet away from them, stood Ramos with Melthuron's soldiers. Quickly, the alien appeared above him and attempted to grab him. The alien felt a strong blow land on its torso as one of the soldiers noticed the alien above Ramos. The force of the blow sent the alien back across the street.

"Unreal!" Greynor said as it witnessed what had just happened. Suddenly, they noticed that they could feel the location of the soldiers just as they had felt the alien before. Their minds quickly shifted to attack mode. Seleece would waste no time at all.

"Now!" Seleece said as she began to fire several blasts toward her enemies.

"Right!" Greynor said as he backed her, throwing several blasts in the enemy's direction. Greynor was quick. He began firing before the soldier had reappeared, and managed to land a hit on him. The force of the blast knocked the soldier backward into the building in front of him.

"Greynor...duck now!" Seleece yelled as she fired several shots in Greynor's direction. She could feel exactly where the solider was going to appear.

Greynor had also anticipated it just like she had, and ducked before the blast hit him. Instead, Seleece's blast hit a soldier who had appeared above Greynor. The blast hit its target, sending the soldier flying into a building behind them, shattering glass as the soldier flew inside. Both quickly ran for cover as the fake humans began to run around, screaming in every direction just as if they were in the real world. The alien quickly appeared behind them, kneeling down behind a parked vehicle across the street.

"That's two down!" Greynor said with excitement, his mind still focused on what was going on around him.

"We have only taken out one of them. The other has not sustained any fatal injuries. Feel my location and back me up," the alien said as it teleported thirty feet away, above where one of the soldiers was standing.

Before they could begin firing, one of the soldiers began shooting at them from above, almost catching them off guard.

"Above us!" Seleece screamed as she felt the soldier's presence. She quickly turned on her force shield, engulfing both of them inside it, shielding them from what could have been decisive blows to their heads. Greynor was anything but unimpressed by her prowess in battle. He could have never reacted so quickly. They continued to take heavy fire from that soldier for a couple of seconds until the alien teleported behind the soldier, dealing a powerful blow with a blaster.

"I think that's quite enough," the alien said.

Suddenly, everything around them began to disappear before their eyes; they were now back in the empty, white void.

"All of that felt so…so real. I still can't believe it," Greynor said as his heart rate began to slow; he was still rattled by the battle that had just taken place.

"Yeah, that was almost too intense," Seleece added.

"We have only just begun,'" the alien responded.

"It was a warm-up, huh? Then let's continue!" Seleece said with excitement.

"I still have much training to provide you both, but for right now we shall return to the real world," the alien replied.

"Why are we back in the real world?" Greynor asked as his eyes adjusted to the walls of their base.

"Because Salvador is about to wake up; I can feel it," the alien said as it pointed toward the end of the room. Salvador was sitting down with his hands still cuffed.

"What in the hell…where am I?" Salvador asked as he noticed his new surroundings. He looked around frantically, still feeling a bit dizzy.

"Don't worry. You are safe with us," the alien responded calmly.

"Why have you brought me here? You have already extracted all the knowledge I have," Salvador said in a low, unenthusiastic tone. His demeanor had changed; he was mentally defeated. He knew there was absolutely nothing he could do.

Seleece found that rather odd. She didn't understand why a solider such as Salvador would be so upset about being captured. "That look, that tone. Something else is wrong," she thought.

"Just kill me now and get it over with. I will be of no further use to you," Salvador said, hoping for a quick death. His face was plagued by defeat; he had given up.

"No one is going to hurt you, Salvador," Seleece responded as she walked over to him.

"That is correct. No one here is planning to hurt you. I require more information," the alien said calmly.

"More information? About what? I told you that I don't know anything else!"

"We need to know when and where you will be meeting with Ramos on the next Earth day," Seleece responded as she kneeled down in front of him, freeing his hands from the cuffs.

Salvador looked surprised to hear that. Maybe he couldn't remember what the alien had done to him.

"Hey! Just what do you think you're doing, Seleece? We can't set him free!" Greynor protested angrily as he took out his blaster and pointed it in Salvador's direction.

"Lower your weapon, Salvador. He won't be escaping as long as I am around," the alien ordered calmly.

"But we can't just—"

"I believe that was an order, Greynor. You better follow it," Seleece interrupted.

Greynor nodded. "All right, but if anything happens, it's on the both of you," Greynor said as he slowly lowered his weapon.

"Now tell us what we need to know, and I will make sure no harm comes to you," the alien said as it looked straight at him, waiting for Salvador to respond. Salvador stayed still for a moment. The alien then stared right at him, patiently waiting for his response.

"All right, fine! Go ahead and read my mind, or whatever it is you do. I won't fight you this time," Salvador responded, sounding defeated.

"So then, what's the verdict?" Seleece asked while the alien looked inside Salvador's mind, its eyes glowing.

"They…they are planning to meet at Earth's congressional building at seven thirty p.m. Eastern Earth time," the alien said as it moved its hand away from Salvador's head.

"Well, isn't that great news," Seleece replied sarcastically.

"Well, yes. Now we know the location and time that we needed," the alien responded. It did not register her sarcasm.

"That's not what I meant by that," she responded.

"What she meant to say was that this is not good news. That building is under constant surveillance. Due to intergalactic law, each congressional house, whether it's Thespian, Human, or otherwise, is heavily guarded by the best security systems in the galaxy. Even more troubling is the fact that each of these government buildings is heavily guarded by soldiers from all over the galaxy. They probably have hundreds of soldiers at each location. If a battle would break out in there, we would possibly be fighting against a small platoon of soldiers; even fellow Thespians," Greynor explained with concern written on his face.

Neither of them wanted to spill any more blood, especially that of fellow Thespians.

"We can't let a battle break out in that location; it would be all over the news. Not only that, but it would be a major crime, one punishable by death. I refuse to fight against other Thespians," Seleece said with great concern.

"That does not matter in the slightest," the alien responded with no concern for any possible consequences.

It seemed the alien did not care about innocent lives anymore. Maybe something had changed. Seleece was somewhat surprised by that. Although she knew the alien wasn't afraid to twist a few arms to accomplish its goals, she never expected it to react in such a manner.

"What? Of course it matters! Wasn't it you who said no life should be harmed? What happened to that?" Seleece yelled back.

To her, that plan was nothing short of ridiculous.

"Think about what you are asking us to do. We would be committing one of the worst possible crimes in the galaxy. We can't just break international law like that. We would be committing treason. We should let Kalduron know about this immediately so that we can come up with a different course of action," Greynor said calmly.

"No," the alien responded, calm yet defiant. "Your laws do not concern me. We will do what we have originally planned, regardless of where this will take place. This is the best course of action to take. Contrary to what you may think, this is not up for debate. I do not wish to harm anyone, but that is not something that we can solely control by ourselves" the alien said without hesitation.

Seleece was growing furious at about his disregard for her fellow soldiers. "Well an order is an order, isn't that right, Seleece?" Greynor said while looking straight at Seleece, trying to diffuse the tension. "Isn't that right?" he exclaimed once more.

"Yes…I guess you are right," Seleece said in agreement, slowly calming down. Greynor was right. They couldn't disobey the alien, at least not yet. Not without Kalduron's approval and a plan to stop the alien from attacking that building by itself.

"I beg of you. Give me a quick death," Salvador said in shame, interrupting their bickering. He kneeled down in front of the alien as he asked one more time. "Please, grant me this request. A quick death is nothing compared to what Ramos will do to me if he finds out I have failed my mission," he said.

"Salvador, you are safe here. They won't harm you as long as we are around; as long as I am around," Seleece vowed.

"Greynor, take him to a holding cell on the floor above us and provide him with some food and water. When you get back we will resume our training," the alien ordered swiftly.

"Right away," Greynor responded as he took out his blaster. "Follow me," he said as he placed his blaster against Salvador's back before walking away.

"We have about twelve hours to train before deployment. Do you think that will be enough time to go through all of the training?" Seleece asked. She had doubt written all over her face. If they were to follow the alien's plan, it could mean the start of war, the one thing she had been hoping to avoid this whole time.

"Don't forget that in the world I created, I have complete control of time and space. In theory, we have all the time in the world," the alien said. "We will have to account for the new variables we have discovered. The simulation will now include the intergalactic soldiers who are stationed there as well as the new location."

"I am aware of that, but...I...I don't want to harm any of the soldiers stationed there; they are not our enemy." Seleece replied out loud, with sadness in her voice.

The alien stared back, completely unmoved. "My primary concern is the whereabouts of Melthuron. If you don't want to harm any of them, don't. I will focus on the mission and nothing more. Let me be clear, I have no desire to cause harm to any living creature, but I will do what I must in order to achieve my goal," the alien responded with a lifeless stare.

Seleece was surprised by the alien's response. She couldn't quite get a reading of its true intentions anymore. "Yeah, but—"

"But what? What are you two talking about?" Greynor interrupted as he walked into the room behind them.

"Nothing important," she quickly responded.

"OK then…I locked Salvador in cell one. I couldn't find any food fit for human consumption, but I managed to get him some water," Greynor said.

The alien seemed pleased. "Good, now it's time to get back to your training. There is still much to go over now that we have new information. Let's get started," the alien responded.

But before they could begin, a red light located on the ceiling turned on and began to flash in fast intervals. Everyone was taken by surprise.

"What is the purpose of this light?" the alien asked as it looked around the room.

The light continued to flash in fast intervals, rapidly turning on and off every couple of seconds and painting the room with alight red hue

"I…I think it's the global alert system," Seleece responded as she quickly put on her helmet. But Seleece wasn't quite sure. It had been many years since such the measure had been implemented.

"The global alert system? Why? This hasn't been used since the civil war," Greynor said.

"What type of message does it convey?" the alien asked.

"Well, it transmits messages to every single device connected to the global network. It was used years ago as a way to communicate messages throughout the entire planet, but why is it broadcasting now?" Greynor added in a confused tone.

Seleece quickly decided to contact Kalduron. If they were right, the alert system should be going off just about everywhere on the planet.

"Sir, are you seeing this?" Seleece communicated through her helmet. There was great concern in her voice. Seleece didn't like this one bit.

"Yes. I have no idea why this is happening. I want all of you to stay put until we know what's going on. Kalduron, out," he responded, ending the transmission almost as soon as it had begun.

Suddenly, a hologram appeared at the center of the room, projected by the base's main computer.

"What's going on?" Greynor asked as he stared at the hologram. At that very moment, all the hologram was displaying was an empty podium inside a building. The universal flag, which contained an overview of the Milky Way galaxy, was hanging on the white wall behind the podium. Out of nowhere, a familiar face walked behind the podium from somewhere outside of the hologram's range.

Seleece's eyes grew heavy with anger as she recognized that face; it made her blood boil.

"Checking microphone...one, two, three. Is the transmission working?" Tei-va asked as she glanced over to the side.

"It's that witch! I don't like this...not one bit. This can't be good," Seleece said as she stared angrily at Tei-va's hologram.

"It's that elected official, Tei-va...what is the meaning of this?" the alien asked as it paid close attention to the transmission.

"I don't know, but I have a really bad feeling about this," Seleece responded in a weary tone.

Tei-va suddenly began talking again, uttering words that would send shockwaves throughout the entire galaxy. "Good afternoon, my fellow Thespians. This is not a drill. We have very important announcements. It is with great relief and pleasure that I introduce to all of you the first Prime Consort of Demora, Dr. Melthuron Doothblier!" Tei-va exclaimed loudly into the microphone.

They couldn't believe it. Those words almost didn't register with Seleece. "It can't be," Seleece thought in disbelief as Melthuron walked over to the podium dressed in the traditional clothes of an elected official.

"No way," Greynor said as Melthuron appeared, waving at the camera with a big smile. Tei-va then walked off the stage, but not before shaking Melthuron's hand.

Meanwhile, the alien just stood there, watching expressionlessly as Melthuron's hologram was displayed right in front of him.

"Good evening, my fellow Thespians," Melthuron said onto the microphone.

The alien suddenly snapped. "We will not waste any time here! Do you know where this is taking place?" the alien quickly asked Seleece as it turned to face her.

"I…I don't know. This transmission could be broadcast from anywhere," Seleece responded.

"Is that a lie? Or do you truly not know where Melthuron is?" the alien responded as it stared deep into Seleece's violet eyes.

"I swear it!" Seleece protested.

Melthuron continued. "On the day of January the second, I, Dr. Melthuron Doothblier, democratically elected leader of Demora, was illegally taken from my office and made prisoner by defector terrorists of Thespian origin. After a top secret joint military operation conducted by the Thespian military and its allies, I was rescued from—"

"This can't be happening…he's going to blame—" but Greynor couldn't even finish his sentence.

"I need to know without any doubt that you are telling me the truth," the alien said as Melthuron's speech continued in the background.

The alien then teleported in front of Seleece, placing its hand on her head to read her mind.

"Stop it!" she yelled out as she slapped the alien's hand away before taking some steps back. "I'm telling you the truth! Don't you believe me?" Seleece asked nervously.

But the alien was not going to stop; it didn't believe her. "This is our chance; do not waste time, Seleece. I apologize in advance, but I will do what I must," the alien said as it disappeared from her sight. Suddenly, she felt a strong blow land on her stomach; the alien had attacked her.

"What the hell are you doing?" Greynor shouted.

The sheer force of the kick sent Seleece flying through the hologram, distorting it as she passed through it before colliding with the wall on the other side of the room. As she fell to the floor, the alien appeared in front of her and lifted her up, holding her against the wall with its left hand locked around her throat. Seleece struggled to breathe as the alien began to read her mind. The alien had been right all along, she knew exactly where Melthuron was, and now the alien did too.

"Hey, what do you think you are—" but Greynor couldn't finish. The alien stared at him.

"We are going after Melthuron...NOW," the alien yelled as it teleported in front of Greynor. "Pick up your helmet. That's an order!"

"Yes!" Greynor exclaimed nervously as he put on his helmet.

"Wait! Please don't do this; there has to be a better way!" Seleece screamed out as she stood up.

"There isn't any other way. We must act now," the alien responded as it disappeared before her eyes, taking Greynor along with it.

Chapter 11

"Where is he?" Greynor asked as his eyes adjusted to the white-coated wall, which stood just a few inches away from his face. They were now somewhere inside Demora's most important government building, the Legislature Chamber.

"According to Seleece's memories, Melthuron must be somewhere in this government building. Begin the search immediately. I will go down this way; I want you to search in the opposite direction," the alien responded as it pointed down one of the many hallways visible to them. The alien's eyes began to glow. Suddenly, tens of thousands of robots appeared out of thin air and dropped to the ground, making loud banging sounds as they fell.

"You brought the battle bots!" Greynor exclaimed as the robots turned on and dispersed in every direction.

"Go," the alien said softly before disappearing from Greynor's sight.

"After being rescued from a ship of unknown origin, and a full investigation led by the intergalactic coalition, the primary suspect for these treasonous acts is none other than Kalduron Golbrook, the supreme commander of Demora's military. A warrant for his arrest has been issued and...what is the meaning of this disturbance?" Melthuron screamed as one of the battle bots broke into the room, smashing the large wooden door wide open. Screams quickly followed as other Thespians that had gathered for the broadcast began to run away in fear as two more battle bots entered the room, both holding blasters in their robotic hands.

"We must keep the transmission going! Our citizens deserve to know the truth!" Melthuron screamed as his soldiers ran to his side and surrounded him on every side, shielding him from any direct harm.

The alien was quick to find him. It appeared out of nowhere, a few feet away from its robots, and quickly registered Melthuron's location. The alien teleported in front of the soldiers, kicking one of them out of the way while simultaneously attempting to grab Melthuron with its left hand. But the attempt was unsuccessful; one of the soldiers managed to kick the alien away, sending it flying back in the robot's direction.

"We are under attack! I repeat, we are currently under attack!" Melthuron screamed nervously as the alien stood up, easily brushing the kick aside as if it were nothing. All of the Thespians that had gathered had been evacuated by Melthuron's soldiers; only he and Tei-va remained. Melthuron quickly glanced over at one his soldiers. "Do it," he whispered. The soldier destroyed the camera with a blast before teleporting back to his master's side.

"Well, well! It's so good to see you again, my tall, beautiful experiment! Tell me, what have you learned so far in this new existence I have given you?" Melthuron asked, grinning wickedly.

The alien remained expressionless as it stared back Melthuron, thinking of its next move.

"Now, now, before we start this little fight, could I suggest a different course of action? How about we don't partake in another pointless squabble you couldn't possibly win. Instead, why don't you just come along with me and we can end this now. What do you say?" Melthuron asked.

The alien, however, had no intention of doing such a thing. "No, I will get what I came here for…at any cost," the alien replied. The alien quickly teleported the rest of the battle bots into the room, surrounding Melthuron and his soldiers with the small army of robots.

The robots quickly raised their weapons at Melthuron, ready to engage. "Oh my, you sure brought the cavalry with you this time, haven't you? Tell me, what is it you came here for exactly? Somehow I don't think you came all the way here because you missed me," Melthuron asked before letting out a big laugh.

"I came here to find the information I have been seeking ever since I awoke in this body. I will not leave here without it," the alien responded swiftly.

Melthuron laughed. "Wait…wait a minute there, my dear experiment," Melthuron said right before the alien executed its next move. "If you wanted to know how to get your soul out of that body, why didn't you just ask me?" Melthuron asked with a nasty smile.

The alien didn't respond; it just stared back at Melthuron.

"Oh, you didn't think to ask? Well, this sure is awkward. I would have told you from the beginning if I had known that's what you so desperately wanted to know. How about you call off your little toys here, and I will tell you everything you want to know," Melthuron said. Melthuron suddenly disappeared as a blast almost caught him and his soldiers off guard. Melthuron, Tei-va, and their soldiers quickly reappeared on the left side of the room, escaping the blast Greynor had fired.

"Oh, and what do we have here? It must be my dear Seleece. Oh how I have missed you! Still as hostile and calculating as ever, I see," Melthuron exclaimed as the debris began to clear.

One of Melthuron's soldiers quickly teleported behind him, kicking Greynor in the head. The force of the kick sent Greynor flying across the room into the chairs placed below the podium, dispersing them all over the room as Greynor crashed into them.

Luckily, Greynor was rather unaffected by the blow and regained his footing quickly, raising his blaster in Melthuron's direction as he used his right hand to remove the now shattered helmet.

"Oh? That's not Seleece. Who might you be, soldier?" Melthuron asked.

"I am Greynor, soldier one zero zero three. Mr. Prime Consort, please stand down and come with us, sir. This is over. You and all of your allies will answer for the crimes you have committed," Greynor replied loudly while keeping his attention glued on Melthuron's soldiers; he couldn't let a single one escape his gaze, not even for a second.

"Greynor? Why I've heard of—." Melthuron was suddenly teleported away from the alien, who appeared three feet above them. The alien managed to touch two of the soldiers while in midair, using Melthuron as a distraction in order to place its energy on the soldiers just like they had planned.

"I can feel them!" Greynor exclaimed as he began to open fire at the two soldiers. Both managed to get away from the blasts just in time, but one of them was met with a strong blow to the chest as he tried to ambush Greynor from behind. As the solider flew backward into the wall behind him, the robots wasted little time as they relentlessly opened fire on that soldier in unison, annihilating everything in that general direction.

Melthuron was somewhat surprised to see this, although he seemed to remain quite calm. "Oh my…that was quite unexpected. What a wonderful performance, Mr. Greynor!" Melthuron said as he clapped slowly.

To everyone's surprise, the soldier suddenly appeared behind Melthuron. Both Greynor and the alien couldn't believe their eyes. One of Melthuron's soldiers was now standing behind his master as if nothing had happened. The soldier's armor had been completely destroyed by the blasts. Just a shoulder piece and his helmet remained latched on to the soldier's green body. But what they were seeing was nothing if not disturbing; one of his arms had been completely blown off. Any other soldier would have died from such a volley of blasts, or at the very least lost consciousness from the pain of losing an arm. But not that soldier; not Melthuron's creation.

"That's simply not possible. Is that soldier even Thespian?" Greynor said as he stared back in disbelief. The blue-colored blood the soldier's body was losing indicated that he was indeed Thespian, but no one could survive such a deadly blow. The soldier just stood there, bleeding out but otherwise completely unaffected. The soldier showed no emotion, no sign of pain...nothing.

"Oh my goodness! It's lost an arm! We have some serious patching up to do when we get back to the lab," Melthuron said as he let out a loud, maniacal laugh.

The alien looked outraged. "What have you done to that innocent life form, Melthuron?" the alien asked as it stared at Melthuron, this time with anger radiating from its bright white eyes.

"Oh? What is this? I thought you were a logical, emotionless being. Yet here you are displaying what I'm pretty sure is anger. What a fascinating creature you are!" Melthuron said in excitement.

The alien seemed to be growing angrier by the second. "Tell me what you have done to that soldier!" the alien screamed out.

Melthuron just smiled back. "What have I done? Why I did whatever I wanted to do, of course. I mean, look at them! In just a few years of research I have achieved what no one else could have ever dreamed of! Just like you, these soldiers are my precious experiments. You are all testaments to my genius!"

It was now quite clear that he held no regard for the life of his test subjects. The alien's eyes began to glow a menacing white as it heard those words. "How dare you…how dare you do this to innocent beings!" the alien screamed. "The souls of living beings…they are not something for you to experiment with! You have caused irreparable damage to them!"

Melthuron could only laugh. "Damage? I gave them a new PURPOSE! To serve their creator's will," Melthuron lashed back. "An experiment such as you should never talk back to its creator. Your insolence stops here," Melthuron said as two of his soldiers attacked the alien head on. Maybe it was anger, or maybe it was instinct, but now the alien was even faster than ever. In what seemed like an instant, it viciously cut off the head of the recently dismembered soldier with its bare hands while kicking the other two soldiers in the chest. As the soldier's took the blows head on, and the disembodied soldier's body fell to the floor, both the robots and Greynor wasted little time in blasting that almost lifeless body into oblivion. They relentlessly fired blast after blast in the soldier's direction without stopping. Debris filled the room as the onslaught of blasts continued, engulfing the entire area in a cloud of smoke. During that very moment, no one could see anything at all.

"Greynor, cover the door with your shield! I sense movement coming from the hallway. We cannot let those innocent soldiers join the battle!" the alien screamed as it appeared behind him.

There were no signs of Melthuron's soldiers in the rubble. "Did we get them?" Greynor asked as he took out his plasma shield from his armor's back compartment. The door was now completely engulfed by his shield. "They are trying to tear down the door! It won't last very long! We need to end this quickly before they break this shield down!" Greynor screamed.

The smoke was now beginning to clear. Two of Melthuron's soldiers were on the ground, apparently unconscious. Melthuron now only had one soldier standing in the alien's way.

"It's over," the alien said as a blaster appeared in its hand.

"We are leaving now!" Melthuron screamed out as his last soldier appeared before him, ready to teleport his master away from the battle.

But before the soldier's fingers could touch his master's body, the alien fired a blast. The soldier had no choice but to teleport away, giving the alien the opportunity it so desperately needed. The battle was over. The alien made contact with Melthuron's throat and firmly grabbed him, teleporting both of them above Salvador.

"You will atone for your crimes against nature, Melthuron. You have lost," the alien said telepathically as it teleported all three of them out of the building.

Chapter 12

Seleece could not believe her eyes. Greynor and the alien were back at base with Melthuron in custody. "I can't believe it! You two actually did it…it's finally over!" she cheered as she welcomed her allies back. Their mission was finally over; they were victorious.

"Take him. I will retrieve Kalduron at once and bring him here," the alien said, sounding upset, still rattled by what it had seen.

Seleece could tell by the alien's look that something had happened.

The alien proceeded to toss Melthuron toward Seleece like a rag doll before disappearing from her sight. "What the hell happened over there? The alien seems…different," Seleece said to Greynor as she caught Melthuron with ease. She quickly secured him with handcuffs.

"A lot," Greynor responded. He was still shocked by what he had witnessed. What he had seen still didn't make sense to him.

"What the hell did you to them, huh? You monster! You will rot in a cell for the rest of your miserable existence; I'll make sure of it," Greynor yelled out in frustration.

"Why don't you go ahead and answer his question?" Seleece asked as she pushed Melthuron against the wall.

"Well you see, I simply—"

"Let him go," Kalduron interrupted. He was now back at base with the alien by his side.

"Sir, yes sir!" Seleece quickly responded as she released Melthuron from her grasp.

"Our deal still stands. He is all yours," Kalduron said to the alien.

The alien quickly appeared in front of Melthuron, lifting him off the ground with ease. "Do not make this harder than it has to be,

Melthuron. There is nothing you can do now," the alien said in a stern voice.

"By all means, do your thing, big guy. I know you will be pleasantly surprised!" Melthuron responded as he laughed out loud, unperturbed by his defeat and capture. Melthuron continued to laugh as the alien searched his mind, completely ignoring the situation he was now in.

"Don't you get it? You have lost, you sick bastard…it's all over!" Seleece yelled back at Melthuron, irritated by his condescending attitude.

"You will rot in prison for all the crimes you have committed, for all the galactic citizens you've killed. Justice will come your way soon enough. You can count on it," Kalduron added as the alien continued to search Melthuron's mind.

Suddenly, the alien's bright eyes began to dim, but the alien's face was now filled with even more frustration. "This cannot be! No! This cannot be!" the alien howled as it exploded with anger.

It viciously tossed Melthuron against the other side of the room in a fit of rage; it was unlike anything they had ever seen. The whole room went completely silent.

"What's going—" Seleece couldn't even finish her question.

"Who are you!" the alien screamed as it teleported in front him. Out of nowhere, it delivered a devastating kick straight into Melthuron's stomach, crushing his ribcage as if it were made of glass.

"Answer me!" the alien screamed again as it lifted the injured Melthuron off the ground. Everyone was shocked.

"What…what happened? What's wrong?" Seleece asked, weary of what the alien would do. She had never seen it like that before. She knew she had to be cautious…there was no telling what the alien might do. "This…this isn't Melthuron!" the alien responded angrily as it firmly held Melthuron up with its left hand.

"What? Of course it's him; look at him! That's Melthuron for sure!" Seleece responded.

"Do NOT question me!" the alien raged back. "This isn't Melthuron! It's an impostor!" the alien responded angrily.

"OK, let's just calm down, take it easy. Please, tell us what you saw," Kalduron said softly, trying his best to calm the powerful alien. "Whatever is going on, we will find a solution, but we can't lose control here," Kalduron said.

"You are right; my apologies everyone," the alien responded as it began to calm down, still holding Melthuron in the air by his neck.

"Good, now just take it easy. Tell us exactly what's going on," Kalduron responded calmly as he placed his hand on the alien's shoulder.

"I searched his mind, and there are no memories of me or his experiments…or anything related to his plans. In fact, the memories I found don't even belong to Melthuron. They are someone else's memories entirely," the alien responded in its monotone voice. Everyone was stunned.

"What? How can that be?" Seleece asked as her voice cracked. If the alien was right, Melthuron had once again escaped justice. The ecstasy of victory slowly began to slip through her fingers as she realized that Melthuron had yet again outsmarted them. "Always one step ahead; that bastard is always one step ahead!" she thought to herself as the same, familiar rage began to take over.

"But how can that be possible?" Greynor asked, equally confused.

"Are you certain of this?" Kalduron asked, remaining composed.

"Beyond any reasonable doubt, yes," the alien responded.

Melthuron suddenly let out a loud laugh as he struggled to stand. He now appeared to be in great pain. He coughed up some blood as he stood up. "Such fools. You will always be one step behind us," Melthuron said before more blood dripped out of his mouth.

"Be quiet!" Seleece screamed as she rushed over to Melthuron. "I'll beat the truth out of you if I have to, you sick bastard!" she screamed.

"That course of action will yield no beneficial results, Seleece," the alien said as it grabbed her hands before she could begin.

"Let me go!" Seleece screamed.

"This course of action will not bring us any favorable results," the alien repeated. "That's not Melthuron."

"Seleece, stop this now!" Kalduron commanded with a stern look.

"Yes…yes sir!" Seleece said as she clenched her fists. Her knuckles cracked as she attempted to suppress her anger.

"Soldier, I'll deal with your…misconduct later," Kalduron said with a displeased look.

"Sir, I'm—"

"Quiet," Kalduron said before turning around to face the alien. "Are you sure about this? Are you sure you haven't made a mistake?" Kalduron asked the alien as calmly as possible.

The alien looked back. "Yes. I don't make mistakes," the alien responded. The alien quickly teleported next to Melthuron and looked at him for a moment.

"And what are you going to do now?" Melthuron asked as he smiled at the alien.

"Something I have never attempted before," the alien responded, its eyes burning with focus as they lit up.

"Ha, ha! And what do you mean by that?" Melthuron asked. This time he seemed a bit more nervous; it was uncharacteristic of him.

The alien remained silent as he focused, and this made Melthuron even more nervous.

"What's it doing?" Melthuron asked nervously as he looked at Kalduron, directing his question at him.

"Seleece, restrain him at once," the alien commanded.

"With pleasure," Seleece responded as she walked up to him.

"No wait, stop! What are you going to do?" Melthuron asked with a shaky voice, growing evermore nervous as the alien stared at him.

"Get off me! Let me go!" Melthuron yelled as Seleece lifted him off the ground with ease, restricting his movement completely.

"I advise everyone to close their eyes," the alien said as it gently placed its right hand on Melthuron's chest.

"It seems the alien is not going to read his mind…this is going to be something completely different," Seleece thought as she took the alien's advice.

"How much this will hurt is entirely up to you," the alien said as its eyes glowed more brightly.

Kalduron quickly closed his eyes as the light overtook the room.

"Damn it, I want to see this!" Greynor said as he placed Seleece's helmet on, hoping it would shield him from the light like a pair of sunglasses; but what he would witness next would be nothing short of inexplicable.

Melthuron began to scream out in pain as the alien's hand went completely through his body, as if it were water. Then the screaming suddenly stopped; Melthuron's eyes began to emit the same blinding white light as the alien's. His mouth slowly opened up.

"Damn it…what the hell is happening?" Greynor exclaimed as the light became too bright, overtaking the entire room. Even Greynor's dark-tinted visor couldn't guard his eyes against the bright light; he had to close them.

"Just what the hell are you doing?" Seleece asked, shutting her eyes as tightly as she could, unable to see anything other than a hint of light that was seeping through her eyelids.

The alien, however, did not respond at all. They both remained completely motionless as light emanated brightly from their bodies. And just like that, it was over.

"You can all open your eyes," the alien said loudly.

Seleece slowly opened her eyes, noticing nothing new in particular. Melthuron was on the floor. He looked unconscious. "What did you do?" Seleece asked.

"Your hand…I saw it…it went through Melthuron's body as if it didn't have any mass at all. I've never seen anything like it," Greynor added in disbelief.

"What was the purpose of that? What did you do exactly?" Kalduron asked calmly, completely unmoved by what he had just heard.

"I had to make sure this person was indeed not Melthuron. I decided to reach in and examine the soul that currently resides in this body," the alien responded.

"The soul?" Seleece thought as the alien continued its explanation.

"I was able to confirm my theory; that is indeed Melthuron's body, but that's not his soul," the alien said.

"Not his soul? But then does that mean that we—"

The alien knew what she was going to say. "Yes, we failed to capture him. Melthuron is still out there," the alien interrupted. "I have underestimated Melthuron completely. His knowledge of souls seems to have expanded beyond what I could have anticipated."

Seleece couldn't believe it…she couldn't accept it. "No! No! No! No! No!" Seleece screamed as she pounded the ground with her fists in a fit of rage, crushing the white tiles as if they were made of plastic.

"Seleece, calm yourself at—" but Kalduron couldn't finish.

Seleece was enraged by their failure. "Shut up!" Seleece screamed back at Kalduron in defiance for the first time

Both Kalduron and Greynor were taken by surprise.

"Lenduin, Caal'dor, and Melron are dead! Dead!" Seleece screamed out as tears slowly streamed down her face.

"Seleece, look at me," the alien said gently before appearing right behind her.

"What!" she responded angrily as she turned to face the alien. As her gaze shifted, she suddenly felt a finger lightly tap the back of her head. "What is this…what's…happening," she struggled to speak as she felt fatigue overwhelm her.

"Just get some rest for now, Seleece. Tomorrow will be a new day," the alien with a smile said as she began to lose consciousness.

Chapter 13

Sunlight began to shine on Seleece's face. She suddenly woke up to familiar surroundings. "What…where am I? What happened to me?" Seleece said in a confused panic as she woke up.

Her Serverbot was standing next to her, ready for instructions. "Welcome home, master Seleece. The whole in the wall has been fixed, and your apartment has gone through a thorough cleaning as commanded. How may I serve you?" the Serverbot asked.

"I'm home? I don't remember anything except…the alien! The alien did something to me!" she thought as she tried to remember how she got there. "Serverbot, what time is it? When did I get back here?" Seleece asked as got out of bed. She let out and long yawn as she rubbed her forehead gently with her right hand.

"It is zero nine hundred hours, master Seleece," the robot responded swiftly.

"What? That can't be!" Seleece said. Seven hours had passed since she had fallen asleep. "Serverbot, how did I get here?"

"Your guest brought you back home last night, master Seleece. You were already asleep when it set you on the bed," her robot responded.

"Good, you have finally awoken," a voice said from behind.

"Yeah I did, no thanks to you. How dare you do that to me! Don't ever do that again!" Seleece responded as she heard the alien behind her.

"But you have been neglecting your sleep for some time. Your body needed it," the alien responded with a smile.

"You're...smiling? That's...new," Seleece said as she walked over to her closet.

"Smiling? I did not notice. I guess I am slowly getting used to emotions and how to express them. It's all still very new to me,"

"I...really lost it back there, didn't I?" she said with a hint of shame

in her voice as she began to put on a new set of Thespian battle
armor.

"What object have you lost? Is it back at base?" the alien
asked.

"No...that's not what I mean by that," she said with a laugh.
"I mean that back at base I lost my mind for a minute...I lost
control," she responded while checking her inventory, making sure
she had everything she would need.

"I don't believe there was anything wrong with what
happened. I am by no means an expert in these matters, but after
being in this body for this amount of time, I am slowly beginning to
understand the way corporeal beings experience and express
emotions," the alien responded.

"I am a soldier. I cannot respond to any situation, no matter
how dire, in the manner I did yesterday. It brings shame to the
Thespian army," she said as she picked up her helmet.

"Even I know that is false notion," the alien responded.

Seleece was intrigued by the alien's response; it wasn't acting like its calm, emotionless self anymore

"You have every right to feel any way you choose; no one can dispute that," it said.

Seleece looked surprised. "This sounds weird coming from you...stop it!" she teased.

"Your soldiers...they were more than just fellow Thespians to you, weren't they?" the alien asked.

Seleece didn't want to think about them; she couldn't. She had to press on, put all emotions aside like the soldier she was. "Anyway, you need to catch me up on what happened after you...put me to sleep, which I'll get you back for later," she responded as she continued to check her inventory.

"Yes, of course. There have been quite a few developments," the alien said as it placed its hand on her head. "Look upon my memories," the alien said. Seleece suddenly found herself back at base without the alien. As Seleece glanced around the room, she saw herself standing at the other side of the room, losing consciousness after being touched by the alien.

"These must be the alien's memories," she thought, with her attention now focused on what the alien was showing her. The alien swiftly caught her before her body hit the ground, picking her up gently in its arms. "I've put her to sleep for now; both her body and mind need to rest," the alien said as it set Seleece down on the floor gently.

"I will discipline her later," Kalduron said in an angry tone, seeming displeased with her behavior.

"That won't be necessary," the alien responded in Seleece's defense. "I don't believe there is any need for such measures, don't you agree, Kalduron?" the alien concluded as he stared down at Kalduron. The alien looked intimidating. Its eyes focused on Kalduron, its stare sent a clear message. The alien was not going to let anything happen to Seleece.

Kalduron was taken by surprise by the alien's defense of Seleece, and he was not about to question it. "Well, perhaps you are right. It's been hard on all of us lately," Kalduron responded grudgingly.

"Hey, wait a minute! If you had the ability to put others to sleep, why the hell didn't you use that earlier?" Greynor asked.

"Mind your tongue, Greynor," Kalduron said.

"I meant that respectfully, sir…err…ma'am?" Greynor followed after his scolding, still confused about the alien's gender or lack thereof.

"If that is a question, I do not require a gender-specific address. I have no gender. To answer the previous question, Seleece was already exhausted, I just took advantage of that fact and helped her body go into rest mode. That's the only reason I was able to do it so easily; this is not something I could easily use during battle," the alien said as it held Seleece in its arms.

"The fact of the matter is, we couldn't be in a worse situation than we are right now," Kalduron interrupted as he remained composed. "Melthuron has played us for fools once again. We fell right into it! That broadcast has been seen by all of Demora. He will no doubt have the public on his side now," Kalduron explained.

"Hell, we even have his body with us right now. It won't look good if we just return him after everything that was broadcast. We would be branded as traitors immediately," Greynor added.

Kalduron nodded in agreement. "Forget a trial. They'll eliminate us immediately if we are found. Melthuron wouldn't risk going to trial, that's why he used the emergency response system. He knew you would try to capture him, even if it was in front of a national audience. And you all fell for it!" Kalduron said, assigning the blame to everyone but himself. "If you had only remained at base like I commanded, none of this would have happened," Kalduron said angrily.

"Do not let anger cloud your reasoning as I just did, Kalduron. A warrant for your arrest had already been issued. I had little choice but to take this gamble," the alien responded calmly.

Kalduron was not happy with the alien's response. After all, he was the one whose reputation had been tarnished on the national broadcast, not the alien's. He was the one who was a wanted man. "It's not you whose life—"

"We don't have time for petty squabbles such as these, Kalduron. We must shift all our efforts into coming up with our next move," the alien responded calmly. The alien's eyes, however, told a different story. They glowed a menacing white, and its stare spoke more loudly than its words.

Kalduron couldn't risk upsetting the alien, not after everything that had taken place. He needed the alien now more than ever. "You are right," Kalduron responded.

After the debacle aired on international television, Melthuron now had all the cards he needed to play his next hand.

"He will declare martial law. I bet that was his plan all along," the alien said.

"Perhaps so. For now, we will have to stay out of the public eye. Greynor, I want you and Seleece to focus on gathering as much Intel on Melthuron as possible. His experiments, his allies, anything and everything you two can possibly find. The more data we gather the better. We will need all the evidence we can get our hands on," said Kalduron.

"I believe I know where we can start," the alien said as it walked to the center of the room carrying Seleece on its shoulder. "Computer, display all known information on the quadrant known as DZ597," the alien commanded.

The computer suddenly turned on. "The quadrant known as DZ597 lies ten light years outside of Earth's solar system. It is home to many gas giants with atmospheres primarily composed of helium," the computer responded as it brightly displayed an overview of the Milky Way galaxy. It proceeded to zoom in to the quadrant, displaying the approximate time it would take to reach it using Demora as the starting point.

"According to the memories I was able to gather from our prisoner, Melthuron's most important lab was located in a spaceship somewhere in that quadrant," the alien said.

"Excellent. Make your way to that spaceship now and see what you are able to find. Greynor will be the only one to accompany you," Kalduron said.

"I am unable to do so at this time," the alien responded quickly. "It seems Melthuron is beginning to understand how my powers work. As far as I was able to gather from the small batch of memories I found, Melthuron made sure the being he switched bodies with spent very little time on that ship. I don't have enough information to be able to feel the exact location of the spaceship."

"I see," Kalduron said.

"I can, however, take us straight to that quadrant," said the alien.

"That is a good course of action to take if we knew, without even the slightest of doubts, that the ship was in fact located in that quadrant. But what if it isn't? What if the ship has moved to another location? What then?" Kalduron asked.

"If so, the plans will be revised and a new course of action shall be taken," the alien responded without any second thoughts.

"That is absurd! We would be wasting valuable time on what could turn out to be a wild goose chase! There has to be a better way. I can't afford to waste any time after everything that has taken place," Kalduron said.

The alien, however, seemed rather unconvinced by his plea. "That is the course of action we will take," the alien responded. "If you wish to use my power in the near future, this debate will not continue. Do you understand me, Kalduron?"

Kalduron was not at all pleased by the alien's response. Greynor remained silent.

"Surely we can come up with a better plan than that. I think we can all agree it would take a significant amount of time and resources to successfully find a spacecraft in such a large—"

"Do not misunderstand me," the alien said as it teleported itself and Seleece within inches of Kalduron. "Your innocence, or lack thereof, regarding any and all charges that this government could bring up against you is not of any concern to me. Our deal is based on taking any means necessary in order to capture Melthuron. That takes priority above everything else."

Normally, Greynor would have come to the defense of his superior, but the alien was sending both of them a very clear message; there would be no debating the issue. The alien's eyes radiated with authority; it would not be challenged by anyone.

"But of course," Kalduron replied as he cowered in the alien's presence. Kalduron had no choice. He had to comply or risk losing a powerful asset.

"I will contact you whenever Seleece ends her resting period. We will need her at optimal cognitive function for the mission. After all, she is the best soldier you have at your disposal," the alien concluded before teleporting Seleece and itself out of base, offering them no time for a response.

"Well…I've never seen anyone talk to Kalduron like that before," Seleece said as her mind shifted back to the present.

"I do not understand what you mean. I merely spoke truth," the alien responded.

"It's just weird to see somebody talk to Kalduron like that. It's not something I see every day," she said.

"I suppose to a being such as you, disagreeing with a superior is not a course of action that is usually taken. I believe it is actually reserved for unusual circumstances, if I am not mistaken. But unlike yourself, Kalduron is not my superior in any way. A being such as me has none," the alien responded.

"And there's the cocky alien I know and almost care nothing about. You gave me quite a scare there for a second with all your new acts of kindness," Seleece teased. But she was thankful; thankful that the alien had stood up for her.

"I'm sorry…you know, for lying to you back then. I should have told you where I thought the transmission was coming from," she said. Seleece then glanced at the picture on her nightstand. "I…I just didn't know what to do at that moment; everything was happening so fast."

But she didn't have to apologize. Forgiveness was already written all over the alien's face. It already knew how she felt. "You didn't tell me because you were afraid of what would happen. I felt it as I read your mind," the alien replied. "If you seek forgiveness, I will provide it."

She couldn't believe it. The alien had really changed.

"The more time I spend in this body, the more I begin to understand how all of you feel. This corporeal existence truly provides a different experience, one which I am slowly getting accustomed to," the alien responded, this time in a rather friendly tone. "I must ask you one question before we join the rest of the group."

"Anything," she said.

"When the time comes for you to decide which of us you will follow, who will you choose, Kalduron or myself?" the alien asked out of nowhere. Seleece was taken by complete surprise. That was not a question she thought the alien would ask. "What do you mean? I'm not sure I understand your question," she quickly replied. But she did understand, she knew exactly what the alien was talking about…she just couldn't admit it.

"I know what you and Kalduron have been plotting. I know he intends to find a way to control me, to use me as his own weapon. In my eyes, he is no better than Melthuron," the alien said as he stared deep into Seleece's eyes.

It was as if the alien were staring straight into her soul. "I don't know what you are talking about," Seleece replied. But the alien knew; it knew how she had been feeling about it for quite some time.

"I am baffled by the fact that while possessing no information about me, Kalduron actually believes he could control a being with power such as mine. Just like Melthuron, that arrogance will prove to be his downfall if he continues down that path," the alien said loudly.

Seleece couldn't believe how much the alien had known all along. It had been aware of their intentions the whole time, and yet it chose to work with them. It had known everything since the very beginning. Seleece could only stand there, frozen with fear as the alien's words continued to shock her.

"Our souls have been linked together many times already. How you could possibly think I was not aware of such a foolish plan?" the alien asked.

Seleece couldn't answer.

"Answer me," the alien said calmly.

But Seleece didn't know what to say. "I didn't…I wasn't…I…I," she struggled to say under the weight of the alien's stare.

"That is not an acceptable answer."

"What do you want me to say? It's true. It's all true! But I don't feel that way anymore. I don't agree with Kalduron's plan," Seleece confessed.

"You still have not answered my question. What will you decide to do when the time comes? And make no mistake… that time will surely come." The alien's expression said it all. It wanted a definitive answer, and they were not going to leave until it got one.

"The truth is, if you had asked me this question yesterday, I would have answered Kalduron without hesitation. But I don't feel that way anymore," Seleece confessed as she walked up to the alien. "I could never betray Kalduron, but I promise you, I will never let him use you as a weapon," she said before locking her arms around the alien. "At this point we are not just allies, we are friends. I would never let anything happen to a friend," she said as she held the alien in her arms.

Although the alien didn't show it, it was surprised. "I understand. That is an acceptable answer," the alien responded without emotion. It stood there for a second, wrapped in Seleece's arms, not knowing what to do.

"I promise you," she said as she let go. "But don't get used to my hugs! I don't just hand them out, you know," she teased as she lightly tapped the alien's shoulder with her fist.

"I'm sure I won't. But we should get going," the alien replied, avoiding the conversation altogether.

"Right, but we should get some food first. I'm starving!" Seleece said.

"No, we are leaving right now," the alien responded as it placed a hand on Seleece's shoulder. The alien quickly teleported them back to base. It was eager to begin the search.

"Hey, wait a...aw damn it!" Seleece said as her eyes adjusted to her new surroundings.

"Does your body require nourishment? Here, take this for consumption," the alien said as it extended its right arm outward toward Seleece, opening its big hand. Suddenly, a bag of frozen food appeared on top of the alien's hand, containing two meals' worth of nutrients. Seleece scowled at the idea of eating such food, especially that kind; it was her least favorite. For the past twenty years, 90 percent of all the food in Demora had been produced by a government-owned entity known as Gael'mar, meaning sun food in old Angro, an old Thespian language that was no longer spoken by the general public. That, along with the military serum, had been the main source of food for Seleece for the past ten years. "And where did you get that?" she asked as she grabbed the bag from the alien's hand. The bag was hot, as if the alien had already pre-prepared it for her consumption.

"I believe you call it a store," the alien responded calmly.

"A store? When did you go to a store?" Seleece asked as she opened the bag. She then pulled out a small, rectangular-shaped food item, quickly shoving it in her mouth.

"Last night as you slept, I made the decision to explore New Jermaxus. I happened to find a store as I traveled throughout the city," the alien said as it teleported to the middle of the room.

"Oh yeah? How did you pay for that? Where did you get the money?" Seleece asked with her mouth full, blurring the words together as she mauled the poorly flavored food. It had been over twenty hours since she had any food whatsoever. She was going to finish it all in one go, even though she found the food less than delectable.

"Money? I don't have such a thing. I just took the item from the store," the alien replied with a confused look.

She almost choked as she heard that; the alien had stolen it. "Wait now," she struggled to say as she swallowed. "You stole it? You can't do that; it's against the law!"

"Law?" the alien asked in apathetic tone. "Perhaps it is against your made-up law. I do not care for such laws. They are not my primary concern at the moment."

"Fine…but don't do it again! Anyway, where are Kalduron and Greynor?" Seleece asked as she walked toward the end of the room, throwing away the empty container into the base's recycling shuttle.

"I have already taken them to quadrant DZ597. They are currently searching for Melthuron's ship," the alien said.

"Then why have you brought us here? We should join them."

"Because we have one more ally joining us. I told him to get ready while I fetched you. He should be here any moment now," the alien said calmly.

"A new ally? Who are you talking about?" Seleece asked. She couldn't think of a single new member to trust with such a mission. After everything Melthuron had broadcast to the world, there's no one Kalduron would trust to bring to their side. Especially after Melthuron ousted him as a traitor. Since he had no political power anymore, no member of the Thespian army would back him.

"Reporting for duty," a voice said, coming from behind the sliding door. A soldier dressed in full Thespian armor then entered the room.

"I...I know that voice!" Seleece exclaimed as the soldier removed his helmet. "Salvador?" she exclaimed in a confused tone as their eyes met. Although her opinion of him had slowly changed as she learned more about him, she still didn't trust him to join them, and with good reason.

"Perceptive as always. I'm glad your eyes are working well," Salvador responded in a snarky tone as he walked closer to the alien.

Seleece was not happy by the alien's decision. "Are you crazy? What do you think you're doing letting him loose like that? He is our prisoner!" Seleece screamed out. She instinctively placed her hand on her gun, but she knew the alien wouldn't let anything happen.

"Yes, he will be joining us," the alien said.

"But why?" she vehemently protested. It didn't make any sense to her. "Why are you bringing a former enemy into our ranks?" she asked, with her hand still wrapped around her blaster.

"Key word being 'former,'" Salvador responded calmly.

"I think you should reconsider; this is a really, really bad idea," Seleece pleaded.

But the alien looked completely calm. "That won't be necessary," the alien replied.

"I have no intention of betraying the alien," Salvador said.

Seleece wasn't quite sure, but it looked like he was telling the truth.

"Yeah? I don't trust you one bit! You betrayed my crew; raised your weapon against my soldiers. You've lost your mind if you think I'm going to work with him," Seleece protested.

"My mind is not los. It has remained constant throughout my existence," the alien said. "I read his mind, his feelings. He has no intention of betraying us at all. As far as I am concerned, I trust Salvador more than your commander. I don't believe we have to discuss that issue any further today, do we Seleece?" The alien's words weighed heavily on Seleece, a weight she couldn't begin to lift from her shoulders. She had no way to argue against the alien when it came to Kalduron. After all, if she was in the alien's shoes, she wouldn't trust him either. It was still a miracle the alien even trusted her in the first place.

"Let's make something clear. We don't have to work together. The only thing I intend to do is enact the alien's will,"

Salvador responded as he put on his helmet. A look of determination was written all over Salvador's face.

The alien had to have done something to Salvador, but she had no time to ponder such things; there was work to be done. "For the record, I am against this decision. But you are the boss. Just keep in mind that from now on, whatever he ends up doing, for or against us, is all because of you," Seleece said.

The alien didn't respond. It looked completely unmoved by her words. It didn't seem her opinion even warranted a response.

"Now that we are all present, let's join the rest of the group," the alien said.

Seleece quickly walked up to the alien, brushing her opinion aside as she put on her helmet. Salvador quickly followed, placing his helmet on as the alien teleported both of them out of base.

Chapter 14

"Welcome back," Kalduron said as he noticed their sudden arrival. He was fully dressed in his Thespian armor. This time, even Kalduron was going to participate in the search. "Oh? And who is this with you?" Kalduron asked, intrigued.

"It is Salvador. He will be working with us from now on," the alien replied.

Kalduron's expression quickly changed. Although he didn't like the idea, he preferred to remain tight-lipped for the time being. "I see. Welcome, Salvador," Kalduron said before quickly changing the subject. "The search is underway. I've sent about twenty drones toward different corners of the quadrant as we previously discussed," Kalduron said as he returned his focus back to their mission. Kalduron then quickly pulled up a hologram of the quadrant. "The red areas highlighted here are the ones we have ruled out already. There were no signs of a spaceship flying there recently," he said as he pointed to each area on the map. "Our best course of action would be to focus our efforts in these areas here," Kalduron said as he used his finger to highlight two different areas of the quadrant. "If we are lucky, we will pick up any sort of signal left by the spaceship in that area."

The alien stared at the hologram for a moment, analyzing everything that Kalduron had said.

"I understand the logic behind such a course of action, but your plan has one fatal flaw," the alien professed confidently. "Correct me if I am mistaken, Kalduron, but your course of action assumes that Melthuron actually physically piloted his ship to its current location, wherever that might be. That's why you are starting your search around the edges of this quadrant, firmly believing the ship traveled to this quadrant from the outside, either from the Earth's solar system or your own, thus leaving some sort of trail behind, which you could use to track its movements. Is my assumption correct?" the alien asked.

"Affirmative," Kalduron responded.

"Well, I have come up with another hypothesis that I believe needs testing. What if Melthuron had his ship teleported to this quadrant by his soldiers?"

It was rather unfortunate for Kalduron, but it was true. Shifting to a new level of thinking was necessary. Melthuron now had the capacity to play by a whole new set of rules. Nothing could be ruled out. Kalduron seemed displeased to be reminded of such fact.

"I see. That notion would have been preposterous not two days ago, but you are not wrong. That is indeed a possibility we can't ignore," Kalduron responded. Kalduron now looked annoyed. "So, what do you propose then? How would we even start such a search?"

Both Seleece and Salvador remained silent. There was no way they were going to get caught up in the middle of these discussions.

"My strategy is simple. We search the least likely areas along with the most likely areas to find him."

Kalduron suddenly exploded. "Oh, well, brilliant! Why didn't you say so? And how are we supposed to know which areas are which when he can teleport? He could be anywhere! That is not a useful strategy at all, Kalduron responded.

The alien remained composed. "I'll make it simple so that even you can understand." The alien responded calmly.

"Observe the quadrant for a moment. What do you see?" the alien said as it used its finger to zoom out of the quadrant.

The whole quadrant was now in full display. Every star and every planet was visible as a small dot on the three-dimensional hologram.

Kalduron stared at the hologram for a moment, but he couldn't see it. To him, it was just like any other quadrant in the galaxy; full of planets rotating around their respective stars. "Spill it already," Kalduron said

"You don't see it?" the alien asked.

"Stop wasting time! What are you getting at with this?" Kalduron asked while staring at the hologram.

"As I said earlier, this quadrant is known for its many gas giants. Most of these have helium as the dominant atom composing their atmosphere. But there is something else in this quadrant that is unique, something I believe is the reason why Melthuron chose this quadrant in the first place. I believe you all refer to it as a Magnetar," the alien said.

"A Magnetar? What the heck is that?" Salvador asked.

"To put it in simple terms, it's a collapsed star that has a magnetic field trillions of times stronger than Demora's or Earth's. That's the short version," the alien explained.

"Putting your little science fact of the day aside, so what? We can't get anywhere near that thing; it's too dangerous. The magnetic field would render all our technology completely useless, let alone what it would do to our molecular structures if we got even remotely close," Kalduron said.

And he was right. It was dangerous to get close to its magnetic field, to such a strong gravitational pull. If the gravity didn't crush them before they got too close, the radiation would destroy their molecular structures before they even knew what hit them.

"That is precisely the point I am making. Melthuron is the most intelligent, calculating being in this galaxy. That's why he surely has chosen to place his ship near that star. The random chance of someone flying near it would be infinitesimally small given how dangerous it would be. Of course, his ship could also be anywhere else, but that's not Melthuron prefers to think, is it?"

The alien was right again. Kalduron was stunned by the alien's logic. He would have never thought of that, not in a million years of planning. "I see," Kalduron responded. His anger was now fading fast. The alien had made excellent points, all of which were slowly reassuring Kalduron that it was possible to find the ship. "Please then, tell us the course of action you wish to take. I will follow your lead," Kalduron said.

Seleece couldn't believe it. Kalduron was actually going to follow the alien's plan without question. Seleece knew quite well that under any other conditions, Kalduron would never follow a plan like this. But that's how desperate he had become.

"I will use my energy to make the drones operable even under the conditions set forth by that star. We will send them all in that star's direction," the alien explained. Suddenly, the alien's eyes began to glow; that was when the drones appeared in the room. They were very small, about two feet long. Their design was simple. They looked just like a gray, miniature version of their ship. What they lacked in size and firepower was more than made up for in speed. Unlike other types of drones more suited to warfare, these were designed specifically to gather intelligence. These drones could travel up to fifty times the speed of light, making them ten times faster than all other military drones. "With more of my energy attached to these drones, I can make them Magnetar-resistant," the alien said. One by one, the alien's energy began to fortify each drone. "Fortunately for us, I am quite familiar with that star. I won't have trouble moving our drones to that area," the alien said before its eyes lit up. Suddenly, all of the drones disappeared before their eyes. "It shouldn't be too long before the drones are done," the alien said.

But all of the sudden, the alien began to struggle to breathe.

"Whoa, hey…are you all right?" Seleece asked as she walked over to the alien's side.

The alien looked tired. "I am all right. It seems I am reaching this body's limit. After all, it takes an immense amount of my energy to protect the drones from the Magnetar's conditions. I require some rest," the alien said as it struggled to stand.

"Don't worry…I got you," Seleece said. She placed the alien's left arm around her shoulders and started walking toward one of the chairs in the control room. "That was some strategy you came up with. I'm quite impressed," she said as she helped the alien sit down in the chair.

"How long will it be until the drones return?" Kalduron suddenly asked.

"Given the size of the area I want them to search and the speed at which they travel, I would say about thirty-four of your minutes," the alien responded calmly.

"And how long until you get your strength back?" Kalduron then asked.

"Of that I am uncertain. This is the first time I've felt this way, but I'll have to manage it somehow. Even if we manage to find Melthuron's ship, without me you will be unable to board it."

"Even if we manage to board the ship, we must be certain, beyond a shadow of a doubt, that we will be safe from the forces of the Magnetar. Will you have the strength to protect us in the same way you are protecting the drones?" Kalduron asked.

"With enough rest and proper nourishment, I don't think that should be a problem," the alien responded.

"Good, then you just rest here for a bit and get your strength back," Seleece said, smiling from behind her helmet. Kalduron seemed to agree.

"Then let's let our friend here rest for a bit. Seleece, come with me," Kalduron said as he made his way toward the door.

"Yes sir!" Seleece said as she quickly followed Kalduron out of the room.

Kalduron was very quiet as he made his way down the well-lit, almost pearly white hallway. He suddenly came to a stop in front of a door and stepped inside the room as the door slid open. Seleece quickly followed. When she stepped inside, Kalduron was waiting with something in his hand.

"You have done well, Seleece," Kalduron said as he extended his hand out to her.

"What do you mean, sir? What is that you are holding in your hand?" she asked. It was a very small, cylindrical container. It was filled with some sort of clear liquid. That's when it hit her. "You have done very well in gaining the alien's trust. I am glad I trusted you with such an important mission. But we cannot ignore this for much longer; we need to place this alien under our control permanently," Kalduron said. Seleece didn't respond; she couldn't.

"The alien is getting harder and harder to manipulate. It's only a matter of time before we lose complete control of this situation. I am entrusting you with this mission," Kalduron said as he placed the small container in her hand. "Only administer this tranquilizer after either of the following two following conditions are met: if we find Melthuron's ship around the Magnetar, administer the drug after we are all safely back on this ship, or if the ship is not found around the Magnetar, administer the drug ASAP while the alien is still recovering. We can't afford to lose such a chance," he concluded.

Kalduron couldn't tell, but from behind her helmet, Seleece was conflicted. She couldn't respond; she didn't know what to say.

"Is that understood, soldier?" Kalduron asked.

"Yes sir!" Seleece replied out of habit.

"Excellent. You have done well. I am proud of you, soldier. I will overlook the outburst you displayed yesterday, but just this once. Don't ever speak to me in that way again," Kalduron said as he walked around her, leaving her alone inside the room.

It had been nearly thirty minutes since Kalduron had left. Seleece had remained in that room the whole time, thinking endlessly of the choice she had to make. Although much had been contemplated as she waited for the drones to return, she couldn't bring herself to come up with a decision. That's was when the door slid open.

"The drones have returned. Report to the control room at once," Kalduron said as he walked away again.

Seleece quickly followed behind him, keeping a short distance between them as they headed toward the alien. "I guess that's that," she thought to herself. Seleece had made a decision.

"Report," Kalduron said as he entered the control room.

"All the data they have gathered are being uploaded to the main computer, sir!" Greynor said enthusiastically.

A few seconds went by before the upload was complete. All of the files gathered by the drones were now visible in the computer's hologram.

"Computer, scan all files for any evidence of a ship," Kalduron ordered.

"Scanning…scanning…complete," the computer said. "Displaying results now."

The hologram suddenly began to adjust and, before long, a video started playing. The video showed what appeared to be a medium-sized ship. From its design, it seemed like it was a simple carrier ship, so its battle capabilities could be small. Kalduron and the rest wouldn't rule anything; Melthuron could surprise them yet again. They would have to proceed with caution no matter what.

Still, Kalduron couldn't believe his eyes; the alien had been right all along. "That must be Melthuron's ship! No one else would be crazy enough to station their ship so close to such a star," Kalduron said as he paid close attention to the video playback. "Computer, give us an overall view of the quadrant and highlight the ship's location," Kalduron commanded. According to the computer's map, the ship was right smack in the middle of the Magnetar's magnetic field. It was now quite clear that Melthuron had found a way to cancel out the star's effects, albeit it was still unknown how he managed to do so. "Now that we know the ship's location, can you take us inside?" Kalduron quickly asked the alien.

Seleece was now quite familiar with the alien and its abilities. She knew the answer to that question already, but said nothing as the alien's eyes began to glow.

"I can't take us inside the ship; I can't feel it," the alien responded. The alien paused for moment. It stared at the map displayed in the middle of the room, contemplating what the best course of action would be. "I may be unable to teleport us directly inside, but I can teleport us to where the ship is located according to this map," the alien responded.

"But how will we get inside? I doubt Melthuron will just let us in! We don't have a team of experts ready to aid us in infiltrating the ship this time around," Seleece exclaimed.

"If I could physically touch the ship, I could do it. Another way would be to teleport us to a room within my field of vision, but the risks involve with that course of action are far too great," the alien explained.

"Why is that?" Kalduron asked with a curious look, hoping to learn more about the alien's powers and limitations.

"If my teleportation were to fail, and I happened to teleport us inside a wall, for example, that would make us part of the wall. We would bind with it on at a subatomic level. In other words, we would die," the alien explained.

"Well, I'd rather skip the dying part if at all possible," Greynor said.

Kalduron was not at all amused by his comment; he looked quite pissed with Greynor's carefree attitude.

"I mean that…uh—"

"Just be quiet," Kalduron ordered angrily. "Damn it all to hell! If only I had more military resources at our disposal, infiltrating that ship would be easy!" Kalduron screamed in frustration. This ship, along with some weapons and food, was all Kalduron was able to take before fleeing his home planet. Earlier that day, the police had raided his home. The Thespian government had voted two hours after the broadcast to strip him of his position, and a warrant for his arrest had been issued shortly after. Kalduron had barely made it out of Demora without being captured. Aside from a few colleagues who still believed in his innocence, the entire Intergalactic Alliance now thought of him as a wanted criminal; it was very hard for someone like Kalduron to accept, but the young Melthuron had completely outmatched him and masterfully tarnished Kalduron's reputation at the same time. Kalduron's entire career, his reputation, and his innocence were all riding on what they could find on that ship; he could not afford a single screwup.

"Master, I will follow whichever course of action you deem best," Salvador said to the alien.

To Seleece, that sight was still strange to see. His new-found loyalty toward the alien was unquestionable.

"I wonder what happened between those two. Whatever it was, it had a big impact on Salvador. Either that or he's being mind controlled once more," Seleece thought. They had spared his life, but that alone was not enough to bring such a drastic change. Whatever the reason, it would have to wait.

"Well, I also place my trust in whichever plan you choose to follow," Seleece said as she shifted her mind back to the task at hand.

"You are the only one who can get us to that ship, so no matter how dangerous, how risky these moves are, I will trust in your judgment," Kalduron said. He had no other choice.

The alien thought about for a moment, silently weighting all of the possible options. "Kalduron, does this ship possess stealth capabilities strong enough to let us get within safe viewing distance of Melthuron's ship?" the alien asked.

Kalduron smiled. "This model was designed specifically for stealth missions. I doubt we will be detected by Melthuron's ship," Kalduron said. "Our biggest problem will be the ship's force field. Even though our Intel didn't catch it, I am positive that ship must have a powerful force field protecting it. We won't know until we come face to face with it," the alien said. The alien then quickly kneeled down and placed its right hand on the floor. A deep breath quickly followed.

"Computer, turn on all stealth mode measures," the alien commanded as it began to focus its power.

"Stealth mode activated. Cloaking online, wave absorbers online, all measures active," the computer replied.

The alien's eyes were glowing so brightly, everyone had to close their eyes. "I will now add my energy to this ship to protect us from the Magnetar. Now that we know where the ship is located, I will take us there," the alien exclaimed as the whole room was engulfed in the alien's blinding white light.

A few seconds went by before the light suddenly subsided. "It is done. We should be safe from the Magnetar for now," the alien said as it walked toward the end of the command room.

There it was, sitting about a half a mile in front of them, Melthuron's ship.

"The ship! It's right there! You did it!" Seleece exclaimed as gazed at Melthuron's ship through the long, rectangular viewing window in front of her.

"Excellent work!" Kalduron said. "Computer, scan the ship directly ahead of us for signs of an energy field," Kalduron commanded swiftly.

"Scanning…scanning…complete," the computer said as it displayed the results up on the hologram. "Level five energy field detected around the target ship," the computer said as it displayed a three-dimensional model of the ship and its force field.

"Level five? We can't catch any breaks," Seleece said as she observed Melthuron's ship. That was the most powerful of the commercial-level energy fields, capable of withstanding very large amounts of damage.

"I don't see any other way," the alien said as it carefully analyzed the ship. "I will go alone first. There's no need to risk anyone else's life," the alien said as it glanced back at them briefly, turning on the cloaking device Seleece had given him back at her apartment.

"Wait! There might be another—" but she couldn't finish. The alien had disappeared. The alien had no way of knowing whether or not it would teleport into wall or onto the floor, but if it was able to successfully teleport inside and leave its energy within the ship, teleporting them back there would be easy.

"Damn it!" Seleece said as her eyes lost track of the alien. But before she could say anything else, a cloaking device turned off in front of her. The alien was back almost as quickly as it had left. Seleece let out a sigh of relief, happy to see the alien back.

"Stop trying to give me heart attacks!" she exclaimed before lightly tapping the alien's shoulder with her first.

The alien stared back at her with a blank expression. "I have successfully placed my energy in that ship," the alien said, completely ignoring Seleece. But the alien suddenly stumbled. It was having trouble breathing again.

"Hey, I got you, don't worry," Seleece said as she grabbed the alien's hand and walked over to the chair beside them. "Just sit down and get some rest. Maybe we should get you some food, water, or something?" Seleece said, not knowing what to do.

"It seems these are the limits of this body," the alien responded as it slowly sat down.

"Sadly, we have no food for you here," Kalduron quickly responded.

Seleece knew Kalduron was lying, but she chose to remain silent on the matter.

"Given the strengths and weaknesses this body seems to possess, I believe I will recuperate at a rather fast rate, so food won't be necessary," the alien responded calmly. "I will just do this instead."

"Do what?" she thought as she saw the alien raise its right arm up in the air. Its eyes grew bright. Suddenly, a white beam of light began to seep out of everyone's bodies. The light traveled straight into the alien's eyes, and in a matter of seconds, the light subsided.

"What was that? What did you do?" Seleece asked.

The alien quickly stood up. It looked refreshed and ready to go. It was a complete turnaround from where it was a second ago. "I simply took back the energy I had placed in all of your bodies. It should be sufficient enough to get us to that ship and back," the alien replied.

"Hey, wait a minute. Are you sure you'll be OK?" Seleece asked with a worried look.

"I'm sure our friend here will be fine, Seleece," Kalduron responded as he walked over to the alien.

"Kalduron is correct," the alien replied as it began to focus its energy. "Everyone, place your hands on my body," the alien commanded swiftly.

Everyone turned on their cloaks. They quickly checked their inventory to make sure they had everything they could need.

"If we are all ready, let's begin," the alien said as they disappeared.

Chapter 15

"What a dump!" Seleece said as her eyes adjusted to the dirty, gray wall that was now just a few inches in front of her. It wasn't long before she began to shiver; it was freezing cold. Even though the alien was naked, as always, it stood still, seeming completely unaffected by the low temperature that was now surrounding them.

"Extreme temperature detected. Adjusting core armor temperature now," their helmet interfaces said. It took a moment, but their suits slowly began to readjust to the low temperature, bringing them to safe levels once again.

"Ah, that's better! It was freezing in here. You're not cold?" she asked the alien.

"No. I've adjusted this body so I would have no distractions by outside sources," the alien responded.

They had appeared in some sort of cold storage area; there were dozens upon dozens of dirty beakers, machine parts, and containers all around them. Some containers were filled with different types of liquid, and others were completely empty. The whole room was a complete mess; it looked as if no one had cleaned it for ages. Their helmets suddenly began to beep.

"My helmet is detecting movement all over the place," Kalduron whispered as he clenched his blaster.

"It is safe to assume that it's the battle bots," the alien whispered back. "Melthuron seems to have dozens of them patrolling the whole ship. I encountered some of them when I first set foot on the ship," the alien explained.

At first glance, it looked as if they had only one way in and out of the room. The only exit they could see was a small door about thirty yards ahead.

"Why did you teleport us into this room?" Kalduron asked.

The alien didn't answer; it seemed preoccupied. It just walked around the room, touching everything in sight. The beakers, the empty containers, the containers with fluids in them, the machines, everything it saw. It seemed like it had no intention of leaving even one speck of dust untouched.

Seleece knew exactly what the alien was doing; it was going to take everything in that room back with them. "I'm gathering evidence," the alien finally responded after a quick round of "touch 'em all."

"I believe you will need as much evidence as possible in order to clear your name of wrongdoing. I believe that is how your courts operate, on physical evidence, if I'm not mistaken," the alien said.

Kalduron didn't seem to understand what the alien was talking about, but it didn't matter much to him. "Very well, do what you must," he said as he carefully walked over to the door with a blaster in his hands. "Everyone, follow my lead," Kalduron said telepathically via his helmet. He was ready to storm out of that room, but as he made his way to the only door he could see, the alien appeared in front of him, blocking his way. "And what do you think you are doing?" Kalduron whispered as the alien appeared, just inches away from his face.

"There's no need to engage these robots in battle. I can easily take them out without causing a disturbance. Just stay here and don't move," the alien said as it teleported out of the room.

The alien's commanding attitude made Kalduron furious, but he chose to bite his tongue for now. The mission was too important to let anything get in the way; there was no time for pride.

Just a few seconds was all it took. That's when they heard some weird sounds coming from the corridor. It was as if heavy things were being dropped on the floor, one after the other. A few more seconds went by before the door in front of them slid wide open, with the alien standing on the other side.

"Follow me," the alien said as it stepped away from the door and into the corridor again.

As soon as they set one foot out the door, they became visible. All of the robots that had been patrolling the hallway were now on the floor, completely motionless. There had been no sign of a struggle; not even a single shot had been fired. Their helmets were picking up no signs of movement in the corridor anymore. The alien had somehow taken out every single one of them in a matter of seconds without letting any sort of physical struggle take place.

"What a showoff," She thought with a smile as she slowly walked past a stream of unconscious robots.

The rest of them quickly followed, avoiding the now unresponsive robots as they made their way down the corridor.

The state of the ship was bad all around. The walls of the corridor were just as rundown as the storage room. It looked as if no one had been around for years.

"My helmet is picking up movement in that room ahead," Salvador said.

It was faint, but the signal in their helmets detected movement down the hall, the fourth room on the left. As they walked toward it, the signal in their helmets became stronger and stronger; someone or something was actively moving about in that room. They were now standing against the wall. The alien placed its left hand on Seleece's shoulder, establishing a connection between them.

"I'll teleport everyone inside," the alien said telepathically. Since Seleece was linked to everyone else via her helmet, everyone else could also hear the alien's thoughts through their helmets.

The alien knew it was better to just teleport everyone inside; it didn't want the door to have to slide open and possibly reveal themselves to the enemy, even if it was low on energy. They then quickly disappeared from the corridor, appearing against the wall directly in front of where they were standing just seconds ago. It was a medium-sized laboratory, but what they found inside was not exactly what they were expecting. There were three unarmed robots, each of them looked busy with their own individual tasks. One of them appeared to be busy building some sort of machine, or perhaps it was repairing it. The other two were busy sorting through boxes that appeared to contain all sorts of things. Some of them contained intricate machine parts, and others were filled with small jars containing all sorts of unknown liquids. The robots were carefully sorting through each box, placing the machine parts on a table in front of them, while the jars were being placed on a lab bench.

"Take those robots out," Kalduron said to the alien telepathically.

"Don't move a single muscle," the alien said as it disappeared.

It all happened in a matter of seconds. The alien quickly appeared in midair, directly above the two robots that were sorting out the boxes. As the alien appeared, it quickly placed its hands on their bodies. As the ship's artificial gravity began to pull the alien to the ground, it dragged the robots down with it. The last robot then turned around as it heard what happened, but it was powerless to do anything.

The alien appeared behind it and lightly touched it with its hand. The robot quickly fell to the ground, completely unable to move. Even the light that was emitting from its artificial eye turned off. All three of them now appeared to be offline.

"Nice!" Seleece thought as she walked over to the alien.

"Quick and efficient…excellent work," Kalduron whispered as he walked toward the alien.

"What exactly did you do to them? Did you turn them off or something?" Greynor asked as it poked one of the robots with his blaster.

"I simply removed the electric energy that was powering their bodies and converted it to a source of energy that this body can use. It's what I have done with all the other robots. I must say I have replenished all the energy I had lost…I now plenty of energy to spare" the alien explained.

"Let's take a look at what they are working on here," Kalduron said. He quickly walked over to the machine the robot was working on. Kalduron had never seen anything like it before.

"What could this be for?" the alien thought as it analyzed it in close detail.

"I can't tell what this is supposed to be…does anyone have any ideas?" Kalduron asked while he inspected every aspect of it.

Whatever it was supposed to be, it was quite clear that it was nowhere near being done. What the robot had built so far just looked like a casing of sorts, perhaps the outermost part of the machine itself. They could tell by the parts the robot had been installing that it was supposed to have some sort of display capabilities, but right now it was nothing but an unfinished mess of wires and metal.

"Salvador, stand guard by the door," the alien said.

"At once," Salvador said as he stationed himself close to the entrance of the room.

"Perhaps we can find the answer inside the robot's hard drive," Kalduron said. He took out a small device from the outermost part of his helmet and placed it inside the robot's head, where the interface of that robot was located. "With this we can steal all of the data stored inside these robots. It will just take a few seconds," Kalduron said.

The transfer completed within seconds.

"Let's take a look here," Kalduron said as he transferred the device back to his helmet.

The helmet's computer quickly gained access to all of the robot's data.

"Computer, sort all files by date of access, starting with the most recent files," Kalduron commanded.

The computer made quick work of the files, quickly rearranging every single file before brightly displaying them inside his helmet. There were millions of files, although that was expected since he took out every single file that was stored inside the robot's hard drive.

"Let's see what we have here," Kalduron thought as he opened the first file. It was some sort of blue print that appeared to be similar to whatever the robot was working on. But Kalduron couldn't make anything out of it; he had never seen anything like it before.

"My helmet is picking up movement out in the corridor!" Salvador said via his helmet.

Seleece quickly tapped the alien on the shoulder, alerting him of the movement, but the alien didn't seem to care; it just stood still. Footsteps could be heard out in the corridor, getting louder and louder.

"Everybody, stand against the wall and don't move," Kalduron commanded telepathically.

Everyone, except the alien, rushed toward the wall.

"What is that thing doing just standing there?" Kalduron thought. It seemed like the alien had no intention of taking cover, it was still preoccupied with whatever that robot had been working on.

"Thirty units offline," a calm voice said, coming from the corridor.

The door suddenly slid open; two robots of the same model walked into the room in unison. They quickly noticed the three robots on the floor. "Thirty-three units offline," one of the robots said.

"Is it communicating with someone?" Seleece thought as she stood motionless against the wall. Her hand was on her blaster's trigger. They were all standing by, ready.

"What the hell are you doing?" Seleece thought as the one of the robots began walking in the alien's direction. The alien didn't acknowledge the robots at all; it continued to stare at the unfinished machine.

The robot continued to walk toward the invisible alien, unaware of what was standing right in front of it. Suddenly the alien appeared behind the walking robot, touched it, and disabled it. The robot then fell to the ground just like all the others had.

"Thirty-four units off—"

The alien made quick work of the last robot. It fell to the ground just like all the others.

"What the hell do you think you're doing? Our cover could have been blo—"

"Will you be quiet for a just a moment? I am doing something of great importance," the alien whispered, cutting Kalduron off before he could finish his sentence. Kalduron was furious. "And what's—"

The alien then vanished. It appeared right next to Kalduron. "Show me the files you have gathered," the alien said telepathically.

Kalduron nodded, still upset.

"It cannot be anything else other than that," the alien said telepathically. "That robot was building a soul container," the alien said.

Those words didn't make much sense. It couldn't be true; souls couldn't possibly exist, regardless of what the alien had said before

"Are you saying those containers can house souls? As in…mine or…anyone else's?" Seleece asked.

"Yes, at least according to the blueprints I just analyzed," the alien replied.

There was no way the alien could have figured out something like that so quickly; it had only taken three seconds to analyze thousands of files.

"That is just pure nonsense. The files here say nothing of the sort. How could you possibly tell?" Kalduron asked.

"I will explain later. We should keep searching every room on this ship. If those robots were indeed communicating with someone, we won't have long before we are discovered," the alien said. Kalduron agreed. "Let's move" he said.

The next few rooms contained nothing but beds, tables, and the like. Since this ship was originally a carrier ship, a few rooms had been designated to house the workers, although none other than robots had been found so far. They had encountered a few more robots along the way, but none stood a chance against the alien. Every room off of that poorly lit, stained corridor had been searched, but no further Intel had turned up. They were now standing at the end of the corridor. A sign on top of the door said 'Docking Room' in Universal. The alien quickly teleported everyone inside.

Just like any carrier ship, the docking room was the biggest room in the entire ship. The ceiling stood at roughly a fifty feet from the ground. There was a lot of activity in that room: robots carrying boxes and flying freight cars moving about, shifting materials from one side of the room to the other. Toward the end there was a small spaceship sitting on top of a platform. Due to its size and design, it was safe to assume it was meant to be a single-passenger ship. It was small and circular with six thrusters sticking out from the side. Two robots were working on the spaceship. It didn't seem as though it would be operational anytime soon since two of the six thrusters were sitting on the ground with other parts all around them.

"There's nobody here either," Kalduron said with disappointment. He needed something, anything that he could use to prove his innocence, and so far there had been nothing. "Search every damn box, every inch of this room for evidence of Melthuron's wrongdoing. There has to be something we can use against him!" Kalduron said telepathically.

There were a total of nine robots in the room, but none of them stood a chance; the alien took out every single one of them in a matter of seconds. It was now safe to begin the search.

"Seleece, help the alien search every box in this room. Greynor, you and I are going to check out that ship. Salvador, keep a lookout for any potential movement," Kalduron commanded telepathically.

Before each of them could start their tasks, something caught the alien's eyes. "Wait," the alien said. It kneeled down and placed its right hand on the floor. "It's faint," the alien said as it attempted to focus. Its eyes began to glow. "But I feel it. There's something, or someone, over there in that direction," the alien whispered as it pointed toward the end of the room.

Anxious as to what it could be, they all proceeded with extreme caution. They walked over in that direction as instructed, but there was nothing but a small storage closet.

"In the storage closet?" Kalduron asked in a whisper.

The alien nodded. Something or someone was in there. They raised their guns. Seleece walked over to the closet and positioned herself on its side. She stuck out her hand and began to count down with her fingers. Three...two...one! She opened it. There was a scream.

"AAAAH! No, please, no more...please, I'm begging, you don't hurt us anymore!" they heard as human fell to the floor.

He was a middle-aged, dark-haired man dressed in a dirty lab coat and black jeans. He had an unkempt beard and looked as if he had not showered in months. He was wearing lab-appropriate attire. Goggles were sticking out of the front pocket of his lab coat. Given all of this, it was safe to assume he had worked in Melthuron's lab.

But the man seemed confused; perhaps he had been drugged. He slowly looked up. "What...what's going on? What's happening? Who's there?" the man asked as he looked around. But he couldn't see anything; everyone was still invisible to him. It was obvious. They could all see it, the fear in that man's eyes. He was Melthuron's prisoner.

"Please don't hurt us anymore!" the man pleaded as he slowly dragged himself over to the wall; he appeared too weak to stand. He was in handcuffs, shivering with fear and covered in cuts and bruises. "I'll do whatever you want; please don't hurt us anymore!" he screamed over and over again as tears fell down his cheeks.

"Identify yourself," Kalduron commanded.

"What…what?" the man said with a confused look on his face.

"I said, identify yourself!" Kalduron screamed out, having no sympathy for the unknown man.

The man seemed confused, disoriented. He looked malnourished, like he had been kept under very bad conditions for a long time.

"I'll take care of this," the alien whispered as the cloaking device turned off.

"Don't you worry anymore, human. We are not here to hurt you," the alien said as it teleported the man's cuffs away.

The human couldn't believe what was now standing in front of him. "I don't believe what I am seeing…it actually worked," the man whispered to himself in a crazy tone.

"Tell me who you are," the alien said as he helped the man stand up.

"I'm—"

"Answer the question or I'll blow your head off right now!" Kalduron screamed with impatience.

"OK, I'm sorry! I'm Dr. Gamelsberg. Please, don't hurt us! We will do whatever you want," he responded as he covered his face with his hands. "Are…are you here to kill us?" he asked in a terrified voice, still shaking from fear.

"Quiet! I'm asking the questions here," Kalduron screamed. "Is Melthuron aboard this ship?" Kalduron asked.

"No. I...I don't know where he is, but he's probably not here... Wait," he said. "You don't work for him?" he asked as he wiped the tears from his face.

"No, we do not," the alien responded.

The human's eyes grew wide with excitement. "We are saved! We are saved," he exclaimed with overwhelming happiness.

The alien placed its right hand on the human. "You appear to be wounded and malnourished. I'm going to help you; don't be afraid," the alien said as it began to heal him. But something was very wrong with that man. It was taking way too much energy to heal him. "Are you able to stand now?" the alien asked as it moved its hand away. The alien had used about three times more energy than it thought the man would need.

"Yeah, I'm...I feel OK now! I can't believe it," the human responded.

"Who else is aboard this ship?" Kalduron asked.

"As far as I know, nobody but us and the robots," he replied. "Have you been sent here to rescue us?" he asked as he stood up.

"Us? Who else is here?" Kalduron asked with a confused look.

He glanced around the whole place, but there was no one else around. Their helmets were not picking up any other signals.

"Oh, I'm sorry. I forgot to introduce you all to my wife," he said with a smile on his face. "I've been in captivity so long, I have forgotten my manners. Honey, it's OK. Come on out. These nice people will get us out of here safely," he said.

"See, my love? I told you to never lose hope," a high-pitched voice said out of nowhere.

Something was happening underneath the man's lab coat. There was something moving underneath it, slowly slithering itself from his back.

"Hi everyone! It's nice to meet you all. My name is Izzy," the voice said.

They couldn't believe what they were seeing. It was some sort of parasitic worm sticking out from inside the man's body. It wrapped around the man's torso, slowly stretching itself up toward the man's face. They were speechless. None of them had seen this type of creature before. It didn't have a face or eyes, just a small mouth full of tooth-like structures. The parasite's skin was the same tone as its host, so it looked as if it were just a big, ugly extension of the man himself.

"Holy crap," Seleece said in complete disbelief.

"What the hell is that thing?" Greynor asked in complete disgust.

"Sir, this man has clearly gone insane. We have to get him to a doctor right away to get that thing removed. It could probably kill him if it's left untreated," Seleece said telepathically.

"Hey! That's very rude! I don't know who said that, but whoever it was, you should apologize to my wife right now," he demanded.

"Oh honey, it's all right. You know how people react when they first meet us. It's nothing new. You know I don't take it personally," the worm said in a happy tone.

"I knew I felt another soul inside your body. Pleasure to meet you, Izzy," the alien said. The alien didn't seem at all surprised or disgusted by the parasite's sudden appearance.

"Everyone be quiet!" Kalduron said. "Listen up, Dr. Gamelsberg. We are taking you under our protection. In exchange, you are going to tell us everything you know about Melthuron's plans," Kalduron said.

"I can keep my energy in this ship. We will be able to return to it at any time if need be," the alien said calmly.

"I'll do whatever you ask of me; I'll tell you everything! Just get us out of this godforsaken prison," the man said.

"Very well. Take us back to our ship," Kalduron said before the alien disappeared, taking everyone with it.

Chapter 16

"What on earth is going on? Where are we?" Dr. Gamelsberg said as his eyes adjusted to his new surroundings.

"I brought us all back here," the alien responded.

The man couldn't believe his eyes. "Teleportation...I never would have imagined such a thing was possible," he responded with awe as he looked around the room.

"See honey, I told you to have a little faith," the parasite said.

"I know, I know, sweetie. You were right, as always," Dr. Gamelsberg responded as he took off his lab coat.

"I am Kalduron, commander of the Thespian army," Kalduron said as he turned off his cloaking device and removed his helmet.

The rest of them followed Kalduron's example, taking off their helmets and revealing their identity.

"These three here are Seleece, Greynor, and Salvador. You've already met the alien," Kalduron said as he set his helmet down on the table.

"Yes. I know who that is. After all, I was the one who created him in the first place," Dr. Gamelsberg replied as he stared at the alien.

Kalduron and the rest couldn't believe what he had just said.

"What? You created him?" Seleece reacted with shock.

"Well, I should clarify. I helped in his creation, sort of…kind off" the scientist replied. "My wife and I are really sorry for what we have done to you. I had no idea what Melthuron had planned. If I had known from the beginning what his intentions were, I would have never allowed him to get this far. Please know that most of what I did was against my will," he said, his voice cracking with regret.

"I will find out the truth. I'm going to read your mind; do not resist," the alien said. For the first time, the alien actually sounded upset as it placed its hand on Dr. Gamelsberg's head.

The alien's eyes began to glow as it read his mind. A few seconds went by. Dr. Gamelsberg didn't appear to resist the alien at all.

"And that's the whole story, down to the last tiny detail," Dr. Gamelsberg said. The alien removed his hand from his head and stood still for a second. "I'm really sorry about all of this; we both are," Dr. Gamelsberg said.

The alien seemed to be shocked. "I...understand," the alien said.

But Seleece could tell that the alien was upset by whatever it had just learned.

"Hey now, don't look so glum white eyes. Every problem has a solution! We just need to put our heads together and figure it out!" the parasite said in happy tone.

The alien stood still, silent. Everyone was waiting to hear what it had learned. But suddenly, the alien disappeared.

"Damn it!" Kalduron said. He would have to wait for another chance to sedate it. "All right, enough of this waiting. Tell us everything you know about Melthuron…NOW," Kalduron howled.

"Right…uh, sorry!" the human replied. "First of all, can anyone tell me today's date? Preferably the Earth calendar. I don't even know how long we have been in captivity."

"It's May tenth in the year three thousand and fifty-three," Salvador replied.

"Fifty-three? I was imprisoned for two years I can't believe I've been gone so long," he responded.

Kalduron was not about to let another second go by.

"Computer, begin recording. You, get on with it…now! From the beginning," Kalduron demanded angrily.

"Right! Right! Sorry! I lose focus easily. Where was I? Ah yes! All right, this all started two years ago. It had been more than five years since I was able to get any funding for my research due to"—he cringed—"what people like to call my 'lifestyle' choice," he said.

"Lifestyle?" Seleece asked.

"He's referring to me," his wife responded. "You see, back home, people don't exactly view us in a favorable light. The only person who grew to accept me and my husband was his sister, and oh was that hard!" the parasite explained.

"As I was saying, it had been five years since I had landed any grant money for my research. I was desperate for money; desperate for any university to fund me. That was when Melthuron came in," he said. He paused.

"Honey, it's not your fault. We could never have anticipated any of this," the parasite responded.

"I know, I know. I was none the wiser at the time. Anyway, Melthuron was the one who contacted me. Me! A nobody astrobiochemist! It was just too good to be true at the time," he said.

Kalduron seemed to be getting impatient. "And why is that?" Kalduron asked.

"Right. You see, among the galaxy's scientific community, Melthuron is like a celebrity. I mean, the guy is a prodigy, even among the most brilliant of minds! He has the type of revolutionary mind that comes once every several generations. When a guy like Melthuron contacts you and tells you he is interested in working with you, well, to me it was like a dream come true! It was the answer to all of my problems. I could never say no to someone of his stature," he explained.

"Once every several generations? Ugh, of course..." Seleece thought to herself.

"It was as if I were in a dream...Melthuron, the most respected scientist in the known universe had contacted me about my research. MY research!" Dr. Gamelsberg said once more.

"Doctor, what was it you researched back then?" Kalduron asked, trying to get him back on track.

"Well, as my title implies, I am a scientist who focuses on the

biochemistry of alien life forms such as yourselves," he responded.
"You see, for the longest time I had a theory that life on our planets,
perhaps life in this galaxy itself, has common ancestry. My life's
work has been trying to definitively prove that beyond any
reasonable doubt," he explained.

"So then Melthuron contacted you. What was it he wanted to
research with you?" Kalduron asked.

"About two years ago, he had come to Earth for a conference
regarding the future of science. It was there that he contacted me
about working for him. We had a brief phone conversation before I
was invited to his home back on your planet, Demora. That was
when he told me he was going to run for the position of Prime
Consort. I must say, I was quite surprised to hear that. Scientists
such as ourselves rarely choose to partake in government, let alone
strive for positions as important as Prime Consort. But Melthuron
had made up his mind…I guess after being engulfed in war for so
long, he truly believed his home planet needed a genius mind to lead
it," Dr. Gamelsberg said.

"Of course that egomaniac would think so highly of himself," Seleece said.

"Seleece," Kalduron said as he stared back at her.

"My sincerest apologies, Commander. Please continue, Doctor," Seleece said.

"Right! Uh, let's see…oh yes. Anyhow, the day I met him at his home was the day he told me something I will never forget. He had made a new scientific discovery, one that he firmly believed could change the world forever. He told me he had definitive proof that souls existed," Dr. Gamelsberg said.

Seleece was not surprised to hear that, none of them were. Souls had been the only topic the alien had talked about since they met.

"Of course I didn't believe him at first, I mean, how could I? I am a man of science. The whole idea of souls existing had been mere mythology for thousands of years back on my home planet.

Needless to say, I asked for proof, and boy did he provide it," he said.

"And what was this proof?" Kalduron asked eagerly.

"Well, the alien of course. The alien's soul, I should say," he responded with regret in his voice. "Melthuron never told me how he discovered the existence of souls, but he had come into possession of one very special soul. The one that now resides in that alien's body," he said with even more regret.

Although she was not surprised to hear such a revelation, it still hit her hard. "So what the alien has said has been true all along. That soul really was imprisoned in that body; the alien wasn't crazy," Seleece said as she teared up a bit.

"Regrettably so. Melthuron had somehow imprisoned that soul. He wanted to study it, understand it…to see if souls could have some sort of real-world application. Only god knows what Melthuron did to that soul before I laid eyes on it," he said as his voice slowly started to break.

"So then, what did you mean when you said you helped in the alien's creation?" Kalduron asked.

"Well, I didn't create the alien's soul, obviously. I…it was me who synthesized the body that the poor soul was imprisoned in! That's why Melthuron wanted my expertise. You see, for years he had tried and failed to make a body that would house such a special soul. He realized that he needed someone like me to help him design a perfect body," he said as tears began to roll down his cheeks. "I witnessed firsthand what it was like to house a soul in a body that it does not belong to," he said.

"What does that mean?" Seleece asked.

"Well, to put it in simple terms, as far as I understand it, and we really just need to put decades of more research into this—"

"Get to the point, Doctor," Kalduron said impatiently.

"Right…well…the souls die," he said with sadness. "Oh god, what have I done!" he said.

It was clear that all of his actions weighed heavily on his conscience.

"I never meant to hurt anybody! That's not what I wanted at all. I just wanted to study it, you see. I could have never—"

But his wife didn't seem to agree. "Honey, you were forced to do it! It's not your fault," the parasite said as it slowly wrapped around his body, making its way up toward his face. "I love you. Always," the parasite said as it kissed its husband on his cheek.

"I love you too," he responded.

"Gross," Seleece thought.

"We have no time for this! Pull yourself together, Doc—"

"Please have a heart," the parasite said. "My husband and I have been imprisoned for two years. Tortured, barely fed, and forced to do things outside the concept of your understanding. You will give him a damn minute!" the parasite said in an angry, high-pitched tone.

Seleece wasn't quite sure what to make of them. The parasite acted as if it cared about its host, but that couldn't be further from the truth. After all, it was just a parasite; a highly evolved, self-aware parasite that had somehow convinced that poor man that it loved him. Even then, Seleece knew the parasite was right about what she was saying.

"Don't you worry now, sir, you are safe with us," Seleece said as she placed her hand on his shoulder in an attempt to console him. "We just need you to tell us as much as possible so we can use all of this evidence against him. We need you. You are the only one who can put that lowlife behind bars for all the crimes he has committed. Please, take your time," Seleece said with a warm smile.

Kalduron decided to remain silent until the doctor was done. Perhaps Seleece's empathic approach would yield them better results.

"Yes…I'm sorry," he responded before taking a deep breath. "During the beginning of our studies, we had mainly focused on studying the state of souls: what they are made of, how they formed, all really interesting questions really. But I could tell by the way he talked that it was more than just studying for him; it was more than just science, it was becoming his obsession," he explained.

"What exactly changed?" Seleece asked.

"Well, at first we made very few advances. After all, this was the first time anybody had ever studied anything like this, we really had no idea what we were doing. As time passed, and little progress was made, Melthuron grew angry, anxious. He started sleeping less and less and working longer and longer hours every day. After ten months of back-breaking studies, we had nothing to show for it," Dr. Gamelsberg said. "It was then that he decided to shift our research in a new direction. I believe that was perhaps when his mind crossed the point of no return," he said as his voiced began to crack again.

"One…one day, he came into the lab with the biggest smile on his face. I had not seen him smile like that in weeks. I thought perhaps he had come up with a new idea; maybe he was going to tackle our questions from a different angle. But that day, he brought with him all sorts of things to experiment with. You name it, animals, robots, and even humans and Thespians! One by one, his robots brought them inside of containers, unconscious. I couldn't tell which ones were alive and which ones were deceased! It was horrible. It turned my stomach. But what really bothered me the most was his smile. I just couldn't understand his smile. He was so happy to bring all of those beings into the lab as if they were nothing but lab rats for us to experiment on. That was when I had enough. My wife and I wanted to leave right away," he explained.

Seleece's anger began to rise to even higher levels as she heard just how ghastly his actions had really been. Nobody could have anticipated how far Melthuron had really gone. "Is there no line he's unwilling to cross?" she thought as he continued.

"But of course he wasn't going to let us go. At that point I knew way too much. So instead he held us hostage and made us work tirelessly day in and day out. In the next couple of months, I began to slowly witness a transformation take place within Melthuron. We saw with our own eyes his slow, grisly decent into madness. As time went by, he—"

"Take a deep breath, honey. It's all over now. Melthuron can't hurt us anymore," the parasite said as it gently rubbed itself against his cheek.

"He began to take joy in what he did. Nothing brought him more joy than to punish me if something went wrong. Toward the end it got even worse. His methods became more…refined," Dr. Gamelsberg couldn't go on anymore. He just stared off into space as his face turned white.

"Doctor?" Seleece asked. "Doctor? Are you all right, Doctor?" she asked again.

"Yes! I'm sorry. I'm going off on such a tangent," he said as he snapped back into the room. "Let's dial this back to the main point. Melthuron had taken our research in a different direction. We experimented on both deceased bodies and living beings to see what would happen if their souls were tinkered with, replaced. That was when I saw his twisted genius. Not in a million years would I have been able to work out everything that he did; all of the technology he developed to manipulate souls, to take them out of their respective bodies. Every day there was some new idea, some new invention he had developed in what seemed like the blink of an eye," he said as he praised his captor.

"What can you tell us about his research, about his inventions? What is his end game? What are his plans?" Kalduron asked.

He shrugged. "I am sad to say I can't help you with those questions. I was kept in the dark since we first met. I was given one task: to help him synthesize a body that could house the alien's soul. I worked tirelessly by his side as he worked on a million other projects. I've never seen someone work as tirelessly and efficiently as he did. He was like a machine that never stopped," he said, pausing briefly. "After almost two years of intense work, every single day, we finally synthesized a body we believed could do the job. That was the body that the poor soul is now stuck in," he said with sadness in his eyes. "That's everything I know," he concluded with regret. Kalduron finally had enough information.

"Are you willing to testify on our behalf in a court of law, Dr. Gamelsberg?" Kalduron asked.

"I have to. After everything I've done, I owe it to everyone I was forced to experiment on. You can count on me," he replied.

"Computer, stop recording," Kalduron said. "I have one last question, Doctor," Kalduron said as he walked closer to him.

Dr. Gamelsberg knew what Kalduron was going to ask. After all, that was the one big elephant left in the room. "What exactly is he...it?" Kalduron asked.

"What do you mean? I told you, it's a soul," he responded.

But that was not the answer he was looking for. Kalduron wanted to know everything Dr. Gamelsberg knew about the alien.

"Cut the crap, Gamelsberg!" Kalduron screamed out. "Why would Melthuron go through all this trouble just to imprison it in that body? Just to study it? I don't buy that for a second!" Kalduron shouted angrily.

Seleece knew the expression on Kalduron's face. Kalduron was right. That part of the story didn't make sense at all.

"I don't know! I only did what I was told! He never shared any of this with me, I swear," Dr. Gamelsberg replied.

Seleece could tell he was hiding something.

"You're lying! Melthuron made more of those things already! Those...those things killed almost every single member of the intergalactic council. They killed my soldiers; they are all dead because of you! Now you are going to stop lying to me!" Kalduron said. The parasite looked outraged.

"My husband is telling you the truth! We have no idea why Melthuron did what he did!" the parasite yelled back.

"I wasn't asking your opinion, I was asking the scientist," Kalduron responded angrily. "Did I just really argue with an overgrown worm?" Kalduron thought angrily as he waited for Dr. Gamelsberg to respond.

"Honey, it's OK. He's right. It doesn't make sense," Dr. Gamelsberg replied.

"Just tell us, Doctor…please," Seleece said, breaking her silence on the matter.

"I was telling the truth. Melthuron never told me anything," Dr. Gamelsberg replied in a low tone.

"You're lying! Now tells us what—"

"You know, it bothers me too, Kalduron," Dr. Gamelsberg said. "I don't know anything else…for a fact. I've pondered this very question for a long time, trying to figure out the answer to that question," he said.

"Even if it's just a hunch, anything you can tell us could help," Kalduron said as he tried to calm himself down.

"Like I said before, the alien's soul is really quite special. It's unlike any other soul I have ever seen."

"Yes, but how! What is so damn special about it?" Kalduron asked.

"Well for starters, it doesn't have a body that goes along with it, or at least that's my theory. As far as my studies can tell, every soul has a corresponding body, a vessel if you will," he explained.

"A vessel?" Kalduron asked, now even more confused than before.

Dr. Gamelsberg looked back at him, unsure of how to answer his question. "Yes, a vessel. Let's see, how can I explain this? Got it! All right, if I were to, let's say, place my soul in your body. It wouldn't survive. My soul would disappear, and your body would break down. That's what I meant by the death of a soul. It doesn't just die, it ceases to exist if it's not in its proper vessel, except for the alien's soul," Dr. Gamelsberg said.

"And why not?" Kalduron asked with a curious look.

"I haven't the slightest idea why. That's still a great mystery. I am convinced of one thing though, that soul is not human and it's not Thespian. It's something else entirely. It's so different from any other soul I have worked with. Sometimes I don't even know why Melthuron wanted to call it a soul in the first place. Although there is one thing I still can't believe, and frankly I can't wrap my head around" he said in a low tone.

Kalduron was intrigued. "And what is that?" he asked in a curious tone.

"We ran our calculations many times, in fact we were so convinced we were wrong, we ran them over one hundred times…but there was no mistake. That soul old… very old. No other soul in the galaxy can be older," Dr. Gamelsberg said with an intrigued voice.

"What do you mean? How old?" Seleece asked.

"It's…Well billions of years old. I know it sounds hard to believe…but that soul…that alien…It's older than our universe…and by a lot" Dr. Gamelsberg said.

Everyone was stunned. They couldn't even begin to react. Silence overtook the room as everyone heard what Dr. Gamelsberg had revealed.

"How...what? No! How can that alien be older than the universe? That's not even possible! Nothing can be older unless..." that's when it finally hit her. That was when it hit all of them.

"Unless the alien existed...unless it existed before the big bang itself" Greynor said in astonishment.

Dr. Gamelsberg nodded. "That's right. That alien...that soul was alive when our universe was born" Dr. Gamelsberg said.

"I'm... I need to sit down," Kalduron said as he pulled up a chair, still unable to wrap his head around what he had just heard.

"And...and you are sure about this?" Seleece asked with a shocked tone.

"It's not just me that's sure about it, Melthuron is sure about it as well. There is no room for doubt anymore. That soul...it witnessed creation itself. Why do you think Melthuron became obsessed with it? That...that cosmic being knows about the creation of the universe! That alien can potentially answer one the most important questions science has ever asked...how the universe came to be." Dr. Gamelsberg answered while contemplating that very notion with excitement. They just couldn't believe it.

"If that that soul is older than our universe…is it…do you think it could have created it…us? The universe? Is it…"

"Only the alien itself knows what it really is," Dr. Gamelsberg said.

"This…this is crazy! It can't be" Kalduron said.

Kalduron was finally getting the Intel he had so desperately wanted, yet he couldn't believe what he was hearing.

"OK… well… do you…uh….do you have any theory as to why Melthuron would want to place it in a body? Why not study it the way it was?" Kalduron asked, trying to get as much information about it as possible. Kalduron now needed something concrete, something that he could use against the alien in order to control it. There was no way he could afford to let it run lose anymore.

"Well, I don't know for sure but—"

"Just take your best guess," Kalduron responded quickly.

"Well, my best guess would be that it was just too difficult to study it in its natural state. The state of that soul radically changes, specially that one. It can go from a highly unstable source of energy to a low energy state in the blink of an eye. Regardless, that particular soul is like an almost infinite source of energy. If we learned to control something that powerful, it could provide energy for eons to come. Only time will tell if it has any limitations at all," Dr. Gamelsberg explained.

Kalduron and the rest could still barely grasp what Gamelsberg had just said; it was much more than they could have ever expected.

As Seleece looked at him, she could not help but wonder what Kalduron was planning to do with the alien if he could somehow control it. Would he possibly use it as a weapon against their old enemies? "With a weapon that powerful, we could take back all of Demora in one day," she thought. That was a possibility she could not ignore. Perhaps that was exactly the same thought that was running through her commander's mind.

"Now if you don't mind, I'd like some time alone for ourselves. I'm a bit overwhelmed right now," Dr. Gamelsberg said in a low tone.

"Oh…Of course, Doctor. Seleece, please escort him to one of the resting chambers," Kalduron said.

"Oh wait, excuse me, but would it be too much trouble to ask for some food? Anything will do. I haven't eaten in a couple of hours, you see," he said.

"We might have some food that humans can digest, but I'm not quite sure," Kalduron replied.

"Oh no, Thespian food is just fine. Really, almost anything will do," he replied.

"I believe we have some food in the eating quarters. Seleece will take you there," Kalduron said.

"Yes sir! Please follow me, Doctor," Seleece said as she began to walk away, with Dr. Gamelsberg quickly following behind her.

"Are you feeling hungry, my love?" Dr. Gamelsberg asked his wife as the door closed behind them.

"You know the answer to that question!" the parasite replied with a smile. "Just wondering what it will be! It's been a while since we ate any Thespian food," his wife said.

A sign saying Cafeteria in Universal stood above the door they were now standing in front of.

"After you, Doctor," Seleece said.

"Why, thank you!" he said as he stepped through the open door. But suddenly he freaked out. "No, no, no!" he screamed as he ran out the door as quickly as he had entered.

Seleece was confused by his sudden outburst. "Doctor? Are you all—"

"Please get them out of there! Please I can't! I CAN'T," he screamed out in fear as he positioned himself right behind Seleece.

Seleece was like a giant compared to him. Standing almost three feet taller, she completely dwarfed the now cowering human.

"I don't understand. What's wrong, Dr. Gamelsberg?" she asked with a puzzled look.

"My husband he's…he's developed a phobia of robots. He can't stand the sight of them," the parasite said.

"Please…just get them away from me! Get them away!" he screamed out. Another scream could be heard from down the hall.

"What's the matter?" Kalduron screamed out as he rushed in their direction, with the rest of the crew following closely behind, with weapons in their hands.

"Oh, it's nothing. My husband has a phobia of robots…sorry about that, boys!" the parasite responded with a smile.

"All Serverbot report to the main control room," Kalduron commanded.

The robots quickly stopped the cleaning they were doing and left the kitchen, one by one in single file. Dr. Gamelsberg was still hiding behind Seleece as each robot exited the kitchen, shaking as each robot passed him on their way to the control room.

"Since we have no idea when the alien will return, we will set course for Demora," Kalduron said.

"Demora? But sir—"

"Take care of Dr. Gamelsberg until we arrive. I have much to contemplate," Kalduron said before he walked away.

"Sir, yes sir!" Seleece quickly responded. "It's all right now...they are all gone," she said to Dr. Gamelsberg, smiling warmly. Anyone who had ever served in the military was aware of the symptoms the doctor was experiencing. Anxiety, depression, all symptoms of posttraumatic stress. Seleece knew what he was going through all too well; that was why she was so understanding. She had seen all of it before, too many times to count.

"I'll go in first just to make sure they are all gone," she said in a soft voice in an attempt to calm him down.

The room was completely empty. "All right, you can come on in! They are all gone," she said from inside the cafeteria.

"Let's get some food honey, come on," the parasite said as it kissed his cheek.

"Yeah…OK," he whispered nervously.

It was small cafeteria, no more than nine hundred square feet. There was no kitchen in the back. Instead, there was a medium-sized, oval-shaped food dispensary machine toward the end of the room in the left corner. They were developed by the military to keep food fresh for long periods. Only military grade, highly processed food full of nutrients suited for a Thespian diet would be found inside; it wasn't anything a human could eat.

"Let's see, it looks as if we have some…ugh," she said.

"What is it?" the parasite asked.

"Oh, it's nothing…I just really hate this type of food. It's all us Thespians get to eat these days," she replied as she looked at the frozen tray. The only food in that dispensary was Gael'mar made, the military edition. It was a smaller portion, and even nastier in flavor when compared with the civilian version.

"I'll take seven if you have them," Dr. Gamelsberg said after he glanced at the small tray.

That was an odd request. "What? With all due respect, Doctor, one portion is enough for a fully grown eight-foot-tall Thespian…and you are human. I'll try to see if I can find anything else that is better suited for you," Seleece replied as she rifled through the old dispensary.

"Oh, no need for that. I promise my husband will finish every bite," the parasite responded in her high-pitched voice.

"All right, if you say so," Seleece responded. She took out all seven of them and placed them all inside the big microwave that stood right next to the dispensary machine. Only a few seconds went by before they were ready for consumption.

"Here you go, Doctor," she said. She placed down each tray one by one in front of the hungry doctor, his eyes almost sparkled with excitement at the sight of the food that was now in front of him.

"Oh, would you look at that! It all looks delicious!" he said.

Seleece almost cringed. "I couldn't find any eating utensils, but luckily for you it should still be quite easy to eat with your hands. I apologize for the inconvenience, Doctor," Seleece replied as she stared at the trays. "No way is he going to eat all that," She thought.

"Oh yes, that won't be an issue at all!" the parasite replied.

Seleece nodded. "I'll be outside if you need anything," Seleece said as she began to walk away.

"Nonsense! Sit down with us!" the parasite said.

"Yes, please join us. It's been quite a long time since I've gotten to sit down and enjoy a meal. We would love the company," Dr. Gamelsberg said.

Although Seleece didn't want to, she grudgingly agreed. "All right." She sat down across from them at the oval-shaped table.

"I can't believe we get to have a full meal! I can't remember the last time we got to do this," he said before taking the first bite.

Seleece still couldn't believe he was about to eat Thespian food. Humans had evolved on a completely different planet and required a completely different diet. Most of the food each species consumed would be uneatable by the other species, but Dr. Gamelsberg was eating the Thespian food with no problem at all. Before she even realized it, he had finished the first portion. Then he started on the second, then the third. Seleece couldn't believe it; it actually looked as if he would finish all seven servings. "I can't believe it," she thought.

"So sorry, I didn't catch your name. What was it again?" the parasite asked while her supposed husband continued to stuff his face.

"Seleece," she responded in a quiet tone.

"Oh yes, that's right! Man...you sure are tall! Much taller than Melthuron, that's for sure," the parasite said.

"Yes, well, we are different species," Seleece replied. "I can't believe I'm having a conversation with a parasite," she thought to herself

"Oh yeah! I forgot to tell you, there are two distinct species on their home planet, honey. Or maybe I told you before; I can't remember," Dr. Gamelsberg mumbled as he continued to stuff his face.

"Oh yes, that's right! I remember now! I had completely forgotten all about that," the parasite said as it continued the awkward conversation. "So, how long have you been in the army?" the parasite asked.

"Two hundred and twelve years," Seleece replied quietly.

The worm's mouth suddenly swung wide open. It quickly turned to face her husband. "Whoa! Honey, did you hear that? Two hundred and twelve years! And you don't look a day over thirty. Good for you! You have to tell me what products you use to stay looking so young!" the parasite said.

"Thespians don't age the same way humans do, honey. They stay looking young and can live for a very long time compared to humans. I once met a Thespian who was three hundred years old, but he sure didn't look it!" he said while finishing the last bite of the sixth tray.

Seleece still couldn't believe it. Dr. Gamelsberg actually ate six portions. She had never seen anything like it before. A talking parasite, a human who could eat Thespian food; it was unheard of. Seleece couldn't stop herself anymore, she had to ask.

"If you don't mind me asking, how can you eat that? And eat so much of it?" she asked the hungry scientist.

"That's reaaly quieat agnr guf ghfla," he responded with his mouth full of food.

Seleece stared.

"Honey...manners!" the parasite said.

He swallowed. "I'm sorry about that! I was so hungry I forgot all about my table manners!" he responded. "Now that's a good question, Seleece. It must be quite unusual to see a human eat Thespian food, but let me explain. You are correct in the fact that humans normally can't digest food from your planet. Given the fact that we did not evolve on your planet, the nutrients we need are vastly different from the one's your food provides. However, I am the one exception to that rule due to my wife. You see, I share my body, my organs, and pretty much everything else you could think of with her. That also goes for her as well. She shares everything her highly evolved parasitic body has to offer," He explained.

"Honey!" the parasite exclaimed.

"Oh, I'm sorry, love. I know you hate the p word. I'm sorry," he replied. "But trust me! Her biology is quite amazing. I published a very long and detailed study about this very subject ten years ago! You should read it if you are more curious!" he replied.

"I'll take your word for it, Doctor," Seleece said.

"Anyhow, I can pretty much digest anything because of her. Now as far as how much I'm eating, well I also eat for two! My wife requires quite a handful of nutrients to stay alive, you see. I guess it would be a benefit if I were ever to partake in an eating contest! According to some calculations I did when I studied this, on average

I need about twenty times more calories than a normal person my size," he said before letting out a small laugh.

"And you still get to keep that beautiful figure…you're welcome!" the parasite replied before kissing him on the cheek.

They really behaved as if they loved each other, like a couple. Seleece was surprised by how well the parasite played her part, but Seleece couldn't find the sight more disturbing even if she tried. "Well, I have never heard of anything like that before," she replied, accompanying it with a fake smile.

"We have a saying back on Earth: there's a first time for everything!" the parasite responded enthusiastically.

"I guess so," she responded, trying her hardest to keep a straight face while talking to the parasite.

"Well, that was really good! Sure hits the spot, doesn't it, honey?" he asked his wife.

"Yes, I sure was hungry! I can't remember the last time we ate anything other than scraps of food," the parasite replied.

Seleece scoffed at the idea of eating that kind of food; she was utterly sick of it after so long. "Kishna Dol alvier," Seleece said.

"Lanor Ga'l alosh," he replied back.

His knowledge of Thespian language took her by surprise; she didn't expect him to know what that meant, let alone respond in the correct manner.

"What? You can speak their language? You never told me that!" the parasite said in surprise.

"Well, I like to keep a little mystery in the relationship," he jokingly replied. "Kishna Dol alvier is an old Thespian saying. It roughly translates to 'may the next meal be as fulfilling,'" he explained.

"Oh! Neat!" the parasite replied enthusiastically. "I'll try to remember that," the parasite said.

"Maybe the parasite controls his mind somehow," she thought. That was the only explanation she could come up with.

"Say, do you guys happen to have any water around here?" he asked.

Her mind snapped back into the room. "I believe so, let me take a quick look, Doctor," she replied as she stood up. She walked over to the food dispensary and opened it. She shuffled things around, looking for any containers with water. "Let's see…ah, here we are. The last one," she said before handing him the bottle.

It was a normal looking water bottle made out of a recyclable plastic material. The mouth of the bottle was narrow like most of Earth's bottles, but square rather than round. The Gael'mar logo, which looked like two half-moons meeting each other at the center, was engraved right at the middle of the bottle. She walked back toward the table and sat down, placing the bottle in front of them. Compared to him, the bottle was huge; it was one and a half feet long and half a foot wide.

"That will do just fine," he said as he removed the black bottle cap off. Using both hands, he carefully placed the mouth of the bottle to his lips and began to sip. Slowly, the bottle gave away all of its water until only drops were visible. Dr. Gamelsberg then let out a sigh of relief.

"Ah! That sure hit the spot, didn't it, honey? I sure was thirsty after all that food," he exclaimed as he set the now empty bottle down on the table.

"You are absolutely right, my love," the parasite responded as it rubbed itself against his cheek. The parasite's behavior still puzzled Seleece to no end. While there had been reports of alien parasites being able to cross into species not found on their planet, she had never heard of a parasite like this one before.

"Seleece, stop being all quiet! Why don't you tell us more about yourself? It's been such a long time since my husband and I have had the pleasure of interacting with anyone other than ourselves," the parasite said.

"Well, there's not much to tell really," Seleece responded. "I'm just a soldier. If you are finished with your meal, Doctor, I've been instructed to take you to the resting chambers," Seleece said as she stood up. Although she was physically present in that room, her mind was somewhere else. She couldn't stop thinking about the alien, about what Dr. Gamelsberg had said.

"Older than the universe" she thought. "If that's true…what are we supposed to do with a being like that? Where do we even begin?" she thought.

"Yes, well perhaps it's for the best. It's been ages since we've gotten decent rest. I sure could use some," he responded.

"Fine, be that way! But you're not off the hook yet! I expect more from you later," the parasite said to Seleece jokingly.

But before they took their first steps, Kalduron walked through the door. "If you don't mind, Doctor, I have a few more questions to ask…off the record," Kalduron said.

"Uh, sure," he responded with a confused look.

"Follow me, please," Kalduron said as he walked away.

They made their way down to the control room once more. As the door of the control room slid open, Dr. Gamelsberg found himself in front of a familiar face. Panic almost took over as he stared at the Thespian who was standing before him.

"Me…Melthuron?" he struggled to say as their eyes met.

Melthuron's feet were in shackles. A large, heavy weight was attached to the end. He was wearing dirty, black overalls, the typical attire of Thespian prisons. His face was covered in bruises; it seemed Kalduron had been busy interrogating whomever Melthuron had switched bodies with. Dr. Gamelsberg was not taking their reunion very well. He looked like he was about to freak out. His face turned white with fear as his hands and body began to shake.

"Honey, it's OK. Calm down; take a deep breath. He can't hurt us anymore. They got him," the parasite said as she tried to console him.

Dr. Gamelsberg didn't respond. It seemed like fear had taken over his mind. He stood still, silent as he stared at his captor.

"Not quite. This isn't Melthuron. Someone by the name of Jess has somehow switched bodies with him. That's all the information I was able to get out of him," Kalduron explained.

"This isn't happening…this can't be…it can't be!" Dr. Gamelsberg screamed out with fear.

"Answer my question," Kalduron replied without sympathy. Dr. Gamelsberg's lack of composure was beginning to irritate him.

"Honey, look at me…look at me!" the parasite said.

He turned to face her. "It's OK! We are safe!" the parasite said as it tried calm her husband down. "Close your eyes and take some deep breaths. I love you. I'm here. Just try to calm down," the parasite said as it rubbed itself lovingly against his cheek.

The parasite's affection seemed to pay off. Dr. Gamelsberg slowly started to regain his composure. "I…I love you too, honey," he responded in a low tone.

"He just needs a minute. I'm sure you all understand. He's been through a lot," the parasite said as it tried to console him. It took a moment, but Dr. Gamelsberg was able to avoid another panic attack. His stare slowly reverted back to normal. "I'm…sorry, everyone. I'll be all right. What…what I was trying to say was that it can't be possible. That has to be Melthuron. I've seen it with my own eyes. I've done the experiments myself. Souls that are placed in bodies that they don't not belong to…well, they die. I…I performed those hellish experiments on living and deceased beings, so I've seen it with my own eyes. That HAS to be Melthuron," Dr. Gamelsberg said with great sadness. The look in his eyes was unmistakable; he was telling the truth. He may have been telling the truth, but that answer didn't seem to please Kalduron.

"The alien was the one who confirmed this. That guy, your damn science experiment, tends to not be wrong given its, freakish powers! So please spare me! You are wrong. Stop wasting my time and tell me everything you know about this Jess person...NOW!" Kalduron screamed.

"The...the alien confirmed it? But...this can't be...wait...if it's true then he...he figured it out," he mumbled to himself as his mind drifted away.

"I said NOW!" Kalduron screamed again.

His screams brought the doctor right back.
"Right...uh...well, I know who that is...maybe. If that's the person I think you are referring to, but I don't know much about her.

She…well, she was Melthuron's secretary, sort of. She ran all of his errands," Dr. Gamelsberg replied.

"Are you sure that's all you know? Think long and hard now, Doctor. Any information that you have could be of great value," Kalduron replied as he stared him down.

"Right…uh, let's see…well, I first met her when I started working with Melthuron, back at his ship. She used to run all sorts of errands for him. Like I said, she was kind of his unofficial secretary. That's really all I know," he replied.

"She is a human, is she not? Jess is no Thespian name. What does she look like?" Kalduron asked.

"It's her nickname. Yes…she is indeed a human. She's about five eleven, brown eyes, blond hair, light skin, like my own. I didn't really have much contact with her other than a few greetings. She ran a couple of errands for me before I was imprisoned. You know, bringing materials, keeping up with the inventory, things of that nature. But after, well, you know, I hardly saw her anymore," he explained.

But Kalduron wasn't buying it. There had to be something else. "There has to be a reason why Melthuron chose her. Think long and hard about that. Why, out of everyone he knows, would he choose her to switch bodies with? There has to be a reason," Kalduron asked.

Dr. Gamelsberg was silent.

"Well?" Kalduron asked impatiently.

But Dr. Gamelsberg remained silent.

"Doctor!" Kalduron screamed.

"Because she loved him! That's why," he replied with agony. "He chose her because he knew she would never betray him. That poor girl, she had great admiration for Melthuron. It was obvious to anyone who spent even a second around her. There's no other reason, at least that I can think of. He's just using her," he said. For some reason, that very topic seemed to bother him greatly.

Kalduron didn't seem surprised to hear this. "Well, that's just pathetic," Kalduron replied.

Dr. Gamelsberg clenched his fist as heard that comment. "If that's all, I'd like to get some much-needed rest now."

Kalduron nodded. "That's all for now. Computer, take us to our first destination. Seleece, take him to the resting chambers."

"Sir, yes sir!" she replied before walking off with him. As they made their way down the hallway, Seleece took notice of how quiet they both were. "Here we are," Seleece said as she stopped in front of a door. "Is there anything else I can do for you, Doctor?" She asked in a polite tone.

"No," he whispered with little energy before rushing into the room.

The blank stare he had said it all; he needed to leave his thoughts and feelings behind. What Kalduron had done to Dr. Gamelsberg was borderline cruel. She had kept her mouth shut during the investigation, but if Kalduron really wanted to check the information he had gathered from that Jess person, he could have easily used the truth serum that had been developed by the military instead of placing a clearly traumatized person in front of his captor without any warning. The truth serum didn't work on humans, but that person was no longer inside a human body.

Seleece was slowly witnessing a change in the commander she had known for so long and respected so deeply. Kalduron would have never interrogated someone like that in the past; he would have never threatened to kill anybody. Melthuron had gotten to him. Melthuron had destroyed his reputation, stripped him of his title, and banished him from his home. Seleece knew what war, or even the possibility of war, could do to someone's mind, especially someone who had been through it before. The lingering threat of war had to be the reason behind Kalduron's slow change. The threat of war must have been plaguing him. Kalduron was known for being a calm, decisive leader—a Thespian who valued justice and fairness above all. But he was slowly changing into someone Seleece didn't recognize. No matter how much she wanted to tell him, she had to remain quiet; there was way too much on Kalduron's mind already.

Suddenly, the door slid open in front of her. "Reporting for duty, sir!" Seleece said as the door closed behind her.

"Take this, soldier," Kalduron said before tossing something in her direction.

She could tell by the clear color of the liquid inside that it was the military serum.

"Sir, yes sir!" she chanted. The syringe pierced her neck; the contents rushed inside her circulatory stream.

"We will reach our target location soon. I will need everyone ready for deployment," Kalduron said as he stood still, admiring the light show that was taking place in front of him. The spaceship was traveling at the fastest speed possible, leaving behind thousands of stars as it moved closer and closer to their destination.

www.ingramcontent.com/pod-product-compliance
Lightning Source LLC
Chambersburg PA
CBHW070345260626
47161CB00001B/24